Christopher J. Finn, born in 1970 in San Antonio, Texas, and raised in Oceanside, New York, was a child with few friends. He was the shy kid, mostly seen off to the side, acting out scenes from movies or a recent story that he read in a book.

It wasn't until his early twenties, sitting alone in his apartment, television off—because he didn't have the money to pay the cable bill—when he picked up a book titled *Battlefield Earth: A Saga of the Year 3000*.

He was enthralled by Jonnie 'Good-boy' Tyler and the Psychlos, but more importantly, he realized writing a story was something he could, and should, do.

Today, 20 years after his decision to learn the craft, Christopher J. Finn sees his dreams come true with *Dorothy and the Glass Key*, his debut novel.

Tycu ye aht k efkwu sn solu rke kow rfkt ye vut ts au.

CRYPTOGRAM

Christopher J. Finn

DOROTHY AND THE GLASS KEY

AUSTIN MACAULEY PUBLISHERS™

LONDON • CAMBRIDGE • NEW YORK • SHARJAH

Ordering Information:
Quantity sales: special discounts are available on quantity purchases by corporations, associations, and others. For details, contact the publisher at the address below.

Publisher's Cataloging-in-Publication data
Finn, Christopher J.
Dorothy and the Glass Key

ISBN 9781641826921 (Paperback)
ISBN 9781641826938 (Hardback)
ISBN 9781641826945 (E-Book)

The main category of the book — Fiction / Fantasy / Epic

www.austinmacauley.com/us

First Published (2019)
Austin Macauley Publishers LLC
40 Wall Street, 28th Floor
New York, NY 10005
USA

mail-usa@austinmacauley.com
+1 (646) 512-5767

For my friends and family.
David Jerry, you're the reason I am here. I bow to you, oh teacher of prose.
Tiffany Finn, I love you and I can finally immortalize what I've been saying to you for years. Read…The…Book…
Janie McFadden—tough, inspiring, compassionate, and too damn far away. I miss you, Mom!

Good Morning, Administrator

Ellen Steward began every Monday morning as Corporate Administrator of Elements of Recovery in the same dull fashion. She'd step inside her office and sort through a slew of backlogged paperwork. Complaints, memos, budget reports, and patient files loomed over her day, as they had every single Monday prior. With one exception—today.

Ellen hung her purse, walked to her chair, and sat. She set her coffee to her left, then eyed her empty desk. No stacks of paper, nothing marked urgent. Just an empty wire inbox with a slim folder placed squarely against its edge.

PATIENT RECORDS—CONFIDENTIAL, stretched across the top in bold, black letters. A corporate memo paper clipped in the upper right corner of the folder read: *Ellen, the board has requested that you handle this case personally. Please see to the patient's administration discreetly and immediately.* The word *you* underlined not once, but twice.

"Hmm. That's odd," she muttered. She took a long swig of coffee and opened the folder. A single sheet of paper sat bound in fasteners—only partially filled out, and she noted this with some agitation—along with a picture. Ellen ran a finger over the name and read aloud, "Dorothy Alston," as she did whenever she wanted to imprint face-to-name recognition deep into her psyche.

Dorothy Alston, an attractive 25-year-old, displayed characteristics Ellen rarely saw when reviewing new candidates, and she's admitted more than her fair share in her decade's long career. She frowned and slouched into her chair, covering part of the photo with her thumb. The girl's eyes, stone-cold and blue, peered into the upper left corner of the picture so fiercely her pupils were barely visible, like a partial eclipse of two moons. Ellen slid her thumb along the slender chin and drooping mouth, then leaned back, absorbing the entire photograph.

Dorothy's head tilted slightly to the right, shoulders jostled, as if someone had propped her up for the picture. The girl appeared vacant, as though her mind was absent from her body. Like a shell, perfectly preserved, but lifeless.

Ellen returned the Polaroid and read the diagnosis. *Persistent vegetative state*. She read this again, just to be sure.

PVS meant no signs of higher brain function, unresponsive to psychological and physical stimuli. The lights were on, yet nobody's home. Her staff wouldn't touch this case. By all rights, neither should she.

Elements of Recovery admitted patients with two types of problems: addiction and physical rehab. The doctors ranged from psychiatrists to physical therapists to standard practice physicians. This girl would need a specialist, which meant Ellen would need to *hire* a specialist. Twenty-four-hour care, bed service, a nutritionist, and specialized medicine would add to her mountain-top Mondays. This woman did not belong here.

Ellen skimmed down the page, shaking her head and letting out a humored sigh when her eyes landed on the name of Dorothy's guardian. Ragesha Dutta, India's premier pill pusher of the 1990s, CEO of Dutta International, and one of Elements' top investors. Ellen had never heard mention of him having any dependents, but then again, she'd never really paid much attention. He certainly piqued her interest now.

She pulled a Montblanc Star Walker fountain pen from her lab coat pocket—a gift she purchased following her latest flop of a relationship—then scribbled Mr. Dutta's name on the back of the folder, preceded by the date and time. She wrote and underlined the following: *Wrong facility? Why here? Why me?*

Ellen sat back, lifted the coffee cup to her lips and wished away the mounting pressure sure to evolve into another fun-filled migraine. Oh, what a day this will be.

The intercom, a series of three speakers fastened to the side of her desk with two applicable volumes—off and mind-splitting—blared, "Ms. Steward, your nine o'clock is here," and Ellen leaped out of her chair and right off her train of thought. That antiquated, overloud squawk-box from hell scared the bejesus out of her no less than four times a day. She vowed to take a crowbar to the damned thing and give her heart a rest. Until then, well, she'd call it a shot of espresso in her coffee.

Ellen knew she had no early morning appointments—Monday meetings were expressly forbidden, and there was no chance, Mary, her personal assistant, would have missed even a late addition to her daily schedule. For Christ's sake, everyone knew this, the Board of Directors included. Monday is paper day! Monday is processing day! That is its purpose! Out with the old and on with the new. What you absolutely did not do, not with Ellen, is hold meetings on a Monday. It screws with her entire routine, and she did not want a pile of backlogged work plaguing her week simply because she's stuck chumming it up with the big wigs over topics easily handled through email, or a simple memo.

Now Mary, who is working on her third year as Ellen's PA and a top-notch pro when it came to penning and memorizing Ellen's schedule; Mary would have contacted her over the weekend had this been routed through the proper channels. No, this came from above, and the only thing to do was pick up the folder and head to the lobby to meet this uninvited thorn in her side. She found the waiting room empty, save for her assistant. Ellen raised an eyebrow at Mary, who merely shrugged.

"I tried to tell him to, you know, wait here. Cute guy and all, little intense for my taste. Millionaires, right? Anyway, Mr. Dutta, that's the guy, he insisted on the Penny Pincher Penthouse, stage left. Even has his own key card! Weird, right?" Mary thumbed toward the elevator and smiled her flawless smile. Not a wrinkle on this one, not for miles. Ellen felt a little twinge of envy. Ah, to be 20 again.

Ellen walked to the elevator, punched the button for the second floor, and inserted a key card. The doors closed behind her and up she went. The 'Penny Pincher Penthouse', as Mary had dubbed it, is a single room within the Elements physical rehabilitation ward—something to do with a multi millionaire's unwillingness to pay his bill after a year of full-time residency. He argued every detail down to the penny, hence the name.

The first floor encompassed outpatient therapy and included a variety of upscale amenities, such as: hot tubs, pools, saunas, massage rooms—the works. The third floor housed the addicts' elite: pop stars and actors who wanted to 'do' rehab in style without the hassle of an overnight stay. The *crème-de-la-crème* of Elements, or resort central if you asked the staff, is where Mr.

Dutta had arranged this impromptu meeting. She guessed he wanted to inspect the accommodations without the usual corporate escort. Typical.

She turned down the west wing to Suite 12—Dorothy Alston's new room if the board had anything to say about it. Ellen inserted her keycard and stepped inside. Her eyes widened, and she could feel her jaw tightening as she scanned her surroundings. Someone had cleared the room of all its furniture and décor! Chairs, tables, even the artwork—gone. All the appliances stripped from the kitchen. This wasn't a luxury suite, it's a damned construction site! Not a great first impression by any stretch. She glanced down at the memo pinned to the patient file and vowed to investigate after the meeting.

Ms. Alston sat in a chrome wheelchair in the center of the room. A tight-knit white throw rug placed beneath her chair extended a foot on either side of the wheels. Ellen noticed an odd insignia imprinted on the rug: a black number three pressed against a lowercase k, with something resembling a skeleton key between them, though the chair did obstruct her view.

The young woman faced a large picture window overlooking the wooded area behind Elements. Standing to the right of the window was an older man, 40 or so, dressed in a black suit, white silk shirt, and maroon tie. He was shorter than Ellen would have imagined, about an inch shorter than she was in her heels. He was trim and attractive, as Mary pointed out, though she could do without the salt and pepper scruff littering his face.

"It is as beautiful as I'd imagined," he remarked with a moderate accent. He turned to Ellen and smiled.

"Mental health begins with serene surroundings," Ellen instinctively dictated, and winced when her words echoed off the bare walls. She'd tear someone a new one for the state of this suite. She strode across the room and extended her hand. "Ellen Steward, Corporate Administrator of Elements of Recovery."

"Ragesha Dutta," he replied and shook her hand. He turned again toward the window, leaned against the wall, and placed his hands in his pockets.

"And this must be Ms. Alston." Ellen approached the young woman, and Mr. Dutta pushed himself off the wall and joined her.

"Yes, this is Dorothy. She's been in my care for many years. I'm hoping you can help where others could not."

"I see," Ellen replied. She mentally rehearsed the contents of Dorothy's folder. Father missing, mother presumed dead. Ragesha Dutta was listed as her benefactor, but not a relative. No mention of prior care. "How long has she been like this?"

"Since we were 14-years-old."

"Fourteen?" Ellen repeated. Nine years. That would mean a permanent vegetative state, not persistent. That's a huge error in charting and diagnosis. Not typical of her staff at all. Still, the paperwork hadn't gone through the usual channels. She guessed the likelihood of these details circumventing her mandated checks and balances to be high. This has board intervention written all over it.

Handle this discreetly…

"Fourteen," Mr. Dutta affirmed. "I have taken her everywhere from Kerala, India, to Milwaukee, Wisconsin. I've retained many specialists to treat her. Shamans from the Americas. The Tawang Monastery Buddhists in China. Taoist alchemy, modern medicine, spirit healers, psychics, witch doctors—all have tried to bring her back to me."

"No progress at all?" Ellen asked. She knew the neurological centers in Kerala and Milwaukee were renowned for treating coma patients. The Rest? Well, she wouldn't fault him for exploring the avenues of the spiritual quack. Hope is its own therapy. Still, if they couldn't help her, then what did he expect to find here?

Ellen lifted Dorothy's arm. She pressed her fingers along the woman's wrist and up to her shoulder. She didn't perceive any muscle degradation. She leaned in, pulled a small penlight from her pocket and swept it across Dorothy's eyes. As she expected, no pupillary response, but no dryness either. No bedsores beneath the girl's. Wham! Tee-shirt, nor a single scar where a feeding tube should have been. She pressed a hand against Dorothy's hip, then ran a finger along the elastic of her sweatpants and brushed along the rim of her cotton underwear. No diaper? Nothing about this poor woman's condition made any sense at all.

"No," Ragesha replied. "She is as absent today as when we were children."

"When you were children?" Ellen repeated. She'd admit she knew little of Ragesha Dutta, his true age included. Judging by appearance alone, she'd say mid to late forties, double Dorothy's age. So…children? At the same time? Not possible.

Ellen moved to Dorothy's side and checked her pulse and blood pressure, both slightly above normal. Her breathing was strong and steady. As she finished her examination, Ragesha moved wordlessly to the suite's kitchenette bar and pulled a pair of stools from beneath the counter. He sat, still silent, and waited until Ellen took the stool beside him. He pressed his hands together in his lap, then turned his gaze to Dorothy.

"Well, Ms. Steward, we were children, and, in a way, we grew up together."

"I don't understand. Are you suggesting the two of you are the same age?"

He continued, "You will understand everything, I promise. It is why I have cleared my entire day, and," he glanced at his watch, pursed his lips, and added, "why I have cleared yours." He turned to the phone hanging on the wall behind him, pressed the intercom, and dialed 117.

"Yes sir," cracked over the speaker. Ellen recognized the boardroom's extension, but the voice on the other end was unfamiliar.

"It's time. Please ensure we are not disturbed," Ragesha instructed.

"Understood," the man replied, then severed the connection.

Ragesha returned his attention to Ellen, cupped his hands on the edge of the counter and swallowed hard. She looked to the phone, the door, the folder in her hands, an uneasiness settling in her gut. A knock sounded.

She rose, expecting, *hoping,* Mary, or another of her staff arrived to greet her with the usual mess of weekend issues. She paused when Ragesha firmly gripped her elbow, coaxing her back into her seat. She glanced from the door to Ragesha, who made no move to answer it. "What exactly is going on here?"

"Dorothy's situation, our situation, can only be classified as extraordinary. You will need to hear and experience it all to truly appreciate the roads we've traveled to arrive at this point in time."

"What do you mean?"

Ragesha slipped a hand into his right coat pocket and retrieved a small wooden box which he displayed to her with an open palm. Ellen inspected the polished woodgrain box, about twice the size of a glasses case.

"Open it," he instructed.

"What is it?"

"Open it."

Ellen pulled off the lid using her index finger and thumb and set it on the counter, keeping her eyes trained on Ragesha, quickly peeking back at the box, to Ragesha, and the box once again. Inside, an elongated stone sat in a red satin foam mold. One end was a cut circle, the other with three prongs. She glanced at the design of the skeleton key on the rug. Then she gazed again at the stone.

"It is the same," Ragesha assured her. "It is a key, my key. The last of three."

"A key to what?" Ellen asked.

"For me, it was an escape from my youth. For Dorothy, it was something far greater. We didn't know this at the time, of course," he added, replacing the lid and sliding the box to his right.

"We were fourteen when we met. And our lives twined together beneath a veil of horrible pain." Ragesha rubbed his chin thoughtfully, then continued, "We were hurting. We longed for an escape. When you search so hard for an escape…" He tapped the key-box. "Sometimes the escape finds you."

Part I

Chapter 1
A Line in the Sand

Dorothy Alston and her father, Peter Alston, crossed the state line from Georgia into Florida. Neither of them so much as glanced in the rearview mirror, but Peter marked the moment with a drawn sigh. His jaw line bulged slightly, and a vein pulsed at the base of his neck.

He swallowed, shifted his weight in the seat, and ran a sleeve under his nose after a brief sniffle. Dorothy could not see his lips beneath the thick black mustache he'd worn for most of his life, but she didn't have to. His white knuckles and watery eyes betrayed his distress, despite his rigid, unemotional face.

She settled against the frame of the open window of her father's truck and ran her finger along the outline of cracked rubber. She brushed over a protruding scar of vinyl near the window's center and plucked at the edges. Dorothy turned her attention outward, viewing the blur of palm fronds along the highway through strands of blonde hair whipping in the wind. Beyond the palms were red oak trees, which paced a bit slower. Past these were fields of tall grass and orange groves, and these barely seemed to move at all.

Where did she fit in this landscape? She knew where she wanted to be: out in the great beyond, past the groves, where time would crawl. Somewhere in a field of sunflowers, between the tick-tacking of cicadas and twittering robins and blue jays, she imagined this to be her new place in her new life. She would exist in an oubliette—rounded in the present, only the present. The past and future were simply unobtainable.

Two weeks ago, Dorothy had friends. She had a home, a mother, and a father. She was an *A* student. Well, mostly—but Home Economics didn't count as a 'real' class. No girl worth her salt paid attention in Home Ec., unless deserts were on the menu.

Her mother and father coexisted during the latter years of her life. She couldn't recall any happy times with them, nor did she remember any sad moments either. They were just…situations. One to the next: every day and everything…the same.

Dorothy's mother loved to cook for the family. She made the best dang fried chicken this side of the Mason Dixon Line. The steaks and hamburgers: just plain awesome. And when her father grilled them—even better.

Her dad worked at the steel mill. Tough job. Dorothy didn't need to see what he did to understand this. His grimy clothes and hands framed an image of total exhaustion, and this told the story well enough. He didn't have it in him to grill, or do much of anything, really.

On one such day, Dorothy's mother had been cooking hamburgers on the stove, filling the kitchen with smoke. Alarms sounded, the three scrambled to silence them, beginning a chain of events which piled up behind her like a line of dominos.

Ten minutes of summer-hot open window air coupled with the three of them waving beach towels at a brand new 1985 Hochiki smoke detector was enough to ignite her father's temper, and he pulled the flipping thing right off the wall. He'd done the same a few months prior when his cigar smoke set off the alarm in the living room.

The first domino teetered.

Her mother contracted the flu the following July. Dorothy was out studying with a friend, and her father was working late, so her mother decided sleep would be the best medicine. She popped a valium, always popped those, but that night, she swallowed two.

Another domino.

Peter, as he admitted later, had not worked overtime that evening. He'd lied to his wife so he could sneak over to the pub for a few quick ones with the boys. A few hours after Dorothy came home from her study date and went to bed, Peter walked through the door into a dark, quiet home. He proceeded directly to the kitchen for a nightcap.

The domino track stacked up quickly from there.

Peter slammed two shots of good ol' Johnnie Black before remembering he had eaten nothing since lunch. Between the four

Buds at the bar and the two shots at the kitchen counter, well, he was past the stage of feeling gosh-darn good.

He pulled a steak from the fridge, oil from the cabinet, and fired up a quick man meal. He wiped his fingers and tossed the grease-soaked rag onto the counter, then moved to the living room and flipped on the old boob-tube for a game recap while his meat simmered. The Braves had beaten Philadelphia in the last showdown, and tonight's game promised to be a real humdinger according to the barstool boys.

He figured his eyes must've grown heavy and he nodded off, forgetting about his dinner.

According to the Fire Chief's final report, the fire began when the unattended pan of gristle and hot oil popped and sputtered into the open flame beneath the frying pan. The greasy towel sitting on the counter ignited, spread to the cabinets, and eventually, the roof and adjacent rooms.

Dorothy woke, gasping for air. Her room was next to her parents' and backed against the kitchen wall housing the stove. She stood—and when she couldn't see the door leading out of her room, she screamed and inhaled thick, brackish smoke. She hacked and swung her arms about; searched for anything tangible to lead her out. She pulled in lungs-full of smoke with each cough, and eventually fell to her knees, then to her stomach. She heard her father scrambling in the living room and wondered fleetingly about her mother, before falling unconscious.

Dorothy's next memory was of her father standing over her, slapping at her face while screaming her name. Her mother was not with them. When she realized this, she mustered her strength and sat up. She cried out for her mom, barely able to hear her own voice over the roaring fire.

The coroner recovered her mother the following morning. A closed casket procession followed the autopsy. And now, sitting in the truck on the way to her uncle's farm in Florida, well those dominos fell. They seemed to chase her down the highway, smacking and clacking across the asphalt behind them.

She'd lost everything. Anything not reduced to ashes smelled like a mix of charred rubber and wood. She could still taste it, feel the heat crawling over her skin, the smoke filling her lungs. Time might heal wounds, sure didn't do a thing for the smell.

Chapter 2
Treasures and Junk

Dorothy said almost nothing during the trip through north Florida, despite her father's attempts to lighten her mood. The open window had thankfully hampered conversation anyway, and Dorothy's impassive shrugs and gestures dissuaded him from an attempt at further—and unwanted mind you—discourse.

A few hours passed between small towns, houses, and plats of land. The landscape held little interest, and eventually, Dorothy shut her eyes and slept.

Her father parked and climbed out of the truck by the time she woke, and she heard the faint baritones of men talking a ways off. She kept her eyes pressed tight and listened.

"I don't know. She seems okay, I guess. But she's different, you know? She's not herself. Christ man, how could she be? How can any of us be?"

"It'll take time, Pete," a familiar voice replied. Her Uncle Al's low, rumbling twang cut through the background of bees, birds, and breeze. "She's young. She'll work it out, just like you will. Time brother, time heals all."

"I need her, Al. She's all I got left, I can't lose her too. Not my Dorothy."

"You haven't lost her, Pete. Now go on inside and get some rest. You've been haulin' ass for hours. Don't worry about Dorothy. I got an eye on her, and I don't think she'll be sleeping long."

"Yeah, I imagine not," Peter agreed with a half-hearted chuckle. "All right, buddy. Tell her I'll be up in a few hours, just need to get rid of this headache."

"Aspirin's in the bathroom. Beer's in the fridge."

Gravel crunched beneath Peter's boots as he walked toward the house, followed by the *creak* and *thwap* of the front door.

Dorothy opened her eyes. She reared, pressing her back against the seat, leaning away from two extremely large nostrils. After her eyes adjusted, she laughed and reached for the scruff of bangs hanging over the face of a curious foal. When Dorothy reached for its nose, it pulled its head through the window and frolicked off.

Dorothy stepped from the car and stretched. The pony pranced about, edged close, then trotted away while playfully flipping its head.

"She's five weeks old. Haven't named her yet, thought you might give me a hand with that." Dorothy turned at the sound of her uncle's voice.

"Uncle Al!" Dorothy chirped, and nestled into his chest. A mixture of relief and sorrow swelled up within and made her eyes water. Her uncle must have sensed this because he hugged her all the tighter.

"It's been a long time, little lady. I'm sorry I missed the funeral. Can't seem to get away from this dang place anymore."

Dorothy nodded. She wasn't thrilled that he'd skipped the funeral, but she understood. She hadn't wanted to be there, why would anyone else? Anyway, he couldn't leave the farm, what with the horses to care for, and she was pretty sure he's couldn't afford to pay anybody to do it. She got it.

"You didn't miss much," Dorothy replied. She stepped out of his embrace and leaned against the wooden plank fence surrounding Al's home and long gravel drive. She inspected the grounds with mild interest, her eyes drifting back to the pony, who was slipping in and out of the round yard outside the stable, tossing its head carelessly.

"I got two fillies, one mare, and a stud named Ulysses," Al said, and motioned toward the pony. "That little lady is his third. Me and the dam's owner cut a deal after the first breeding. She'd get the first two, I took the third. Probably could've gotten a stud fee," he said, kicking at a pebble. "Didn't want one, I guess." He laughed. "Your dad always said I had as about as much business sense as a lame mule. Still, I sure do like that mare. She's the one neighing like a stuck pig on the other side of the ranch."

Dorothy lifted her head. Odd she hadn't heard the braying before Uncle Al mentioned it.

"My partner's trying to clean her. She gets a bit ornery around her filly. Gets a might frantic away from her too. Mothers…" he startled and jerked his head apologetically.

Dorothy shrugged. Apologies followed her everywhere these days, though half the time she couldn't figure out what anyone was sorry about. Yeah, Mom died, it sucks royally, but does everyone have to tip-toe on the wound? Does every slip of the tongue deserve an *I'm sorry?* She didn't think so.

"Anyway, how 'bout a tour? I think the last time you were here was, what?"

"I was eight."

"Right! A lot has changed since then."

Dorothy considered this. If she said no, Uncle Al would usher her into the house. She wouldn't have the rushing open window air to serve as a barrier between herself and her father. She wasn't in the mood for his droopy-eyed apologies and inevitable excuses.

"Sure, okay. Right on," Dorothy said, and her uncle beamed with excitement. He motioned to the stable opening, and they proceeded inside.

The tang of cypress surprised Dorothy, and at the same time, refreshed her. It overshadowed the stench of dirt and manure outside. Eight pens lay before her, four on each side, deep stain highlighting the grains in the wood. Wrought-iron gates stood well above her head with a u-shaped opening extending from the height of her chest to a top rail, connecting one end of the building to the other. She paused, stricken by the simplistic beauty of the structure.

"Been runnin' four pens while I finished the stable. Took a hit, but it's been worth it. Stock likes it too."

"I bet," Dorothy agreed, and peered into the first pen on her right. She scanned over countless boxes and splintered wood— presumably from the old stable—tools and piles of junk lining the floor. She moved to the next stall and smiled.

"The filly was born in this one, wasn't it?"

Al chuckled. "I've got a foaling area for birthin', offers a bit more room. This here is Sassy's pen, though. That's her mother, in case you were wondering. Over in the far corner, on your left, is Ulysses' stall. Not quite as pristine as the rest of 'em." Al rubbed his chin. "Come on out back, have a look at the stock."

They stepped into a grassy field surrounded by a trim-cut oak fence. The usual jumps and fancy barricades used for show ponies lay haplessly about, though Dorothy suspected there might be a method to the madness. A riding path stretched along the perimeter of the property and hooked around what Al called the arena, with a show pen at its furthest point. Six paddocks surrounded the arena, set within the outer perimeter of the trail.

Al led Dorothy to a gate facing the first paddock, crossed the hardpan trail, and propped his elbow on a fence post. Dorothy climbed up the top rung of the fence and swung her feet over, using her uncle for balance.

The mare and foal casually ambled around the paddock, mother grazing, filly suckling. The mother nuzzled the filly on occasion, trotted away on others. The foal never left her side.

Al sighed, pulled the white Stetson from his head, and wiped his brow. "These August days just seem to get hotter every year. I imagine Georgia's the same way."

Dorothy agreed. "Yeah, maybe not as wet. Always feels damp out here. Like a steam bath."

Al chuckled and pointed to the tree line beyond the paddock, at a gathering storm in the distance. "That's your bath right there. Think it's hot now, wait till she gets here."

"She?" Dorothy asked.

"Rules of the south, little lady. Anything with the potential for damage is named after a woman, thunderstorms included."

"Mom would've smacked you for that."

Al laughed and shook his head. "She was a spitfire, that's for sure."

"She used to be, I guess. Maybe before Dad started working at the mill." Dorothy said. She hadn't wanted to talk about her mom, but now that she was, it didn't feel so bad. There wasn't anyone worth talking to back home. Her friends either didn't care or didn't know what to say. As for her father? What could she say to him?

"I'm not so sure she was much of anything at the end."

Al turned and looked at Dorothy. She met his gaze for a moment, then moved her attention back to the horses. "Things were bad?" Al asked. "What about your dad? Bad with him, too?"

"I guess. They didn't talk much at the end. He's always too drunk to notice anything goin' on around him," Dorothy blurted. "The only thing he sees lately is the bottom of a glass."

"That's a might deep for a fourteen-year-old."

"Yeah, I suppose. Guess, I don't really feel 14 anymore."

"I imagine not. Crap like that has a way of adding years up here." He tapped the side of his temple. "Imagine how your father must feel."

Imagine how he must feel? What difference did that make? She knew good and well how he should feel! Guilty for one thing. She hadn't said this out loud to anyone, but she felt it deep down. He should cringe at every meal, choke at every whiff of smoke. Just like she did.

"I guess," Dorothy replied.

"Anyway, back to your little friend here. You got about a month, I reckon, before school starts. What say you pick up the reigns on our little filly? Maybe fix up her new pen." He shrugged. "Even name her if you like."

Dorothy watched the filly prance about her mother and smiled. Something about the young horses' energy lifted Dorothy's spirits. Maybe it was the innocence of the happy little foal, or the obvious bond she had with her mother. Whatever it was, she wanted to be a part of it. So, she agreed.

Al mopped his forehead again. He raised a hand and waved, dropping his hat on the post next to the gate. His partner, Isais Santiago, approached and slapped his shoulder. He greeted Dorothy by tapping a finger to the brim of his cream-colored Stetson, then leaned on the gate between them.

"Whatcha need, boss?"

"I told you to stop calling me that. You're an equal partner here."

Isais winked at Dorothy, "Sorry, boss."

"You remember my niece, Dorothy?"

"*Si,* yes I do. Glad to have you here at our happy little ranch!"

"That first stall," Al interrupted. "What do you think about the foal taking it?"

"Mare might not like it."

"After she's weaned."

Isais shrugged. He poked Dorothy's heel and smirked. "Boss, I tol' you not to turn the pen into a closet."

"I know, I know." Al snatched his hat off the rail and slapped the side of his leg.

"I'm just sayin' boss, you work too hard. Now you got to work hard again." He elbowed Dorothy, and she dropped her head and hid a grin.

"Isais, I'm just askin'…"

"I'm just sayin'."

Al brushed his hat against his leg. His cheeks flushed red and he pursed his lips. He ran his hand along the scruff of his cheeks and chin, then turned and stomped off toward the house. Isais and Dorothy suppressed a laugh.

"He hasn't changed much," Dorothy noted.

"Yeah, he's a good guy, though. Bit of a temper on him, like an over-ripe jalapeño," he said. "Hey, I'll teach you how to set him off. Always good for a laugh."

"Won't he get mad at you?"

Isais looked up at the sky and raised a hand to the brim of his hat to mask the sun from his eyes. "He's kind of mad all the time. Sometimes, he's up here." He raised a hand over his head. "Other times, he's down here," he continued, and tapped his knee. "I try to keep him right around here." Isais placed his left hand under his chin, and his right hand over his belt.

"Until he storms off?"

"He's not much of a rancher. But he's good with the books and he can build stuff. And besides, you didn't look like you were ready," he said. Dorothy raised a brow and considered his dark eyes inset in his rounded, tan face.

"Ready for what?"

"Talking," he replied casually, then motioned towards the barn. "Come on, I'll show you the stall. Then, maybe you can help me bring in the horses."

After helping Isais pen the stock, Dorothy wandered around the farm, alone, until dusk. She soaked in the acrid smell of manure and found—after a while—it didn't bother her as much. The afternoon seared on, raising the temperature from bake to broil once the thunderstorm blew through. Dorothy was a sweaty mess when she finally succumbed to the weather and slipped inside her new home.

"Hey, hey, little Gray!" Al greeted. He motioned toward an island at the center of his kitchen and pointed to a tall glass of tea. Dorothy thanked him. He offered to fire up the grill if she was hungry and Dorothy quickly declined, opting for a banana.

"This place is beautiful," Dorothy remarked. She sipped her tea and scanned his—their—home. Thick, barrel-like timber framed the outer walls, connected to thinner trunks along the ceiling. Rough-cut wood panels lined the conjoining living room walls, and the floor a polished oak. The kitchen—apart from the cabinets—had small cut white tiles outlined by thicker hunter green tiles along the edges of the floor. Above that? Wood, wood, and more wood. He certainly had a thing.

"Decorating is kind of a passion of mine. Don't tell your father."

"Where is he anyway?"

"Went in for another nap. You still hungry?" Dorothy shook her head. "How 'bout a tour then? Not often I can show off my handiwork."

"I'm kind of tired, actually. Could we do it tomorrow? I just want to end this day."

"Fair enough," Al replied. He led Dorothy through the living room, around a couch fashioned out of some large branches with flakey, peeling white bark. She crossed a thick pile throw rug, brushed her hand along a rounded plank bordering the hallway, and followed him into a smaller room on the right.

Large cedar logs framed the wood planks sitting above a polished hardwood floor. Against the far-left wall was Dorothy's bed, donned with pillows and a thick white comforter. A small table stood next to the bed, and a four-drawer, aged white dresser sat beneath the window which overlooked a paddock. She stepped inside and sat, springs groaning beneath her.

"Smells funny," Dorothy commented and brushed her hand over a white doily sitting beneath an alarm clock.

"It's the cedar," Al replied, and tapped the wallboard. "You'll get used to it. Might even like it after a while."

"I guess. Kind of smells like a closet," she said, kicking off her shoes and bouncing on the mattress. The coils squealed and the loose headboard tapped the wall in three quick thuds.

"I finished the headboard, last week. Haven't had the chance to bolt it into the bed yet. I can pull it out if it'll bother ya."

"It's okay. You really made all this?" She ran her fingers over the polished grain arching up to the center of her bed, and down to the post aligned perfectly with the edge of the mattress.

"Made just about everything in this house, smelly walls included."

"You're really good; I wish I could build stuff like that."

"I can show you some tricks. Plenty of time left in the summer," Al offered. He looked to the floor, frowned, and crossed his arms. "Listen, little Gray, I know you and your dad have some...problems to work through. Just give him a chance. He's gonna work through it, and he'll need your help to do it." Al's evident discomfort made him seem more like a kid than an adult. Dorothy liked it. She smiled and half-nodded, and he returned the smile. He wished her a good night and closed the door behind him. She shut her eyes and slept.

Dorothy rose with the sun beaming through the curtain-less window. She found the shower, washed, dressed, and ran to the barn before her father woke, and guessed her uncle would be off working the ranch.

She crossed the grass along the round yard, pulled the stable doors open, and wiped the sweat already beading along her brow. It was going to be another scorcher.

Isais greeted her from the far arena where he and Ulysses were fighting over who was getting a bath. The mare and her foal weren't in view, but she could hear them prancing about the paddock.

She entered the stable her Uncle Al meant for her to clean, then leaned against the Iron Gate and soaked in the size of the task. She stretched out her foot and tapped a line of storage boxes towering above her head. A wall-to-wall mess of cardboard and junk.

"Hey, little miss!" Isais called, and Dorothy stuck her head around the gate. "Standin' around lookin' only makes the job bigger!"

Ulysses tossed his head and sprayed Isais, who stepped back and cursed good-naturedly. Dorothy laughed and slipped back inside. She sighed, braced herself, and worked.

She stacked the first few rows of boxes outside the stable doors. After a few hours and periodically throughout the day, her uncle and father would appear to transport Dorothy's stockpile from the stable to the garage, connected to the main house.

Afterwards, Al asked Peter to help with a few repairs along the perimeter of the property once the last of Dorothy's boxes had been stowed away.

He gave Peter a quick refresher on how to saddle a horse, mounted Ulysses and Sassy, and trotted from her view. Isais led the foal to the arena where he could keep an eye on her, then proceeded to clean the stalls.

Dorothy started in on another round of boxes, gradually uncovering a decrepit old dresser set along the left wall between 30 or so smaller boxes. She cleared a four-foot section in front of the dresser, tugged at two suitcases stuffed beneath the legs, and gave up when neither budged. She'd have to clear the next round of garbage off the top, she supposed, maybe ask Isais to lift the dang thing.

"That dresser was your father's when he was about your age," Isais commented. He handed Dorothy a glass of tea.

"He lived here?" Dorothy asked after pulling a long sip from the glass. Her body cooled and she licked her lips, suddenly realizing how overheated she had become. Isais handed her a clean dishrag.

"You need to drink more water, miss. Heat's like a rabid dog out here; it'll nip ya good."

"It's tea."

"Same thing," Isais replied. He kicked on a pair of fans at either end of the stable, which did little more than convey the hot, sticky air into the barn.

"Did Uncle Al make that too?" she nodded toward the dresser.

"I think his father may have. You want to look inside? I bet he still has lots of stuff in there."

Dorothy grinned. The thought of uncovering hidden treasures, *old* hidden treasures appealed to her. More importantly, she might see what her father had been like as a child. Was he a troublemaker? Had to be, right? No one grows up all normal, then pops the top on the nearest bottle once they spring into adulthood. Uncle Al said Mom was a spitfire. She thought it safe to assume her father was as well. Besides, she wanted a story, something embarrassing to hang over his head, like the ones grandparents told the grandkids, the funny, embarrassing stories which reduced mom and dad down to the humans they were. She never met her grandmother on his side of the family, so she never heard about his youth.

In Macon, her friends told stories of their parents doing gobs of drugs, or hiding frogs in their pockets, or getting sprayed by skunks and having to take tomato sauce baths. She'd asked her father for a few stories from his childhood, but he'd always replied with the same dismissive grunt. "Just your average, boring kid."

She turned to Isais; he nudged her, and she stepped away from the dresser, suddenly nervous.

"You do it!" she whispered and stepped behind his large frame. Isais pushed her forward. "Go on, dodo! Them boxes ain't gonna bite ya."

"I can't! I'll get in trouble!"

"Bah! I knew you was chicken. I'm going back to the horse poop, you're no fun."

Dorothy frowned and scratched her left collarbone, or *itch-n-twitch* as her mother used to tease. She dropped her hands to her side and approached the dresser.

Was it her nerves dancing like a spring chicken on a hot bed of coals? Was it Dad? She wasn't exactly sure why this potential porthole to her father's past made her so nervous. Might have something to do with the tinge of excitement prickling her insides, when she should be laying knees to tits in mourning. Still, a little dirt on dad might be just what the doctor ordered.

"Open it," Isais hissed. He leaned back and comically scanned both entrances, then motioned for Dorothy to continue. "Hurry, while no one's looking!"

"What if nothing's in it?"

"You going to find out by staring at it? You the wrong sex for x-ray vision, Superman! Use what you got!"

Dorothy stood motionless, then shifted her eyes about questioningly. Isais wiggled his fingers at her. She stomped her foot with resolution and turned her attention to the dresser.

She tugged once, again, then pulled at the top drawer. It wouldn't budge. She yanked at the other drawers in turn.

Isais pointed and roared with laughter. "I nailed it shut a year ago!"

Dorothy grunted and slapped his arm. "You're an ass!"

"Got you laughing though," Isais replied, then pointed to the boxes sitting on the dresser. "Those are your pop's. See what's in 'em."

Dorothy picked up the first, a faded shoebox covered with a child's doodling. She pulled the top open and sat on the dirt floor next to the dresser. Isais struggled to squeeze his frame in next to her, only managing by shifting her toward the back of the pen with a gentle backhand to her hip.

"That's your dad, I guess?" He asked as Dorothy raised a small stack of faded Polaroids and inspected the first: a small child, hair parted in the middle, dressed in cotton shorts and a striped t-shirt. She recognized Uncle Al's house in the background, though the paint seemed darker in the picture.

"I think so. Wow, he's so young."

"He wasn't much younger than you when he lived here, from what the Boss Man says, anyway. Your mom lived down the road, maybe a few miles."

Dorothy perked. "Could you show me?"

"Sure, I guess. You sure you want to walk around the neighborhood with a fat old Mexican at your side?"

"Better you than him," she muttered. If Isais heard, he said nothing.

Dorothy flipped through a few more pictures. She lifted another of her father, one where he stood next to another boy and a small girl. She wore her hair in pigtails and dressed in a knee-length skirt, topped with a cowboy hat. The boys, standing with their backs to each of her hips, held toy pistols in each hand.

"I think this is my mom."

"Man, that's an old one. Must be in the fifties. It's 1986 now, so that's…a hundred years ago, right?"

Dorothy shot Isais a look. He nudged her and chuckled, then pulled himself to his feet. "You keep looking, sweetheart. I need to get back to work. Let me know if you find anything interesting, okay?"

Dorothy agreed and placed the pictures back in the shoebox. She slogged through the next ten boxes, labeling their contents as she went. Old toys, rocks, and piles of pictures of her father and mother in their younger years. Her uncle had snuck into a few shots, too. She smiled happily, and a tear dropped onto the picture above her mother's shoulder. Dorothy ran a finger along the outline of her mother's cheek, then her own. It was as if she were looking in a mirror; seeing herself and her mother—as if the two were one.

"Wow, look at Dad," she whispered, noting the gleam in his eye, one she hasn't seen since he took the job at the mill, long before she entered middle school. She missed this version of her dad. She missed the teasing and playful banter—often directed at Mom—and boy, did that drive her crazy. Then there's the trips to the creek past old-man Langley's farm off State Road 44, just a few miles away from her old home. He'd teach her how to track game, fish, and cook from campfires built from nothing more than a few twigs and kindling. They were good times.

They had been inseparable their entire lives, her mom and dad, and Dorothy recalled days where her mother would sink in her seat, smile at her father, and say they were 'two peas in a pod' or 'horses of the same color'. Yet, somewhere and somehow they lost that magic spark, or time simply pushed them in opposite directions.

Dad's working days eventually drifted into the nightshift, and sometimes they didn't see her father at all. Even his time off created a myriad of problems for him, and if he didn't hit the bar after work, he'd soak up a six-pack before crashing on the couch. Dad slept there quite a bit, and barely moved off the thing during the weekends.

Mom struggled during those days. Dorothy recalled moments where she'd stare out of the kitchen window and whisper, "Come back to me, Pete." Dorothy didn't understand what was happening, not then. She watched as her father drifted slowly away, and her mother helplessly observed from whatever shore she stood upon. She felt her pain, and it coincided with her own. Together, Dorothy and her mother vowed to rebuild their family.

"We are the foundation, Dorothy. We are the strength, and we will hold this family together. You and I. Your father will see that one day, I promise you."

He never did.

Dorothy pulled a small wooden box off the dresser, one she had spotted earlier and had been planning to save for last. It looked too pretty to be a child's keepsake—what with its smooth grain finish and copper hinges. A treasure chest for sure. Maybe it was jewelry, she guessed, or something Dad had purchased for her mom years ago! She couldn't wait, not for this, not with such a mystery lingering. She placed the box in her lap and carefully opened the lid.

The key—or maybe not, the thing was hella-big for any door she had ever seen—was made of smooth pink glass. Along the stem, there was…some kind of writing, maybe? Very faint. The bow was smaller than her fist and the stem stretched the entire length of her hand. The front base of the key had to double the size of any lock she had ever come across, even those peepshow skeleton key numbers. She took the glass from the case and it weighed so heavy in her hand she needed both to hold it steady. She lifted it and peered through, marveling at the distorted orange-pink gate, boxes, and floor.

She decided this must have belonged to her mother. It was too pretty and pink to be her dad's. He was not a man who enjoyed a whole lot of color. Blue, black, or Johnny Cash black. So…her mother's, right? Dorothy returned the key to the box, leapt to her feet and ran to her room. She hadn't noticed the change in weight from key to box, nor how the box with the key inside weighed less than a feather.

The following three hours passed in a blur of hazed, transcendent thought.

Dorothy's mind slipped in and around visions of grand doors and a prince behind each. She like the idea of a nobleman falling hand over foot, just something so romantic about strange lands and royalty within, and the poor little farm girl sweeping him off his feet. Maybe it was the other way around.

She imagined—as the key-holder—she had been the focus of a royal courtship, where prospective suitors vied for her hand in marriage and a chance to hold her grand glass key. Good golly Ms. Molly, she sure could use a bit of pampering this week.

The afternoon settled into twilight, and the rustle of stable activity stirred Dorothy from her enchanted visions. She walked to the window and watched as her father, uncle, and Isais penned the horses. They each shouldered a few of the boxes Dorothy left outside of the barn, and headed for the garage.

Dorothy's father was smiling. His demeanor had changed, and she didn't like the way he was swaggering around like nothing was wrong. Two weeks didn't seem like enough time for him to start acting all normal.

She recalled the shoebox picture and frowned. Dad, even as a child, spent all his time with her mother. That was like, thirty-plus years together—maybe more, and double or triple her age. He must still be hurting. She should forgive him. But shouldn't he wear his sorrow like a badge? Did he earn the right to smile?

Dorothy slumped into her bed, opened the grain box, and pulled the key from its padding. Its weight doubled instantly; this time there was no not-noticing. She set the key on the comforter and ran her finger along the small, almost indiscernible nicks on the stem—and noted something odd. The key left no impression against the down comforter, even though she could barely hold it in a single hand. It felt like it weighed about ten pounds. She pressed a finger along the key's face and the cloth sank. She lifted the key, and the weight bore down in her hand so much she needed her other hand to keep the first from shaking. She raised the key, and dropped it to the bed. It landed as it should, even bounced on the comforter.

Dorothy pressed against the mattress and the key tilted toward her hand, then slid on top of her index finger. The glass seemed to push against her skin. She pulled her hand away, fearing and feeling as if it might cut her. The mattress snapped to its former shape and the key sat on top as if it were floating.

"What an odd little thing you are," Dorothy commented.

A knock at her door caused her to jump, and she painstakingly slid the key under her pillow. She winced and shook out a burn racing up the length of her arm.

"So weird…" Dorothy whispered, and then called, "Come in!" Her father entered, and she immediately sat up straight.

He sniffled and his mustache twitched. She guessed it was time for another uncomfortable conversation. Game on, little horsey, game on. She thought of her parents as children, the happy years between the sad, then vowed to bite her tongue.

"Missed you today, think you might have enjoyed it."

"Fixing fences? Oh, no-can-do, amigo," Dorothy replied.

Her father settled into the chair. Seemed a bit relieved if his twitching mustache had anything to say about it. "Well, maybe not the fence part. Riding those horses, I mean. Man, I tell ya, it's been a long while since I felt this good."

35

"A few weeks at least, right?" She averted her eyes guiltily and found herself staring at her pillow and the treasure beneath.

"Well...well yes, Dorothy, a few weeks would be about right. How long are we going to go on like this? I can only say how..."

She snapped her head and glared at him. "Don't!"

So much for the vow.

"Dorothy, sweetheart. It was an accident! I don't know what I can do."

"Can you bring her back? Can you turn back time? Can you put down the beer for once? And don't tell me you have, because I smell it!"

"Yeah, I had a drink! So what? That doesn't make me any less of a man, or any less your father!"

"Sure made you less of a husband though, didn't it?" Her words struck the air like a brick and she felt hot tears welling up. Her lip quivered and she met her father's red, watery eyes. He took a breath, held it, licked his lips, and stood. He paused for a moment, then moved to the door. He did not turn around.

"Honey bear, I know you are hurting. We both are. One day we are going to have to move past this and be..." he paused. "Be a family again!" He shook his head, turned, and closed the door.

Dorothy fell into her pillow and wept. She wrapped her hand around the key, pulled it to her chest, and murmured "I'm sorry" over and over. She realized with a sudden, odd gasp, that it wasn't her father she was apologizing to. Maybe it should have been, but deep in her gut she knew these tears were not meant for him. She cried because she was embarrassed. She cried because she wasn't the person she should have been when sitting so close to the glass key.

"What a weird thing to think," she whispered, closed her eyes, and slept.

Chapter 3

Dorothy and the Glass Key

Dorothy woke to an empty house the following morning. She sat up, panicked for a second when she couldn't find her key, then relaxed after she ran her hand across the smooth barrel resting beneath her pillow.

A white shirt and a pair of shorts sat on the foot of her bed, along with packaged underwear and tank tops. She inspected each, and though she might have preferred the cotton stirrups she had seen in the latest IN magazine, she supposed jean shorts and a white t-shirt with the words, CHOOSE LIFE, written in bold pink letters across the chest wasn't too bad. Probably more of a message from her father than a fashion statement.

Parents…go figure.

Dorothy dressed and practically hauled her key into the kitchen—fricking thing seemed like it gained five pounds overnight—and was pleasantly surprised to find a plate of sliced apples, oranges, and pears sitting beside a note that read, *Take it easy today, buttercup.* Dad must have bugged out after last night, and she was glad for it.

She poured a glass of juice, grabbed a fork, and nibbled on her breakfast, going after the pears first, then the apples, and two slices of orange. She looked down at her shirt and frowned.

Choose life. A day like today and only a few months ago, Dorothy would have begun her morning in a similar fashion. Mom would have prepared breakfast and Dad would've left for work over an hour ago. Dorothy would drag her boom box to the kitchen and drop in the latest mix tape that her friends had made for her. Wham! Had topped the latest cassette, and more often than not, both Dorothy and her mother would sing along, even dance if the mood struck them.

Looking back, those days were carefree and easy, though at the time the mounting problems of her early teen years had certainly seemed weighty. There had been boys to evaluate, fashions to accumulate, and piles of music she needed and didn't have the money for. Her mother and father did what they could to accommodate her, and she realized this now—but then, there was never enough. She wished she could thank her mother for all she had done, and the fact that she couldn't made her feel sick.

She shook off the thrum of sadness, not wanting to ruin the rest of the day, and turned her attention outside. The grass sparkled with dew, and glimmering droplets of condensation fell from the stable's planked roof. Isais popped into view from time to time, bustling about with sacks of grain or bales of hay.

She was disheartened to see Isais moving about on the far side of the stable. Dorothy had planned to continue her search through the stockpile of old boxes in her little pen project, and she wanted to pull a few pictures of her mother for keepsakes. She needed to be alone for this, well, mostly alone. Dorothy tapped her key and smiled.

Isais's proximity to the stable presented a problem. Dorothy wanted to bring her key with her, but the dang thing kept getting heavier and she could see no way to hide it from Isais. The glass key took a substantial—visible—effort to move it from one area to the next. Questions would arise, judgments made…she simply couldn't risk it.

The only way she could conceal the key was if she put it in its box. The feather-light box—with or without the key inside.

Dorothy poked the key with her fork. It moved effortlessly, as it normally should. She tried again with her finger and could scarcely nudge the key an inch across the table. The effort turned the skin under her fingernail white, and she had to rub out a slight numbness along the base of her palm. She propped a spoon under the key and slapped the handle against the table. The key launched into the air, flipped, and landed as if the item only weighed a few ounces. She picked it up again…anvil heavy.

Dorothy wondered if this should concern her. It was obvious this fantastical object reacted to her touch, but why was anyone's guess. She supposed she should be cautious, maybe even afraid. But she wasn't. The fricking thing was cool—*hella*-cool!

"I wonder if it does that with everyone?"

To find the answer, Dorothy would have to let somebody else hold the key, but she really didn't want to do that. This key was hers and hers alone, and she rather liked keeping it a secret. What if the key decided she was giving it away? She wouldn't have that, no-siree Bob-ski. Dorothy ran to her room, grabbed the box, and hefted the key inside. She headed for the stable whistling a modified version of *Careless Whisper* while tossing the box from her left hand to her right.

Isais met her at the stable and engaged in a bit of small talk. Dorothy kept her replies short and pointed. She wasn't trying to be rude, but she really felt to the need to shrug him off. She wanted some alone time sorting through things she'd come to think of as hers. Isais seemed to get the hint. You got to love the guy, he's got a sense, you know? Yesterday with the talking, today with the me time. Some people are just that way, and she was happy he was one of them.

When he stepped out, Dorothy pulled her key from the box and set it in her lap. It settled heavily, leaving an imprint in her exposed thigh. She slid the key so it rested on her denim shorts and sighed when the pressing weight lifted.

Over the course of about an hour, Dorothy presented several of her favorite pictures to the glass key and explained what her mother might have been doing at the time. Of the 50 or so Polaroids nested within six shoeboxes, only 24 pictures included her mother, and only seven where she had posed by herself. In one particular picture, her mother stood next to one of those awful grandma-type bicycles where the wheels were as tall as truck tires and the seat as large as a couch. She wore shorts above the knee and a blouse with ruffled sleeves. The wind must have been blowing hard that day, as her hair was suspended horizontally across her forehead and eyes. She wasn't smiling, but still, she was beautiful.

Something nudged her shoulder and Dorothy snapped about, ready to tear Isais a new one for scaring the crap out of her. The foal jumped backward and anxiously trotted into the arena. Dorothy jumped to her feet and chased after the filly foal while holding the glass key to her chest.

She ran to the doorway and stopped to catch her breath. The key bore her hand into her chest to the point where she could barely hang on to it.

"What is with you?" she asked, gripped tighter, suddenly stumbling beneath its weight. She dropped to her knees. Her arms burned something fierce and she leaned against the wall, hoping the angle might increase her leverage. She gasped for air as the key settled into her torso. Her ribs felt like the squealing coils of her bed, strained and ready to crack. She slid down the wall and trembled, wanting to scream but unable to pull in even the slightest drop of air. The lights above blurred into a halo of white haze, fading to gray, then black.

Her hands dropped helplessly to her sides, and she pulled in a deep, full breath. Thoughts fluttered into a dim gray cloud. Slowly, her mind cleared and refocused. She looked down her chin to see the glass key sitting innocently on her stomach, caught between folds in her t-shirt. "Whoa," she whispered. "Right. The skin. You'd think I'd know better by now."

The foal and its mother galloped to the far side of the arena and slipped behind two brick pillars linked by two diagonal planks. Dorothy reached under her shirt, wrapped her hands around the glass stem, and climbed to her feet. She ran outside and slowed when nearing the panicked horses.

"It's okay, I promise," Dorothy soothed and raised her right hand. "It's just the key gets heavy when I touch it, that's all, nothing to worry about. I'm okay, you're okay…"

Dorothy took a step and the mother reared, then slammed her hoof against the ground. Dorothy lifted the key buried in her shirt, and the horse repeated the warning.

"I get it, the key is wigging you out. I'm going to put it away, see?" She slid the key along her midsection, grabbed the cloth from the back of her shirt and worked the key into her pocket, hoping the same rules applied to her shorts. The bit pressed against the small of her back and pulled her down. She tucked her shirt in, straightened, and pressed the key deep into her pocket.

The mother and her foal vanished. Dorothy spun in a circle, thinking she would spot them by the house or any of the six paddocks surrounding the farm. Her mind clouded into a whirlwind. She couldn't tell where, or if she was standing. She reached for the column to her left and grasped at the air in its stead, falling to the ground against what felt like concrete. She yelped as skin pulled from her shoulder. She rolled and winced while warm blood trickled to her elbow. She pushed herself to her knees, swatted her pocket and ran her hand over the outlined stem. Still there, pressed tight against her rump.

Dorothy stood and stumbled backward. She wiped a mix of black soot and blood from a scrape stretching along her shoulder to the base of her elbow. Black soot, where she had just been standing on lush green grass. Beneath her feet and at least five feet in diameter was a charred circle cut into thick, overgrown greens which reminded Dorothy of something akin to hollowed bamboo. Wildflowers peeked above the knuckled shoots of grass. Tiny pink, purple, and red flowers set upon string-like stems appearing almost invisible, as if the petals were floating. She lifted her gaze. There were thousands of them, hovering from the edge of a vast forest on her right to another on her left.

Dorothy whirled about searching for some sign of familiar landscape.

The trees around her uncle's farm were a mix of oak, pine, and palm. They were tall for sure, though she gauged this always from a distance. She may not have lived there long, but she was smart enough to know what creepy crawlies lurked in the Florida wilds. A list which included a multitude of large spiders with extremely large webs.

The trees here were different. Bigger, and shaped like overgrown Christmas trees with needles the length of her arm, and tufts of frilly pink hair at its top. She glanced to the sky, a blue sky, thank God, but not the same color blue as home. She couldn't describe it exactly, maybe deeper? Like water color, all patchy with dark and light splotches haphazardly placed. She turned. No sun?

Dorothy pulled in a breath and found the air fragrant and fruity. She closed her eyes and felt a slight flush in her cheeks. Her fingertips tingled.

"Wow." She squatted on her heels and smiled. She wasn't sure what was in the air, but she wouldn't mind bottling it. It charged her with each breath. She felt faster, stronger, like The Bionic Woman.

"Okay, so, where the heck am I?"

Dorothy recalled the drive to her uncle's farm and the sunflower fields she imagined beyond the orange groves along the interstate. This field was like that, only better. This place was a dream.

She stood and scanned the surrounding forest. Looked like a whole lot of the same, so which direction she chose probably didn't matter. She took a step and jumped back when the wispy wildflowers parted to avoid her feet. She knelt in a fit of laughter and poked at a tiny, pink, clover-looking flower. It poked her back. She pushed her finger into a tiny pink rose, then a red daisy. Each sprang back at her with equal force.

Dorothy burst into laughter, sprinted toward the tree line, and yelled as loud as she could. She leaped into the air and hit the ground, laughing as wildflowers parted beneath her feet. She ran, pumping faster, leaping farther, and screaming louder. As she grew winded, she became energized. When she made it to the tree line, panting in a fit of ecstasy, she turned and roared into the field at the top of her lungs, raised her hands, and jumped!

A deep growl echoed in reply, and the air grew suddenly heavy and still. Dorothy's arms dropped to her sides. She turned toward the forest, instinctively crouched and listened. A grumble emanated from the dark hollows between the frilly-pines, followed by a clicking tut-tut-tut to her far right. Another to her left. Leaves rustled a few yards deep and directly in front of her. She took a step back and a low hissing sound froze her in her tracks. She whimpered.

Pssssst! Another hiss, and this one seemed close. Dorothy looked frantically around for a stick, a fallen branch, anything she could use as a weapon. There was nothing, only those quirky wildflowers and a key too dang heavy for its own good. She pulled in a breath, ready to scream for help.

A boy stepped into her view. He raised his hands, then brought a finger to his lips and shook his head. He pointed toward the forest, and then motioned for Dorothy to crouch low. Dorothy crawled toward him and mouthed a "thank you".

He wore a thick cap, kind of like a baseball cap but different, made from a brown denim, much like his shorts which extended past his knees. His cheeks were ruddy and freckled underneath a layer of dirt plastered over his pale skin. Small patches of blond hair escaped from his cap like shoots of corn silk, and he wore long, white socks pulled all the way up to his knees.

He said nothing, just motioned to the ground and waited. They heard another clicking, fainter this time, deeper in the woods. The boy abruptly stood, turned, and walked along the tree line as if nothing had ever happened. Dorothy watched the trees cautiously, then ran to catch up when another grunt startled her.

"Shhh, you'll just bring them back," the boy said. His accent was strong and foreign, like the television shows on the BBC, Monty Python, or Benny Hill.

"Are you British?" Dorothy whispered. He nodded.

"You're an American," he replied, then laughed softly. "You talk like a cowboy."

Dorothy considered this, unsure if she should be offended. She lived on a ranch and worked in a stable—well, kind of, it had only been a day. She wasn't exactly farm bred and corn fed, but she was born and raised in Macon, so southern by default. She shrugged and gave a little laugh in agreement.

"What was that?" Dorothy asked, looked over her shoulder to be sure nothing was following them.

"Don't know, I've never actually seen one." He turned and offered his hand. "Charles W. Cuthbert the Third, at your service," he stated proudly. Dorothy giggled, gripped his hand, and replied with equal vigor, "Dorothy Elaine Alston…the First, I think!"

"You know, you're the first person I've seen out here," Charlie said, then recommenced walking along the tree line. Dorothy glimpsed a reflection of white from his trousers and noticed a polished stem with a familiar looking bit poking out of his rear pants pocket.

"You have a key!" She exclaimed, reaching for her own, and then pausing as she remembered the weight.

Charlie stopped and whirled around. "You have one?" he asked, and Dorothy nodded enthusiastically. He stuck a finger through the hole and pulled it out for Dorothy to see.

The barrel, a trite shorter than Dorothy's, doubled hers in diameter. It looked like bone, only shinier, and the bit sat perpendicular to the bow, unlike Dorothy's key. Charlie spun the key around his finger a few times, then reinserted it into his pocket as if he was holstering a pistol. Dorothy turned so she could display her own without touching it. She lifted her shirt slightly and extended her rump to avoid pressing the key against her skin.

Charlie's eyes widened, cheeks colored, and he quickly turned.

"It's just up here," he blurted, and ran forward. Dorothy watched quizzically, then shrugged and chased after him.

He turned into a small clearing in the cut of the tree line. Dorothy ran to catch up, then stepped back in surprise. Charlie smiled.

"This is my home away from home." He hopped over to a thick, olive-drab tent erected between two giant frilly-pines. Three canteens rested against a peg to his right; lanterns, military helmets, and bullet casings to his left. Two wooden chests—*antiques,* Dorothy thought, sat alongside another pair of trees. The objects each rested in a small, charred circle like the one beneath her own feet when she'd first arrived.

"Wow, this is incredible. Did you find all of this?" she asked before inspecting the helmets. "This looks really old, I bet you could get a mint for it!"

"I could get more than a piece of candy, believe you me! My last helmet fetched me those lanterns above you." He pointed to a pair of oil lamps framed within a cross-hatched cage, each with an oversized iron handle hooked over a cut-nail in the bark of the tree. "They're really worth something at home," he said, ran to the chest, popped the top, and pulled out a thick, wool towel wrapped around another one of his treasures. "This is worth even more! I could get a whole uniform if I wanted!" Charlie carefully unwrapped the towel and revealed a stainless-steel Luger. He presented it to Dorothy. She thought she recognized the odd shape of the gun, noting the numerous times it appeared in her father's old war movies.

"Hey, it's a Luger, isn't it?" she asked. Charlie offered her the weapon with a smile. Dorothy aimed the gun at the trees behind the tent, then turned toward the woods where she'd met Charlie.

"Let those clackety-clack monsters near me now!" She sounded a few gunshots, bucking the gun as if firing it, then clumsily flipped the pistol from one hand to the next. "Is everything you own old?"

"It's not that old," replied Charlie, who then retrieved the pistol and returned it to the chest. He perked up suddenly. "Hey, I've got some candy, are you hungry? I always get hungry when I'm here."

He pulled something called a Marathon bar and a Baby Ruth from the trunk, presented them to Dorothy, who cringed, raising her hands to object. She didn't even know what a Marathon bar was, and the Baby Ruth…wow, how old was that thing? The wrapping looked like paper, and the wording—*Rich in dextrose!* (whatever the frig that meant)—seemed as out of place as, well, this whole freaking place. She crinkled her nose and warned Charlie he had better not eat it either.

He inspected the bar, smelled it, and shrugged. "I traded them yesterday, can't be all bad. It's from you Americans, isn't it?"

"I guess. But it looks kinda…I dunno, old."

"Old? Are you mad? This is perfectly good chocolate!" Charlie defended.

"Mad? Me? No, not at all! Sheesh don't freak-out! Just trying to help, you know."

"Huh?"

Dorothy sighed, raised her hands and shouted, "Freak! Wig out! Just take a pill man!"

She raised her hands to her lips, suddenly wary of the volume of her retort.

"It's all right, seems like they moved on," Charlie said, glancing at the trees. He walked back to the trunk and sat on it. Dorothy took a seat beside him.

"Sorry," she said. Charlie nudged her amiably.

"Can I see your key?" he asked.

"Sure. Could you hand me a towel or something?" Charlie nodded, slipped into his tent, and returned with a wool cloth. Dorothy gripped her key with the towel and handed both to Charlie. He picked up the key, flipped it about, then grabbed his own and set both down on the towel. They leaned forward simultaneously.

"Where do you think they're from?" Dorothy asked.

"No idea. I found mine while digging through Mrs. Caldwane's attic. That's our neighbor. I was looking for pieces of the doodlebug that hit her home last year."

"Doodlebug?"

"It's a flying bomb," he replied—a bit too casually. She figured he was fibbing.

"I found mine in a stable," Dorothy said.

Charlie eyed her with a teasing smile. "I knew you were a cowboy."

"Cow-girl," Dorothy corrected, then giggled. She leaned closer to Charlie, ever so slightly, and they inspected the keys again. Charlie lifted Dorothy's glass key without difficulty. She frowned, feeling almost betrayed. Why did the key like him and not her?

"Doesn't it feel heavy to you?" Dorothy asked. Charlie spun her key, flipped it up into the air and caught it. He shook his head.

"I can barely lift it," Dorothy slumped, and Charlie returned her key to the blanket. He smiled and tossed his ivory key to her.

"Try this one, it's as light as a feather!"

The bone struck above the collar of her shirt, at the top of her sternum. The blow was immediate and hard. Dorothy recoiled and collided with the trunk of the tree behind her. She bounced off the bark and onto the ground. She gasped, arched her back and grit her teeth, fighting off a mix of white flashing lights and a wave of dizziness.

Dorothy blinked as the pain subsided, seeing Charlie kneel over her, saying something in a panicked voice, though what he was saying hadn't quite hit the level of comprehension. She waited until the two versions of his face melded into one, then sat up carefully. Charlie rolled over onto his back, slapped his forehead, and thanked God repeatedly.

"Wow, that was freaky," she said.

"That was bloody terrifying!" Charlie looked Dorothy over, wide-eyed. He pointed below her neck. "That's going to leave a nasty bruise," he said. "I'm sorry, I didn't think I threw it hard!"

"Well, keep digging, Watson," Dorothy half-teased, rubbing her tender skin, then itch-and-twitching her collarbone. "I guess the keys just don't like me." She reached for Charlie's key lying in the scorched dirt beside her and found that she couldn't get her fingers under the barrel. Charlie leaned over, lifted the key, and returned it to the wool towel, then lifted the glass key.

"If I threw this at you, would it do the same?"

"Only if it touches my skin," Dorothy coughed.

Charlie lifted his chin, and chucked her key at his own neck. It bounced harmlessly into his lap. He shrugged, and returned it to the towel.

"Well, I guess when we are here, I can hold the keys," Charlie offered proudly.

"You're the Key-master!" Dorothy roared. "That makes me the Gatekeeper!" She thought the roles were reversed in the movie, but she couldn't help but feel pleased with the comparison. She turned toward the woods, then winced as a burn eradiated from her bruise. She frowned. "I hope those things out there aren't *Zuul.*"

"Who?"

"*Zuul*...you know, Ghostbusters? Don't you ever go to the movies?"

"Mum doesn't have money for the theater. Not after…" He drifted for a moment, looking at the sky, then the ground. She thought his eyes glistened a little bit and she turned away so he wouldn't be embarrassed.

"We should get going, it's going to be dark soon, and I don't like being here after dark. Besides, Mum will have dinner ready, and then she's got to go to work."

"You can leave…you know, here?" Dorothy asked, and perked, despite the pain under her chin.

"Of course. You think I live here?"

"I don't know," Dorothy replied. "It didn't occur to me until now."

"And that didn't scare you? Well, aren't you a brave one. I was about stainin' my trousers when I first got here." Charlie said. His eyes were wide, skin flushed, as if he was sincere and embarrassed at the same time. She found it cute.

"I guess I was scared," Dorothy lied. The clackety-clack monsters, or monkeys—or whatever they were—darting through the woods certainly gave her a scare, but now, sitting with Charlie in their little otherworldly camp, she felt quite comfortable.

Charlie asked her to stand and picked up her glass key. He pointed to the bit, turned her so she faced away from him, then paused.

"Promise you'll come see me tomorrow."

Dorothy smiled, and her cheeks warmed. "I will."

"The bit—that's the end of the key—up to come here, down to go home." His voice pitched a little as he said this. Dorothy bit her lower-lip, smitten over someone—anyone—paying this much attention to her.

"Close your eyes," he said, and she trembled. She felt the key slide down into her pocket.

She waited a few excruciating moments, opened her eyes, turned, hoping their lips might meet upon a chance proximity accident. She slumped and frowned a little.

The stables, the foal and her mother, even Ulysses stood in the surrounding paddocks.

She was back at the ranch.

Chapter 4
So, Doctor, Give Me the News

"So, you're saying Dorothy believed she transported herself to...what? Another dimension?" Ellen asked. She mentally summarized Dorothy's case: kid has an alcoholic father, loses her mother, home, and all her belongings in a fire. That'd be hell on any adult; God only knows what a child's mind might concoct after such an episode.

Ellen had been pacing behind Mr. Dutta as he told the story. She stopped now, and turned toward the comatose girl, full of pity. What an awful ending to a tragic story.

"You know, I think we could both use some coffee. Or tea, I do prefer tea," Mr. Dutta stated, flat out ignoring her question.

"You mean I'm not locked in here?"

He confidently shook his head and motioned to the door. "If you are not interested in Dorothy's past at this point, I am not sure you will ever be. Just tap on the door, I've two men posted outside, and they will see to your needs."

"Still a prisoner then."

"You can leave at any time. My men are here for me, and to see that we are not disturbed."

When she didn't move, Mr. Dutta strode past Ellen, opened the door, and spoke quietly to the men outside. He returned to the stool at the window and Ellen looked at him expectantly.

"Did Dorothy return to Charlie the next day?"

"Oh yes! And many days following. And this was both wonderful and tragic. You see, as her bond with Charlie grew, her love for her father faded. I don't think she knew this at the time. Love—new love—has a way of sheltering a person from the world, or worlds in this case. Charlie had lost his father, and Dorothy her mother. Both felt as if the world was crashing down around them. But they had an escape in each other."

Ellen understood this to a degree. Children can, in extreme traumatic situations, regress into their own imagination, often inventing playmates or guardians who relate to their woes. Sometimes this can be healthy, others…

"How did her father respond?"

"Not well, I'm afraid. Guilt is a cancerous monster, Ms. Steward. It does not allow forgiveness; it does not allow a person to see anything other than their own remorse. So rather than addressing his daughter's turmoil after her mother's death, he turned to the bottle.

"Dorothy's father drank; her uncle tirelessly worked. Isais was sympathetic but remained neutral when it came to the dealings over Dorothy's past. These were all the ingredients she needed to slowly abandon one life for the next." He turned at the sound of a gentle knock at the door. "Ah, tea time!" He clasped his hands together, then dragged the stools back over to the bar as a heavyset man dressed in a dark suit, white shirt and, go figure, a maroon tie, entered carrying a silver tray. Who was this guy? India's version of the Godfather?

While Ragesha's man poured tea into two Styrofoam cups, Ellen circled Dorothy and knelt before her. She pressed her hand against Dorothy's wrist, searching her eyes, hoping there might be a small piece of her still hiding within. Could she have regressed so deeply into her mind that she simply could not find her way out? If so, then what? God, she wished she had a cat scan or MRI to look at.

Dorothy blinked, and Ellen's skin rolled with gooseflesh. "Where are you?" she whispered. "What world have you lost yourself in?"

"Join me, Ellen. You must be hungry."

Ellen pushed Dorothy's frizzed hair behind her ear. She had hoped the girl might blink again, or follow her movements, even if only for a fleeting moment.

"I took the liberty of ordering a few sandwiches from the hospital's menu. Ham, turkey, roast beef, and one with all three. There is coffee, orange pekoe tea, and water of course." He smiled.

"You're not eating?" Ellen asked. Mr. Dutta shook his head, lifted a cup of black tea and sipped.

Ellen picked up a turkey sandwich, took a bite and set the halved piece back on the plate. "So, when do you come into all of this?"

Chapter 5
Ragsy

School was two weeks away. New clothes appeared almost daily now, and Dorothy's father seemed to have acquired some small sense of taste. She had four pairs of cotton leggings, fashion-worthy shirts and shorts, the works. When she returned from yesterday's visit with Charlie, a backpack was waiting at the foot of her bed next to a pair of ivory-white flat-top Adidas. Nice.

Her father had picked up a night job, worked around the farm during the day, and drank himself into a stupor when in between. She didn't ask what the new job was, and he didn't tell her. She thanked him for the clothes, and that was that.

Upon returning from Charlie's World—she didn't know what else to call it—she'd eat and sleep. She didn't see much of her father and didn't really mind. As long as he provided. Little of her home world—except for the foal—mattered to Dorothy. Leaving mattered. Charlie's opinion mattered. His wide-eyed reactions to her cutoff jean shorts mattered. He mattered.

Though puzzling, Dorothy found Charlie's curiosity about her clothes simply adorable. The feel and look of her shirts and pants amazed him, often inquiring about brand names and why the band members depicted on her concert tees dressed so scantily.

She wasn't sure what he meant exactly; they looked normal to her, but he was from England, and therefore strange.

She had questions of her own about the odd clothes he wore. Why were they so thick? What were they made of? And what was with all the wool? At first, she thought it to be a British thing. Her father used to say those "Brits were behind the times". Now she wasn't so sure. Today seemed like as good a day as any to ask, so she wrapped the glass key in one of Charlie's towels, dropped a bunch of fruit into her backpack, and ran out the front door.

Uncle Al and Isais waved, she waved back, slipped into the stable where she offered Alice the foal—now rightfully named— the first of three apples.

"I'm off to the rabbit hole," she whispered. Alice nudged her. Dorothy offered the second apple to Alice's mother, then tossed the third to Ulysses and flipped him the bird. The bite marks from her last feeding still ached, and she wasn't about to offer the grumpy old monster-goat a second helping of her palm.

She sauntered over to her uncle and Isais who were busy replacing posts along the arena.

"Little miss, off to the woods again?" Isais asked.

"You're not hanging around the lake, are ya Dorothy? Gotta stay away from the lakes around here. There are…"

"Alligators everywhere," Dorothy finished. "I don't go near the lake, Uncle Al."

Isais heaved a long four by four from the bed of Al's pickup and set the beam into a hole Al had dug into the sandy earth, then paused, wiping sweat from his forehead.

"Grab a bag of concrete, would you Isais?" Al asked. He dropped three full blades of dirt into the hole and set a two-foot hand level against the post.

"No more boss, you used too much on the last post." Isais replied and nudged Dorothy. She rolled her eyes.

"I'm going to jet; you guys look busy." She turned and marched away from the tirade her uncle would soon unleash upon Isais.

After a short walk on a curved footpath through fields of sticky sandspurs, she stood in the center of a new charred circle. Dorothy unwrapped her key and slid the butt end into her jeans pocket, then closed her eyes.

She blinked, and there was Charlie.

"Did you bring the oranges?" he asked. He pulled her key from her pocket, walked to the center of the camp, and set it on top of the trunk next to his.

"Of course," she replied, and tossed him an orange. He peeled it part way and bit into its center. Juice ran down his chin and he laughed, then put the rind in his mouth like a boxer's mouthpiece. He growled. Dorothy rolled her eyes, but she couldn't keep from smiling.

"What about you? Did you bring…"

Charlie handed her a cloth satchel wrapped in a red ribbon. She unraveled the ribbon, peeled back thick cotton wrapping revealing a crumpet covered in strawberry jam. She bit into it. Wow.

After breakfast, Dorothy looked about, and, after realizing she was the only one with a lick of taste in this camp, this *entire world,* would therefore redecorate their drab home away from home. Charlie objected, citing ownership. "My camp, my rules." Dorothy dropped to the floor, and sulked.

"Men are sensitive little weasels my dear, and the one thing they cannot stand is to see a miserable woman. This is how we test them. Remember this, Dorothy, it's called a lesson of the heart. If a man cannot bend to your emotional desires, he's not a man worth having at all." Mom's wisdom, and it certainly worked.

Charlie caved quickly, all things considered, and they discussed how they would, or rather could, liven up the campsite. She considered the pom-pom pink approach, even had an idea where she could purchase such bright oddities like end tables, lamps and the like. She chose against it. Two reasons: First, she didn't want Charlie to feel uncomfortable. He was a good friend; a tolerant friend and if pressed, he'd settle on whatever Dorothy suggested. Not much of a challenge and certainly no fun.

Second, she wouldn't say she hated the color pink, yet, outside of blush and eye shadow, it held little appeal to her. Pranking Charlie with carnival colored furniture would be fine for a while, and the two had shared many jokes over the past few weeks, but in the end she'd hate it as much as he would. Besides, it didn't fit. Nothing of color seemed to blend here, only contrast. So, she shelved the contemporary glamorous concepts and set her sights on creature comforts.

She couldn't think of anything to bring, at least anything her uncle wouldn't miss, and explained how she'd lost everything during the fire. Charlie understood, citing his own troubled times, though there was enough debris laying about that he'd been able to swipe a couple of chairs, and thought he might even grab a table. He decided he wasn't comfortable pulling something so big with him. He didn't explain why. The chairs were what led to Dorothy's next question.

She squatted next to one of them. Three angry holes in the seatback sure looked like bullet holes to her. Nicks on the legs, and deep scores of charred wood stretched across the seat like aged scars. It didn't take much of a detective to see these marks weren't from regular wear and tear.

"Charlie, what year is it?"

"I thought we agreed it was year 100. I like year one better, but I guess you have to have a zero or two to make it official. Have you come up with a name yet? Charlie's World feels funny to me."

"No, I mean what year is it where you are from?" Dorothy asked.

"You said we shouldn't talk about home."

"Yeah, but now I kind of want to know."

"Well then, it's 1946. Do you want to know what town I am from?" Dorothy nodded. "Lewisham, just outside of London," said Charlie.

He's fourteen in 1946. God, she wished she had paid more attention in Social Studies. Something had happened over there, more than just the war. What was it called? A blitz-freeze? Bliz-creed? Only blitz she knew anything about had something to do with football.

"Those doodlebugs you mentioned, they were German bombs?"

Charlie lowered his head and nodded. "Flying bombs."

"Oh, you mean missiles," Dorothy murmured. He looked up. "Never mind. You come here to escape, don't you? Whatever is left there, you're running from it."

"Isn't that what you're doing from your time?" Charlie asked.

"You knew?" she asked, and Charlie pointed to her Walkman cassette player and headphones. "Oh, right. I guess you wouldn't have these in your time, would you?"

"We don't have much of anything, honestly. Mum's always working, but…that's just the way it is, I suppose. She did say you Americans were helping us with money now that the war is over, so thanks for that. Do…do things get better for us?"

"You mean for England?" She thought for a moment. She honestly didn't have a clue. Heck, she wasn't sure she could point to England on a map. Somewhere near a boot by the water? She decided things must be okay or she would've heard *something* about it. "Sure, I guess. I mean, y'all put out some hella-cool bands! Ozzy Osbourne, Tears for Fears, and my dad always listens to the Beatles. They were slamming back in the day! So, can't be all bad, right?"

Charlie stared at her blankly. "They were really popular," Dorothy amended. "Do you think there are any other keys out there?" she asked, quickly changing the subject. Charlie shrugged, picked up both keys and sat, placing each in his lap. He lifted Dorothy's glass key to the sky and commented on the hue of purple shining through what had normally been a lightly colored pink.

"I don't know." He closed one eye and spun the key in all sorts of directions. "I did wonder though, since my key is perpendi…per…crooked, and yours is straight, on what would happen if…"

He placed her key on top of his, and when the bits met, he vanished. Dorothy yelped, but before she could move or even think, Charlie reappeared.

"Together. Maybe it makes…" he pressed his key on top of hers and disappeared again. Dorothy stared, bug-eyed.

"Type of key," Charlie re-materialized. "See look…" Gone again.

"Charlie—" Dorothy began, but there he went again.

"Of fits like this, even like this. If I…"

"Oh, for crying out loud!" Dorothy dropped her head into her hands.

"Not as well…"

"CHARLIE!" she hollered, and he turned to her, wide eyed. "Do it again, but look at me. Don't—"

He touched the keys together, vanished, reappeared, leaped away, and fell into his tent. Dorothy laughed.

"What did it look like?" she asked.

"I don't know, you disappeared and I…"

"Freaked out?" she finished, and he nodded excitedly.

"Shall I do it again?"

"I want to see too!" Dorothy whined and dropped next to the keys. She reached for hers, then paused. "I guess I can't do it, can I?"

"I can," Charlie replied.

"Yeah, but…"

"No, I mean, maybe if we hold hands, we could go together?"

"Why Charlie Cuthbert, are you flirting with me?" Dorothy teased in an exaggerated southern accent. His face turned bright hot red and he raised his hands in protest. Dorothy smiled and took his hand. She felt the heat racing to her own cheeks then, but didn't mind it.

"I'm kidding, Charlie. Together, just like always."

The color drained into a few red splotches on Charlie's cheeks. His palms were damp and she could feel his pulse racing. They interlocked their fingers, and he lowered Dorothy's key onto his.

There had been no rush or light-headedness, only a sudden shift of scenery from the oversized wooded areas of Charlie's World, to the stunted landscape of this new one. Dorothy stood and peered over at a canopy of wide-trunked trees with tear-shaped leaves, some the size of her head. Vines drooped from the branches and were laden with small orange fruits hanging just inches from the ground. They looked like tiny pumpkins hovering over a field of ankle-high bluish grass. Dorothy knelt and brushed her fingers along a blade twice the width of her finger. Unlike the purple, red and yellow wildflowers of Charlie's World, these offered little diversity in the drab, near-colorless backdrop. Even the sky appeared faded, like a pair of old, worn jeans.

"Can I have my hand back?" Charlie whispered. Dorothy blushed and quickly dropped his hand.

"Look at the sky," she pointed, "it's almost the same color as the grass."

Charlie's eyes wandered over the horizon and down to their feet. He tapped Dorothy's shoulder, then pointed to her shoes. A few strands of the blue-grass around the perimeter of the charred circle had turned the same brilliant white as her new Adidas. Dorothy hopped away. Within a few moments, the color faded into the blue-green of the sky.

"Chameleon grass and pumpkin trees. Sure, why not? Makes sense," she said, and pointed to the dwarf bonsais-looking trees framing a field nearly half the size of Charlie's world.

"What's next, Lilliputians?" he asked and guffawed at his own joke. Dorothy raised a brow, and he nearly choked on his own laughter.

"Don't you people of the eighties read?"

"I've got a whole stack of Teen Beat and Bop mags, if you must know. Now be quiet for a sec. I want to know if there are any of those clackety-clacks lurking in the trees."

"We could probably just kick them if there are, doesn't look like anything big would live here," Charlie commented, tapped Dorothy, and pointed to her right. She could see fireflies off in the distance blinking about, on and off. The colors varied; some were a brilliant blood red, others the common green she was used to, and others seemed almost purple. They pulsed wicked-bright.

A flash of white caused Dorothy to jump behind Charlie. She wasn't sure what she saw, if anything at all. It blew by so quickly she might have imagined it, if not for the accompanying thwap. Charlie turned, and she pointed toward the nearest set of trees sitting a few dozen yards away. They inched closer.

Thwap-thwap-thwap!

Dorothy slipped behind Charlie and gripped his shoulders. He looked at her, raised the combined keys in his hand, and quietly simulated a separation. She nodded, then dug under his linen shirt and wrapped her hands around his waist, momentarily smitten.

Another snap from the tree line pulled her back to reality.

Dorothy shook him and pointed once they covered half the distance to the fat Bonsai-trees. They dropped to their heels and listened. A faint rattle, and then another thwap. He looked to her, and she wiggled her hand while extending her arm.

Charlie mouthed, "A fish?"

She shook her head, and whispered, "Snake!"

Charlie's eyes widened. He placed his free hand on top of Dorothy's glass key.

They paced to a dozen or so feet from the nearest set of dwarf trees before Charlie stopped and knelt. The grass turned to a drab brownish color—a good match for Charlie's pants—and faded into green, before turning white, matching her sneakers, creating an oddly blended circle around them. She knelt beside him. Charlie touched her cheek, then pointed to a nearby 'pumpkin' tree. She flushed, and her hand rushed to her cheek, where his had been. She dropped her hand to her side when she spotted what Charlie was looking at.

A fist-sized, pulsating bubble sat along the midsection of a nearby trunk, milky white, and with a string-thin thorn poking out of its center. The thing wobbled, then suddenly shot into an adjacent tree, slapping flat against the bark. Two large black dots appeared, scanned about, then vanished as the creature's body puffed out again into its rounded, dot-candy shape.

Charlie dropped his hands, stood, and laughed. "That's the neatest thing I've ever seen!"

She gripped both his shoulders as he tried to move toward it. "Are you insane?" What is it about boys and insects?

"It's just a bug," he said. "A really neat looking bug! Come on!" He inched closer, plucked a long blade of grass, and poked at the thing.

"Charlie don't!" Dorothy pleaded. He giggled when the two googly black eyes reappeared, circled, and settled on him.

"It's cute! Come and see," he shouted, but as he turned back, the thorn lashed out and struck him in the chest. He lurched backward into the grass, writhing, screaming in agony. Dorothy gave a little yelp and ran to his side.

"Get it out, get it out!" He raised his arms, balling his hands to fists while arching his back. The white blob sat against his vest, stretched along his midsection into a hole ripped in his shirt just below the ribcage. A small trickle of blood appeared below the wound, then vanished when the blob pulsed. It was drinking his blood!

The two beady black eyes reappeared and settled upon Dorothy. She gasped, grabbed the keys—hoping she could separate them—fell forward under the weight and collapsed onto Charlie's chest. Her hands thrust into the creature's jelly-white body and it erupted like a water-balloon, splattering milky goo over her hands, arms, and face.

She slid her fingers away from the keys with tremendous effort, and Charlie drew in a hard, deep breath. He rolled, coughed, and curled into a tight ball, both keys firmly gripped in his right hand. Dorothy wailed his name and frantically rolled his body. She patted about his chest and shoulders, unable to see through the haze of tears clouding her vision. She gave up, sank into his lap, and cried.

A gentle hand pulled her away. She turned, alarmed, and found herself face to face with a thin dark-skinned boy, a wild mop of black hair covering his eyes and forehead. He wore a stained white tank top over grimy green shorts, and thong sandals.

"I need to check him. Quickly, please." Dorothy backed away, dazed. The boy leaned over Charlie, and Dorothy spotted the dual-pronged bit sticking out of the back of his shorts pocket. A wave of relief passed over her—a key meant a kid, just like the two of them—and she watched as the boy tore open Charlie's shirt to look at the wound. "It's good, only a little stinger. That means it was one of the smaller ones. He should be all right," the boy said, pulling a knife from his pocket.

Dorothy lunged at him and frantically reached for the blade, but he shoved her to the ground, gave her a hard look, then turned back to Charlie. A golf ball-sized boil had formed where the blob had struck Charlie's chest and it oozed a clear liquid around the embedded stinger. "They are poisonous," the boy said calmly, "but not deadly if you get to it in time. We have to cut the stinger out, but only a little. I need your help."

Dorothy tried to gather her wits, but the tears kept coming. She peered into the stranger's dark eyes. He touched her shoulder. "It's going to be fine. Please, hold his shoulders. I'm just going to poke a hole around the stinger. It's got a hook," he said. She slid to Charlie's side and rested a knee on one shoulder, leaning over and pinning the other with both hands. The boy pressed the tip of the knife against the wound.

"Wait!" Dorothy yelled. "The keys! He'll drop them, and we'll both vanish to who knows where!"

"Well, pick them up."

"I can't, if I touch them…it'll be bad. Trust me. You grab the keys. Give me the knife."

He paused for half a beat, then handed her the knife and pulled the keys from Charlie's hand. "Keep them together," Dorothy instructed. He nodded, raised the keys to his chest and positioned his knees over Charlie's shoulders. He moaned and vacantly looked about, then haplessly focused on the boy. "Things are getting dark," Charlie moaned. "You look funny."

"I'm over here. Hold still." Dorothy slid the knife under the thorn embedded in Charlie's chest. She drew a breath, pressed the blade into his skin, and pulled the thorn.

Liquid oozed from the wound and stained his shirt yellow. She winced and sneered, then covered her nose. Thing smelled like a rotten egg.

"Good job. Do you remember which tree the worm came from?" the boy asked. Dorothy nodded. "Good. Shouldn't be another near that one, so go to the tree and cut the fruit at the stem. Don't pull it!"

She stood, scanned for the tree, and did as he told her. She cut the fruit above what looked to be fern-green colored braid. She let loose the vine and turned, then did a double-take to confirm what she thought she saw. The vine fell upward into the sky, snapped, bounced, and straightened, as if gravity had reversed itself. She looked again at her catch, and discovered it was no fruit at all. It felt like the skin within the rind of an orange, as if made of wet paper. She knelt beside Charlie and the new boy.

"Cut a slit along the side, then place it over his mouth. It will counteract the poison," he instructed.

Dorothy ran the knife through easily, and placed the pumpkin-bag fruit—or, well, whatever it was—around his mouth and nose. Charlie drew a breath and the bag flattened. He coughed.

His eyes grew brighter, and he smiled wide. "Hello, pretty lady," he said distantly, looked at his hand and giggled. "I've got four hands! That is so melba-cool."

Dorothy inspected the bag, grimaced, and tossed it over her shoulder. The boy leaned back and sighed. "He'll be all right."

Dorothy wiped her eyes. She hadn't realized how much one little, innocent act could go so wrong. Other than the clackety-clack tree monsters, which they never saw anyway, the place seemed like paradise. She never expected anything like this could happen to either of them.

"He'll be okay, I promise. He is just a bit fruit-drunk," he assured her. Dorothy nodded.

"Thanks. I'm Dorothy, by the way. And he's Charlie."

"My name is Ragesha, Ragesha Dutta," he replied, adding, "You have keys, too, I see." Ragesha looked around for a place to set the keys down. Seeing nothing, he lifted the bottom of his stained tank-top, ripped a thin band off the bottom, and tied the keys together. He looked to Dorothy for approval. She shrugged, and closed her eyes.

"Heck of an idea, chum," Charlie complimented, and swatted at Ragesha.

"Rest Charlie," Dorothy soothed, and he dropped his head to the ground, turned, and poked absently at the peach-colored grass next to his head, then toward his chest, where it blended to brown, matching his vest.

"Do you have a campsite or something?" Dorothy asked. Ragesha thumbed over his shoulder. "Good, help me with him. I don't want to be around if another one of those milk-bugs slaps by."

Ragesha agreed, and together they pulled Charlie to his feet. He smiled. "You're like a princess," he said. "A really tan princess." A little spittle hit his chin and dribbled down to his chest.

"Over here, Charlie," Dorothy groaned, amused. He turned with wide eyes, looked back at Ragesha, then to Dorothy. "You're much prettier than your twin," he said.

She rolled her eyes. "Yeah, thanks."

It took a good hour to drag-carry Charlie to Ragesha's camp, and upon arrival, Dorothy discovered that it held a great many similarities to their own. He had constructed a tent, pegged to a tree and made from patches of ragged cloth. A heap of baskets and burlap bags sat a few yards away from the tree line. She could certainly understand that. The deflated sacs of three pumpkin-fruits had been discarded on her left. The entire campground sat on the same, black-charred earth as their campground, though his was noticeably bigger.

Charlie had recovered most of his wits by the time they reached camp, and when Ragesha and Dorothy sat him down, he managed to stay upright on his own. He and Ragesha exchanged introductions.

"I guess all these places have little quirks about them," Charlie noted. He pressed his shirt against his wound, winced and sighed. "How did you know the pumpkins would do that?"

"I've been coming here for some time. There's not a lot of food back home, I just wanted to see if I could eat these. They looked like pumpkins, so I tried them. Found out what the gas does," he smiled at Charlie, "by accident." He stretched his hand out for a high-five. Charlie slapped it and pointed. Dorothy slumped, and shook her head.

"I couldn't eat them, obviously. So, I wandered into the woods hoping to find something like a stream, or a different kind of fruit. One of those white bugs stung me. Didn't bother me at all," he said, then pulled his knees to his chest. "A few days later, another hit me, just like it did you." Ragesha pulled the front of his shirt up and pointed to red puncture above his stomach. "When I started feeling woozy, I put one and one together."

Over the next few hours, they swapped stories from their different homes and times. Dorothy noted how well the boys seemed to hit things off, and after a while, she resented the feeling of being outnumbered. All things considered though, she guessed two boys would be better than two competing girls. Charlie asked, "Did you find any water or food?" Ragesha shook his head.

"We have to bring food from home too," Dorothy added. "You're Indian, right? Where did you learn English? You speak it very well."

"But, I don't! I was about to ask you how you knew Bengali," he replied.

"We don't," Dorothy said. Charlie nodded in agreement.

"That is so...weird," Charlie mused, then suddenly sat up.

"Are you from Dorothy's time? What year is it? I live in 1946, and Dorothy in 1986."

"1966 for me. You're American, and you're British?" he asked. Both children nodded. "How did you get here? My key only takes me to this one spot."

"My key took me to Charlie's. We just put them together, and whammo! Here we are."

Ragesha looked at Charlie, questioningly. "She talks funny." Charlie nodded.

"Hey! Can I see your key?" Charlie asked. Ragesha pulled the key and set it on the ground.

"Is it stone?" Dorothy asked, peered at the ragged surface of the bit and stem. It about split the difference between Charlie's and Dorothy's keys, size-wise, and looked like it was carved out of rock.

"Yeah, I guess," he said, picking up the key, and motioning as if he was going to toss it to Dorothy. Dorothy yelled and lurched backward, Charlie vaulted between them. Ragesha jumped to his feet. "What'd I do?"

"It's all right, they just hurt her for some reason. She can't touch them."

"Even her own?" Ragesha asked.

"I have to wrap it in a cloth or something."

"Do you know why?" Ragesha asked, his tone dropping considerably. She shook her head, then motioned him over, displayed her index finger to him, and hovered it over his key.

He nodded, and she tapped the bit.

The weight difference was immediate and overpowering. Ragesha struggled, lost his grip and the key crashed into the ground with a sharp thud, then settled into its previous state. Ragesha looked at Charlie, who said, "You can pick it up now, only lasts while it touches her skin."

"That's incredible," said Ragesha.

"For you maybe, freakin' sucks the big one for me." Dorothy exclaimed, shamelessly pouting.

Ragesha again turned to Charlie. "She means…" Charlie began, and Ragesha cut him off.

"No, I get it. I was wondering, do people really talk like that in the future?" Dorothy raised a brow. "Like what? Like me? Of course they do!" she snorted.

"You said that you went into the woods?" Charlie asked, quickly changing the subject. Ragesha nodded. "Did you make it through? What did you see?"

Ragesha pointed to the tree line on the opposite side of the field, then thumbed over his shoulder. "I entered there, and came out here."

Dorothy laughed. "You went in a big circle? You dummy!"

Ragesha, solemnly, shook his head. "No, I did not. I went in there—he pointed across the field—and wound up here. Twice."

"Well…" Dorothy began, stood, and looked both areas over. She guessed that the diameter of this field was a football field's length, at least. She could see beyond the initial tree line—she stood taller than most of the big-leafed bonsais—and didn't see the horizon. He must have gotten turned around somewhere and circled the field, right? It was the only thing that made sense.

"How long did it take you?" Charlie asked.

"I'll show you," Ragesha replied. He walked past his tent, and though Dorothy couldn't see him, she heard the snap of his pocket knife and guessed what he was doing.

A vine fell upward, snapped, and rested, suspended above the tree. Charlie gasped.

A few minutes passed, and Ragesha hollered from the opposite tree line, jumping up and down. Another ten and he emerged behind the tent. He sat, tossed the pumpkin sack to the side, and Dorothy watched as it drifted slowly to the ground like a balloon with a small leak. Charlie and Dorothy stared at him.

"Whoa. Do you think Charlie's World is the same?" Dorothy asked.

"You named the field after yourself?" asked Ragesha. Charlie shook his head and cocked a thumb toward Dorothy.

"Ah," Ragesha said, as if this answered all the questions in the world.

"What's that supposed to mean?" Dorothy asked. The boys eyed each other and then fell over backwards, laughing.

"It's where I found him, the name is just sensible," Dorothy defended herself. She felt a hot anger welling in her gut.

"Hey," Charlie said while catching his breath, "have you figured out what year it is here?"

Ragesha thought for a moment. "Well, I just arrived a few weeks ago, so I'd have to say year one…right?"

Charlie nodded to Dorothy, "Year 100 for us."

"Well, you can't just say it's 100. That's silly."

"I can say whatever freaking year I want! And if you don't like it, you can shove it right up your old wazoo and make it whatever year you want, Charlie!" Dorothy rose to her feet and stomped off toward the center of the field. She had to, she was boiling mad, and it was either walk away or slap him. She might still, if he said year one…

"Hey, Dorothy! We can call it 'year of the temper tantrum' if you like!" Charlie shouted, followed by a loud slap. He high-fived the twerp!

Dorothy balled her fists. The boys froze and glanced at each other, then scrunched together so their shoulders touched. She stormed back to Charlie, breathing heavy, fuming over the teasing this red-hot lame narbo—that's 'dork' for these two idiots—and his new dweeb-o-rama buddy had decided to lay on her. She turned to Ragesha and demanded to see his key. He presented it to her, and Dorothy pressed her fingers against the bit and pushed him to the ground. She held her hand lightly against the stone, keeping the weight on him.

"Now say you're sorry!" Ragesha pushed against the stone key, but the weight was too much. He whined an apology, and Dorothy backed off.

"Now, you two listen and you listen good. When we are here, together, it's the three of us. Three freaking Musketeers, got it? You two dweebs want to play best buddies, you do it alone!" Dorothy pointed at each of them, and asked if they understood.

They nodded, and snapped to attention.

"Okay then, here's is what we are going to do. Charlie and I are going home, and you, *Rag*-sy, you are going home as well. We are going to meet here tomorrow, same bat-time." The boys raised their eyebrows but dared not interrupt. "And, we are going to run some tests on these keys of ours. I will tell you right now, Ragesha, I don't like your world. I don't like your milk-bugs, and I don't like you!"

Dorothy steadied herself, took a breath, closed her eyes and added, "But I am willing to give you a chance to make it up to me. Tomorrow, you're both going to be perfect gentlemen. That means doors open, yes ma'am and no ma'am, all the things we ladies expect from you rude knock-ups. No teasing, no more little-boy prep-tard antics!"

"There are no doors out he…"

"I said gentlemen, and I mean gentlemen," Dorothy interrupted. "Charlie, pick up our keys and send us home. I don't want to hear any lip from you, either. If I do, I'll pluck one of those milk-bugs off the nearest tree and stuff it up your nose!"

Charlie gave Ragesha a half-wave, looking a little sheepish. He picked up the keys and untied the string. Dorothy turned, folded her arms, and waited. Charlie pulled the keys apart, and they snapped into Charlie's World. Then, a whirl of dizziness, and she was home, key stuffed in her back pocket, bit pointing down. The sun had recently ducked behind the barn and shadows stretched for miles. She could hear Ulysses neighing about his paddock, and Isais trying to coax him into the stable.

She took a breath, and made for the house, pulling the anger she felt and redirecting it toward her father. God help him, if he said anything but 'goodnight'. She slipped into the barn, wrapped her key in a rag hidden behind a washing tub near a hose on the wall, and returned it to its box on the shelf above.

Chapter 6
The Divine Test and an Open Door

Dorothy's father wasn't home, and she was glad for it. By the time she walked into the kitchen, sat at the island where he'd left her supper—now cold—she was spent. It was a crap-tastic day, finally at an end.

Her uncle hadn't said much. "Hey-ya kiddo," was about the extent of it, though he did eye her a bit more than she cared for. There's got to be a conversation looming on the horizon, and the thought of having to explain herself was just too much. She just wanted to eat dinner and veg-out on the couch. Was that too much to ask for?

"You all right? You look madder than a three-legged dog trying to bury a bone in an icy pond."

Dorothy glared at him, "It's turd."

"Well, I don't want to refer to my niece as a turd, if that's all right with you," he mused and dropped his plate beside her. "Whatcha think about that?"

"It's 'bury a turd on an icy pond', not a bone."

Al nodded, cut a piece of steak, took a bite and dropped his silverware. He reached across Dorothy and removed the steak knife clutched in her left hand, spun the blade around so it faced her plate, and not the ceiling. He patted her on the head, smiled, and proudly returned to his dinner. Dorothy looked at her right hand, turned her fork to match the knife, cut herself a slice of meat, and leaned back in her chair. She let out a little laugh and her uncle's eyes sparkled.

They polished off their dinner in relative silence; such was the way in her family. Dorothy helped clear the table without being asked. She hoped her uncle noted this as her way of saying she was sorry. It had been one heck of a day.

After dinner, Al scooped out a plate of vanilla ice cream for Dorothy, then poured himself a cup of coffee. He stood by the stove and smiled, waiting. She met his eye and rapidly turned away. Unfortunately, once you know the attention is on you, it's so very hard to ignore. She glanced at him, looked away, repeated, then sighed and firmly asked, "Okay, what?"

Al chuckled, and sipped his coffee. "We need to do something about that." She looked at her uncle with curious reproach. What was in his head? Had to be about her dad, and if it was, she'd nip the stitch right out of him.

"About what?"

"The bug crawling up your butt. What's up with you? About your dad, is it?"

"No, not about him," she replied. "Couple of friends giving me grief is all."

"Friends? Here?" Her uncle rubbed his chin, "I didn't think there were any kids out here, not for a few miles at least."

"Charlie and Rags," she replied, shortening Ragesha's name to avoid explaining how an Indian boy came to live in the rural sections of Ocala.

"Rags? What kind of name is that? And what trouble are they giving my favorite niece?"

"Well," she began, and again had to sort through her experiences and choose what parts to divulge. She wanted to tell him everything but suspected that it might lead to a few unanticipated judgments on her mental state. Something sure to lead to a potential grounding. School was right around the corner and she hadn't solved the mystery of the glass key. Time locked in the house is time wasted.

"Me and Charlie, he's the boy I normally hang out with now, see, me and him were solid just yesterday."

"Solid?"

"Super tight, good friends," she added, and he nodded. "Then along came Rags, the little turd. He's so annoying, and oh-my-God when the two of them started high-fiving and picking on me, I just wanted to slap the piss right out of them both!"

Al lowered his head and smiled. He pulled a stool next to Dorothy, grabbed a spoon out of a glass jar at the center of the island, and pilfered a little ice cream from her dish. He laughed. "Darlin', that's just boys bein' boys."

"It's stupid," she scoffed.

"I'll do you one better. That's boys bein' boys—around you." He waggled his eyebrows.

"Me? What the heck did I do? All I was doing—"

Her uncle placed a hand over her forearm and shook his head. "It doesn't matter what you were doing. It's who you are. You are a young lady, and young men just act like…" he paused for a moment. "They act a bit goofy. It's like a cog. You know what that is? Little wheel inside a clock?" He slapped her shoulder, as if this quip explained the secrets of the universe. "Well, normally they run fine, until someone throws a wrench in 'em."

"Are you calling me a wrench?"

"Well no, sweetheart," he said and paused again. "Not exactly."

"So, I'm throwing a wrench? I don't get it, I didn't do anything," Dorothy said.

"You're not a wrench and you're not throwing a wrench. You're not throwing any tools at all. You're the girl, and they are the boys, and boys and girls just act differently when around the opposite…" he paused, considered, and wiped the sweat from his brow.

"You're not making much sense," she replied. Thoughts of Isais giving her the thumbs-up popped in her head, and she began to giggle. Uncle Al must have taken this as a rub against him and dropped his hands to the countertop.

"I…I don't even know what the heck I'm sayin' anymore."

"Well…you are a boy," Dorothy pointed out. She grinned wide. He looked at her, returned the smiled and agreed.

"Well, I am at that. I'm going to go see if Isais got that stubborn horse back in the barn. Your father said he'll see you in the morning; he's pulling a double. Asked me to tell you that he loves you, wanted to be sure I told you that. Well, I told you." Al leaned over and kissed her on the forehead. "If those boys give you any trouble, you let me know. I'll show them how to behave." He smiled, and nearly tripped over his own feet trying to race out the door.

"That would be difficult, you know," Dorothy replied once her uncle was out of earshot. "Run on down to 1946, if you would. Oh, you'd have to cross an ocean, maybe dodge a few Nazis along the way, but go ahead and do that for me, set those boys straight. Whaddya say? What? You only see the one boy? Oh, right, the other is floating around 1966. Pop the doors on that old time-machine, she's going to get some serious use tonight!" Dorothy dropped her head into her arms and laughed.

The ridiculousness of the story was also the appeal. Here she is, just a little ol' girl from Georgia—well, Florida now—and she holds the keys to the universe. Just a quick slip into her pocket and, whammo! Off to a new world. Add another key and blammo! World number two! So, what happens when they combine all three? Will they find a fourth kid lurking in some far away land? More questions popped into her head, and she had decided she had better start writing them down.

Her first question, being the most obvious, was *Why the pocket?* Why does the key work when you slide it—freakin' bit up or down—inside your back pocket? Is it only the back pocket? She recalled both Charlie and Ragesha storing their keys in theirs, and if her memory served, it was the right back pocket. Same for her.

Why are the fields safe? This question had sort of snuck its way into her head earlier today, at least until the doofuses started in with their wise-cracker remarks. Charlie was the one who told her the camp was safe, at least he assumed as much when they met. Ragesha hadn't directly said the same, but his camp was pulled away from the trees, toward the center. Next question, the follow-up humdinger: *What is beyond the trees and is something trying to keep us out?* She didn't care to find out the answer, at least not in Charlie's World. Just hearing those clackety-clack monsters was enough to deter her from venturing in there. But other worlds, like Ragsy's for instance. Were the milk-bugs natural there, or a set deterrent? She wasn't sure how she might find the answer. Still, good question for the boys to work out, and maybe they'll focus on something other than picking fun at her.

Dorothy flipped the page, and sketched the three keys. She numbered them one, two, and three. Beneath those numbers, she wrote: one, three and two. She continued down the list, starting the next row with three, one, and two. She did this until she had six possible combinations using all three keys. You could add six more, if you combined only two of the three keys. Twelve worlds in all. Freaking 12, and all 12 belonged to the three of them.

If the glass key goes to the bone key's world, is there another key that takes someone to the rock-key world? One world, two keys. It made sense, she supposed, why else would she have met Charlie in Charlie's World and not jump to one of her very own?

What does it all mean? Dorothy paused there. The question was a summary of all questions. What is this key, where did it come from, how does it work, and how did it get here? She was getting a headache. She also felt...small. It made her want to run to her father with all her questions and uncertainties. Relinquish her responsibility and let him be the responsible one. This was one of his functions, one of his main functions.

But no. Not this time. She would not run to him or anyone else. This would be her puzzle to crack, and no one, not her father, not her uncle, and certainly not those dweebs sharing the ride would take it away from her. Dorothy dropped her dish of melted ice cream into the sink, and retired to her room.

She rose around 9:00 a.m. the following morning, dressed and stuffed some fruit, canned meat, bread, peanut butter, jelly, and candy into her school backpack, along with some of her new clothes, toilet paper, deodorant, and a bar of soap. She wanted to be a little more prepared this time. Whether the boys had realized it or not, they'd set up their camps for extended stays, should some unexpected event keep them from returning home. She simply took this a step further and packed her belongings in a convenient carry-on.

Dorothy slipped out the back door and pulled the key from the box using a thin handkerchief. As she'd hoped, the cloth prevented the key from weighing heavy against her skin, and now the key fit nicely in the front pocket of her jeans. She pulled her hair into a tight ponytail before stepping off the porch, and slipped the key into her back pocket. The black patch that remained in her wake, well, that'd be Uncle Al's problem, not hers. She anticipated a bit of walking today, and it wasn't going to start at the ranch.

As usual, Charlie was waiting for her when she arrived. She turned, and he took her key without speaking, though she caught him eyeing the jeans she'd picked out. Boys…

She dropped her bag next to Charlie's trunk and called him over to the center of the camp, where she unfolded her handkerchief and laid it on the ground between them. Charlie placed both keys on top, again without a word. He was anxious, almost too eager to please, and she knew it. She guessed he was feeling pretty bad about the day before.

"I'm sorry, Charlie," Dorothy began, hoping an apology might help cut the tension. Boys had trouble with those words— pride and all—and she did, too, to a degree. But if they were going to adventure together, pride would have to take a back seat. "I didn't mean what I said last night. I mean, I did. Just not the way I said it."

"It's all right. I thought about it last night—most of the night actually—and I think…I was just a little scared."

Dorothy perked. "Scared? Because of the milk-bug?"

Charlie nodded, paused, then shook his head, and said, "A little bit. Well, a lot when it happened, but after, I think I was scared because of Ragesha. It's always been us, me and you, together, like you said. I thought I was being funny, like that man you say you like, Benny Bill?"

"Benny Hill. He's goofy and kind of fat, and you're nothing like him."

"Right, well, I guess I was just upset. It's still us, together, right?"

"Of course!" Dorothy exclaimed, and her uncle's words, *Boys will be boys around you*, echoed in the back of her mind. "It's always us Charlie. You're my friend…I think my only friend." Hearing the words out loud, turned her mouth to cotton. "I come here to see you! Everything else, that's the icing on the cake."

He smiled, leaned over, and kissed her on the cheek. The ensuing rush of heat and tingling butterflies dancing around her stomach invigorated her, and she beamed. He noticed—had to have noticed—and turned his attention back to the keys. They sat in awkward silence, until Dorothy remembered her notes, and pulled them from her pocket.

"Before we go see Ragsy, I wanted to show you this," she said, turning the paper over to display her drawing of the three keys and the numbers beneath.

"What's this?" he asked and dropped to his belly.

"Do you remember how you put the keys together? Which one did you put on top?"

"My key. It's a bit smaller than yours," Charlie replied.

"Always?"

"Yeah, I guess. Why?"

"It's a theory of mine, and I want to test it today," she said. Charlie sat up. "I think if you place my key on top of yours instead, we'll visit a new place."

"Really?" he asked, and without a second's hesitation, placed Dorothy's key on top of his, and vanished. Dorothy sighed and laughed.

He snapped back thirty second later, and nodded vigorously. "Sand in that one, a lot of it. No trees, just high dunes. I didn't see anyone there, and I had a good view of the field."

"So, there's another field like this one? Like a bowl, and we're in the middle?" she asked, and he agreed, it was. Dorothy pulled a pen from her backpack, and wrote *Desert* next to the one-two combination, and *Ragesha* next to the two-one combination.

"If we find more kids, we'll put their names next to the combinations."

"I wonder why you came here rather than your own world," Charlie pondered.

She flipped the paper and pointed to the same question where she'd written it.

"I think we share this place, so we can join keys and travel to a new one."

"So," he began, and slowly pieced the puzzle that Dorothy had solved the previous night, "that would mean Ragesha's World would have another key-person?" Dorothy agreed.

"And the desert place, that might have two kids as well!" Charlie reveled, then flipped the paper over. "And this is all the combinations you came up with?"

"Twelve in all."

"So, we could potentially meet…twenty-one new people! Do you think they'll be our age?"

"Probably. Two for two, right?"

Charlie dropped his head for a moment, lifted the keys, one in each hand, and bounced them lightly as if comparing their weight. She suspected he wasn't, and figured he needed a moment to consider. This was heavy, adult stuff. She was certain that he had considered showing his key to his mother. And she was equally certain he chose against it. After all, he wasn't alone, and coincidentally, neither was she. They had each other. Together, they could tackle anything. She felt this with such certainty, she didn't need to hear it.

"Do you think that we might be, what is the word you say? 'Screwing' with something we shouldn't?"

She thought for a moment, then pointed to the keys. "Well, we found these, right?" He agreed that they had. "They weren't given to us. We felt we needed to look in a certain place—my barn, your neighbor's busted attic—and we found them. Two 14-year-old kids who knew, kind of without knowing, that if we put the key in our pocket, we'd go someplace. And here we are. I bet if you ask Ragesha how old he is, he's going to say 14, just like us." Dorothy concluded with a triumphant smile.

"So, what does it mean?"

Dorothy stood, extended her hand, and pulled Charlie to his feet. She motioned to the keys, and he raised them, bone over glass. "It means: we were meant to do this!"

They laughed, and he pressed the keys together.

"I was starting to wonder if you were coming." Ragesha was sitting in the center of his camp. He didn't stand when they arrived, only lowered his head, and tossed a pebble of molded black dirt.

"I told you we would," Dorothy replied, and reached for her backpack. She grumbled, and turned to Charlie. "I left my bag back at the camp."

"I'll get it," Charlie exclaimed, and pulled the keys apart before she could protest. She braced for a moment, unsure if she would go with him or be sent to her farm, or worse. She stood tall and waited.

"Do you still not like me?" Ragesha asked.

"I do not dislike you today, if that is what you're wondering. But the day's still young," she added with a smile. He smiled, too, looking relieved.

Charlie popped in wearily, and groaned when he spotted Dorothy sitting beside Ragesha. He looked up at the sky and fell to his knees, dropping the recovered backpack at his feet. Ragesha questioned Dorothy with a glance.

"There's one more test out of the way," she proclaimed, pulled the paper from her pocket and noted: *Need to be touching to travel. Can be left behind if someone takes the keys with them.*

"I didn't…"

"I know," Dorothy replied, and punched Charlie in the arm after he sat. "Don't do that again," she threatened, and he nodded solemnly.

Dorothy proceeded to explain her theories to Ragesha, and when she concluded, she asked his age. As expected: fourteen. He'd also found his key by a chance encounter while doing something else.

"The police raided my village, and my brother told me to hide in the garbage dump. I picked up the key when I heard gunshots. Looked like a big rock, so I thought I could throw it if I needed to. I put it in my pocket—"

"Bit side up," Dorothy added.

"Yeah! And here I am."

"So, you need your key-mate," Charlie said. Ragesha shot him a puzzled look, and Dorothy jumped in. "You need two keys to travel anywhere else. Me and Charlie in his world, and you and your person—whoever that is—in this one."

Ragesha looked over Dorothy's drawing while she passed around fruit from her pack; banana to Ragesha and an orange to Charlie. Ragesha wiped his hands on the back of his shorts— same shorts he had been wearing the day before.

Dorothy wondered if he had a change of clothes, clean underwear, heck, something to entertain himself with at home. What happened in 1966? This would have been 20 years ago, and she didn't think her school covered such recent topics. Her social studies class brushed over World Wars I and II. She had no clue what Ragesha was going through. She supposed she could ask, but it was personal—home personal—and she didn't want to delve that deep into either of the boy's lives outside the key-worlds. History started in Charlie's World, year 100. It continued here in Ragesha's, year one.

Year one, how stupid did that sound.

"You think we can add my key to yours? That's what your picture shows, if I am reading it correctly. Your key is one, Charlie's is two, and mine is three?"

"How come I'm two?" Charlie protested.

"My list," Dorothy responded. "In order of appearance."

"Do you think we should?" Ragesha asked.

"Could be other kids out there, you never know. More kids means more keys."

Ragesha added, "And more keys means more worlds. But don't you think there might be a limit on the places you visit?"

"I don't know. I thought there might be a kid who has lost his key, or had someone do what Charlie did to me when he went and grabbed my backpack."

The boys glanced at each other, then looked to Dorothy, quizzically.

"Taking both keys with you, and leaving me behind," she clarified. They nodded.

Ragesha paced in front of Dorothy. His eyes never left the sheet of paper. His expression reflected how Dorothy had felt the night before, lost between rational thought and imagination.

"It has to be better than what you've got going on here, Rags," Charlie coaxed.

Ragesha nodded.

"I'm not afraid of going, Charlie. I want to make sure I come back. All the way back." Ragesha turned, and spun again, motioning to speak, then stopping himself. Looking at him, his stern-lipped face beneath furrowed eyes, she wasn't sure he was telling the truth. Dorothy took a risk and spoke her thoughts.

"Or, we might find a place worth staying."

Charlie perked up and slapped his knee. "Like the lost boys in *Peter Pan*!"

"Except I'm a girl, and there are three of us." Dorothy corrected. "I don't much care for the three musketeers, either. If you ask me, I'd say we're the Three Key Children," Dorothy drew the number three on her paper, then a capital K with its back against the three. Now, if they did cross paths with others like themselves, they had a banner of solidarity to fly under. Charlie must have thought the same, for he grabbed the pen and drew a shield-like crest around her drawing. Ragesha added a sketch of Dorothy's glass key behind the letters, and the three of them smiled at the result.

"I have one condition," Ragesha added. "We three must agree on all decisions. No matter how big or small, it has to be…" he paused, trying to think of the word signifying their unity.

"Unanimous," Charlie offered.

"I agree," Dorothy said.

"Me, too," said Charlie.

Ragesha concluded by reaching his hand forward, palm down. Dorothy placed her hand on top of his, and Charlie put his on top of both.

"The Three Key Children," Charlie commented while nodding. "That's…"

"Righteous," Dorothy interjected, and she wiggled her fingers around an air guitar. Ragesha smirked, stuck his tongue out and mimicked her. Charlie shrugged, and joined in.

He picked up the combined glass and bone keys, and since they were already bound, offered them to Ragesha. Dorothy placed one hand on Ragesha's shoulder, and one on Charlie's. Ragesha flipped his stone key, smiled—a little nervously—and said, "Three Key Children." He placed his key on top.

Chapter 7
Open Minds and Open Hearts

"That's quite a tale, Mr. Dutta." Ellen was on her fourth cup of coffee, fighting caffeinated jitters and an overwhelming urge to curl up in a corner and sleep. She needed a break, just a few minutes to process all the unusual, outlandish happenings between Dorothy and the Three Key Children.

She started by asking for a pair of comfortable lounge chairs from the two behemoths guarding the door. They responded politely, and cordially asked for a few moments to locate members of Ellen's own staff to fulfill the order.

Furniture, she wanted to add and decided against it, which would have been readily available had these goons left the suite furnished, as it was intended. Really though, what was the point? She's knee deep in the den of insanity, led there by an eccentric millionaire tied to the supernatural, or an overabundant supply of his own drugs.

When two orderlies—accompanied by Ragesha's men—entered the room, Mr. Dutta paused his narrative, nodded to his men, and pulled the chairs over to the window. Ellen took advantage of the distraction and slipped to the bathroom to compile her thoughts.

Ellen was fully convinced by this point that Ragesha was a paranoid schizophrenic and in serious need of medication. The only reason she allowed him to rattle on was in the hope that she'd learn something about how all of this lunacy connected, or caused Dorothy's current condition.

However fantastical his tale was, this woman was real. Her coma was real. If Ragesha had built his entire fortune around caring for Dorothy Alston, then it was likely that he felt some sort of responsibility for her condition. If Ellen could figure out how they knew each other, outside of this mythical land of Id he's concocted, she might be able to get a sense of what actually happened to Dorothy.

She washed her hands and reemerged from the bathroom. Mr. Dutta was standing beside one of the chairs, looking thoughtfully out at the woods, now bathed in the bright light of the late afternoon sun. God, had they been at it this long? It only seemed like a couple hours.

He rolled Dorothy's chair so she sat to his right and took a seat. Ellen's chair was at his left, cocked slightly, so she was facing him.

Mr. Dutta folded his fingers under his chin, peered thoughtfully out the window, perhaps deciding what to tell her next—or perhaps fabricating it, as the case may be. Despite her doubts, Ellen had to admit she was enjoying the story. She was curious as to what road he'd take from the key-ports to Dorothy's current vegetative state.

She took a seat next to him and set her coffee on the floor by her chair. She hadn't really wanted it, just needed something to reach for when she felt uncomfortable. She had the coffee in hand more often than not.

"I imagine you have many questions," Mr. Dutta opened. He did not turn to face her.

"Most can wait, though I am curious about the keys. Why the pockets? It seems so…out there. I mean flipping them one way, then another? Home and Charlie's World?"

Mr. Dutta laughed. "Yes, strange to be sure. I'm not sure if I have a proper answer for you. There is a purpose to the keys; I expect that's your next question. But as to how they work; well I have my own thoughts on the subject, but that's not important right now." He shook his fingers, as if a revelation occurred to him, and looked thoughtfully at Ellen. She forced herself upright, though she wanted to turn away.

"The keys—these few that we have found, and the many we have not—are meant for children. You see, Dorothy had rightly concluded that each child who came across a key, did so while in a time of great hardship, and the key itself was drawn to them. The same way a pet might sense sadness and sink into your lap. Nature can be unforgiving, but those who survive in her world can learn to forgive. I think the key-worlds were created for this purpose. A forgiving world for the downtrodden youth throughout time."

"You think the keys have some kind of consciousness?"

"Not in the sense of cognitive thought. But instinct? Yes, I do." He affirmed this with a raised brow and a nod. "Just as I believe it was instinctual for each of us to place our keys in our pants pockets, bit up or down. I think the keys responded to our desire to escape. In my case, it was the year prior to the Naxalbari uprising. We had very little. Our farms grew smaller and drier each year. Land was taken, and we, meaning my village, were ready to take it back.

"My father shot someone the day I found my key, and the police scoured the village looking for him. I hid and I cried. I don't even recall picking up the stone key. Well, I do not recall much of that time, but we will get to what I remember and what I do not remember, and of course, why. What little has come back to me has done so in fragments. I can say with certainty that I did not see the key, only that in one moment, I did not have it, and the next I was placing it in my pocket. A simple, innocent," he raised a finger, "instinctual act."

"You weren't afraid at all when you…crossed?" Ellen asked.

He thought for a moment, then said, "If I was, it was only for a moment. Remember, I was a 14-year-old boy hiding from men shooting guns. Relieved, yes! Scared? I think I was more frightened of going home. I was worried that the police had found my father and gunned him down."

"Did they?"

"Yes. They arrested my mother, and shot my father dead. They left his body in a ditch, and my brother and I had to bury him."

"That's horrible!"

"That was India. So, you can imagine the bond we three shared," he said, and touched Dorothy's hand. "We became fast friends."

"Seems like you and Charlie shared a similar past."

Ragesha nodded. "Yes, I imagine he might have had a similar go of it. England in the forties was no place for a child."

"Why isn't Charlie here with you? Is he still wandering about in his own world?" she asked. "I don't mean this to sound sarcastic, and if it comes across that way, I do apologize. But wouldn't Charlie's presence here solidify your case?"

He broke into a gut-laugh, and leaned forward in his chair. "Ellen, is that what you think this is? An attempt to con you? Force belief upon you?"

"Isn't it?"

"To what purpose would it serve? Dorothy's treatment? I don't need to convince you of her plight to have you care for her." He shook his head, and clarified, "No. I want you to understand. I want you to feel. Then you can treat her, and I think you will put as much of yourself into her care as I have.

"To continue, I would estimate it has been well over 30 years since my adventure with the Three Key Children, and I dare say, even I question my limited memory. Most of what I recall to you now derived from interviews and interrogations within my village, my remaining family, after the fact. Dorothy is the only piece of my past I can recall with absolute certainty.

"I question everything—until I hold my key. Then I question nothing. I want you to understand why I have dedicated my life to Dorothy, and why she sits here, like this, when I know she should not."

"So, something happened to cause this," Ellen asked, pushing toward the crux of the story.

"Yes. And I will tell you this with the utmost certainty. Had I known then, what I know today, I would have never pressed my key to theirs."

Chapter 8
The Explorers

"Wow," Charlie exclaimed. Dorothy merely choked in agreement. Dumbstruck by the smell of ammonia, and God did her eyes burn, she found herself struggling to stand. Ragesha tapped both their shoulders, covered his mouth, and motioned to the ground. Dorothy dropped to her knees and took a breath.

"We're in another bowl," Ragesha said, and gestured to the perimeter of the field. Cracked, drought-ridden earth flaked in all directions beneath the dark haze of clouds above. The trees stretched out like dark skeletons against gray-green smoke. Everything here was dead.

"You should record this," Ragesha instructed, and tapped the paper gripped tightly in Dorothy's hand. She snapped out of her stupor and, next to the three-over-two, two-over-one key combination, noted: *Windex Land. Do not return.*

"Doesn't look like anyone would want to stay here," Charlie commented.

Ragesha slapped him on the arm and pointed behind Dorothy.

She turned and found she could hardly focus. The air burned at her eyes, even down here under the haze. She wiped at her lids and squinted. She thought she saw something.

"Is that a camp?" Charlie asked, and the two crawled toward it.

"Seriously? We're crawling over there?" Dorothy asked. Ragesha tilted his head upward, as if to remind her of the ammonia, and scrabbled forward along the ground.

Dorothy sighed and folded the paper into her pocket. She hunched her shoulders up around her ears and followed the boys on hands and knees.

They'd covered 50 yards or so when the dense ammonia-mist cleared enough to see an outline of a small camp. A tent, a few boxes, some tools, and a lantern sat a dozen or so feet away from the edge of the ominous forest.

Bare trees jutted from the ground like broken shards. Huge branches lay decaying beneath them, cracked, and splintered.

Ragesha arrived at the campground first and motioned for the others to hold back. He then called Charlie to his side. They began to whisper, nod, and shake their heads.

"What is it?" Dorothy asked and gasped, placing her hand over her lips. It sounded as if she were speaking under water. Her voice lurched forward, then stifled, as if the fog were swallowing it up. The boys waved her over.

"What is it?" she repeated in a whisper. Ragesha pointed to the ground toward a tarnished metal ring in the charred dirt. It looked like the base of a key.

Charlie slipped his finger through the ring, and pulled.

"Looks like a skeleton key," he whispered, and brushed it clean. He measured the length by placing his four fingers along the shaft, and again. The double bit resembled two small houses sitting against one another.

"It looks like a normal key," Dorothy commented. She reached for it, then withdrew.

"Go ahead," Charlie said, and offered it to her. "Then we'll know, right?" He turned the key over so it would fall clear of his body. Dorothy pressed a finger against the bit, along the base, then snatched it from his hand. She shrugged.

"Guess it's a normal key," she said.

Ragesha shook his head. "It's too big. Look," he placed the key next to their three. It was the same length as Ragesha's.

"But Dorothy can pick it up," Charlie added. Ragesha turned a worried eye to them both. "Yes," he said solemnly. Dorothy felt her gut seize up.

Ragesha hadn't come outright and said it, but she sensed it. The key was here, and there was no one holding it. She could only think of three things: the kid abandoned the key and went with another child—though she thought her touch would still affect it in this case. Someone or something abducted the kid—again, same thinking applied. Or the kid had died.

She looked to the others. They scanned the camp and forest, not looking for movement, but for a body. Seeing nothing, Dorothy turned her attention to the camp's furniture. Wooden chairs, a trunk, vinyl tent, all items typical of most eras between Charlie's and her own. She'd call many antiques, not that she was an expert by any stretch, but she thought that she could distinguish between old and new well enough.

Something here had caught her eye though, and she crawled to a black storage box.

The material was familiar yet strange. Square at the top, four or so feet long with two triangles cut into the lid. Well, not triangles exactly, the tops were cut off. She thought back to her math class, and tried to remember her shapes. "Octagon, pentagon, parallelogram, square!" she sang, "Triangle, rectangle, trapezoid...TRAPEZOID!" she clapped, and pressed her finger against both sunken trapezoids.

The box had hinges with plastic slides for clasps. She read the words *Dee-Zee,* after wiping the sticker on the nameplate clear. She guessed this had come from the future. Not distant, she had seen boxes like this on trucks all around Georgia. But, maybe within a decade or two.

She slid the latches and opened the box, then sank. She picked up a key resting on top of a plaid, folded blanket, and set it on the ground beside her. She hadn't hesitated, hadn't worried about it weighing her hand to the ground. She knew it wouldn't.

"Another glass key," Charlie pointed out. "Looks just like yours, except blue."

"No mistaking it." Ragesha said, but he looked at Dorothy, as if he was hoping he was wrong. Dorothy shook her head, eyes downcast.

"But both keys are here. What does it mean?" Charlie asked.

"It means that we need to leave," Dorothy replied. They formed a circle as Ragesha unwrapped the tattered bits of shirt holding the keys together, gripped tight, then opened his hand. They did not fall apart. He flipped the keys, rolling them along his palm.

"They're not breaking apart," he said, and handed the set to Charlie.

"Maybe they're different here." Charlie turned the key vertical and held the group an inch from the ground. He looked to Dorothy and nodded. The keys slammed into the dirt as she touched the bit. The bond held, and the falling keys left a small divot in the ground.

Traveling keeps the keys together, Ragesha noted on Dorothy's paper. "We're going to need a binder at this rate. So, what do we do? Pull them apart, go home and start over?"

"Jenga?" Dorothy offered. Both children turned to her. "It's a game where you stack blocks, then pull one of the loose ones out," she explained. She instructed Charlie to push at his key in the center, then pressed her hand into his. Ragesha wrapped around Charlie's back, and reached for Dorothy's free hand. He pushed, and his key slid beneath Dorothy's.

The next landing was more of the same. Oversized dead trees, charred black land, no signs of life. They didn't see a campsite, didn't want to look for one, and quickly ran the next combination, sliding Dorothy's glass key around Charlie's, which then swapped with Ragesha's, creating a combination of two-over-one, one-over-three.

Fragrant orange blossoms scented the air. Lush green grass stood taller than their ankles and stretched for miles, broken up in places by groves of trees with tremendous canopies. Dorothy thought she could make out the silhouettes of birds flying among them.

She saw rock formations that touched the clouds, and mountain ranges so tall that they disappeared above them. She could see sunflowers and wildflowers to her left. Pink daisies, three times the size and twice as brilliant as anything back at home. Thick grass swayed like grain, and insects, glorious, buzzing, normal-sized bees everywhere!

"Now this is more like it!" Charlie hollered, stretched out his arms and fell into the lush grass. Ragesha grinned and did the same. Dorothy hesitated, inspecting their surroundings cautiously. It looked beautiful, sure, but she couldn't relax. Not just yet, not with those two abandoned keys tapping at the back of her mind. Two keys, two lost children. The boys didn't see it, or maybe they did and just didn't care, but she couldn't shake her uneasiness.

There was proof of the danger here. She supposed this would be true during any of her visits from Charlie's World to Ragesha's. Yet, between the clackety-clack creatures and the milk-bugs, which were absolutely dangerous, she never felt threatened. But now… "Two keys," she whispered.

"Do you think there's food down there?" Ragesha pointed. Charlie jumped to his feet, peering at the closest oasis. Before Dorothy could protest, the boys broke into a run, pushing and screaming.

Dorothy shook her head. Not this time, no way. She's going to check this place from top to bottom and document every dang bug and bird before settling down. She looked at the boys, now a few dozen yards away.

"My key!" she shouted, and took off after them. She caught up to Charlie first, and yelled, "Charlie, you stop this minute!" He was too far gone, enamored by the chase, the birds, and the small animals scampering out of his way. She couldn't see what they were, just little tufts of mauve hair appearing above the grass as they sped by, vanishing before she got a good look.

They passed plants with giant cup-like leaves, deep red and yellow along the stems. The leaves were as tall as she was, coated in a thick gel which flashed white as she passed. They ran, and the birds flying above the oasis, grew—and they grew. Crow squawks turned to screams and rolled along the swaying grasses. And those damned boys pressed on, not seeing, and not caring.

The trees looked like a variation of oak trees from home, though the trunks were as wide as a house and smooth as stone. The leaves shimmered in the breeze, and when they did, she caught hints of orange and deep cobalt.

Ragesha stopped a few hundred yards from the tree line, flopped to the ground, and caught his breath. Charlie tumbled in beside him and Ragesha punched his arm.

"I win!" he said, and Charlie flipped him off before rolling to his back.

"That's only because you run all the time!" he countered.

"And you don't?" Ragesha teased.

"I used to," Charlie replied between heaving breaths.

Dorothy took a seat next to them and fell back, gasping for air. She had prepared another tongue-lashing—these two dorks sorely needed it—but oh, she needed a breath.

And water, yeah, she needed water something fierce.

She pulled a water bottle from her backpack, took a sip, then recapped it. Charlie stretched out his hand, but she held up her own, index finger extended.

Ragesha tapped Charlie on the shoulder, and nodded toward a tree to their left, its trunk about the size of the stable back at Uncle Al's farm. Brilliant orange fruit dangled beneath long needles resembling porcupine quills. Naturally, Ragesha wanted to jump right over there and grab one. Doodle-bug Charlie, unsurprisingly, agreed. He wanted a drink of water first, and began to whine when Dorothy refused to give it to him.

"You two," she began, sank, and drew in a long, deep breath, slowing her heart rate from a gallop to a trot. "Are IDIOTS!" She threw the water bottle at Charlie.

"What? Look around you, Dorothy! This is everything we were looking for! Paradise!" Ragesha exclaimed. "That's got to be food! And if you think about it, if there are other kids like us, with keys, they would be here, not one of those other places."

Charlie upended the bottle, swallowed, and offered it to Ragesha. "He's right. Given a choice between Charlie's World and here, I'd go here."

"But the keys? Two stops back, remember? Two keys, for two kids?"

"Come on, Charlie," Ragesha ignored her. "I'm hungry. I want to know what those taste like."

Dorothy's jaw dropped. Hadn't they learned anything from the milk-bugs? The missing children? Holy whiskers, Batman! Get a clue! They were in over their heads, and apparently, she was the only one who knew it.

Ragesha pulled Charlie to his feet, and they brushed off their shorts and stepped toward the tree. Dorothy stomped her foot and screamed, "HEY!" They turned. "I don't agree with this. So, you can't do it! Three or nothing, right?"

The boys slumped and shuffled back to Dorothy. She sat, and they joined her.

"Come on, Dorothy, look! It's good; I know it's good. I can almost taste it!"

She calmly swung her pack and handed it to Ragesha. "If you're hungry, I brought food."

He shook his head and pointed at the grove of trees.

"I want that," Charlie said. Ragesha agreed. The orange fruit, double the size of a grapefruit, did look tempting. Seeing it made her mouth water, and she could practically feel her body inching toward it. She had to remind herself of the childless keys before she snapped back to reality, and she tugged on Charlie's shirt.

"Don't. I don't like it."

Charlie sank and looked to the sky. "What's not to like? Look at it!" He wrapped his arm around her shoulder. Ragesha, quick catching on, did the same, and the boys stepped toward the tree, forcing Dorothy to do the same.

"Happy fruit," Charlie sang.

"Tasty fruit," Ragesha followed.

"Stop it." Dorothy wriggled free and jumped back.

Ragesha laughed, slapped Charlie's arm, and proceeded to taunt Dorothy.

"Scaredy-cat, watch your back! The big bag man will snatch you back!"

Charlie chuckled and joined in, repeating, "Scaredy-cat! Scaredy-cat!"

They stepped to Dorothy and lifted their hands, as if they planned to tackle her.

She backed away. "Come on, cut it out!"

"Oh, scaredy-cat wants us to stop, Charlie Brown. What do you say, shall we drag her there? I get the feet, you get her hair!"

"Don't call me that," Charlie replied.

"What's the matter, Charlie Brown? Little Dorothy got you down? Shut up and grab her!"

"Ragesha, please!" Dorothy entreated. She couldn't remember which boy had the keys, and she turned to each of them in a panic.

"I said, don't call me that!" Charlie grabbed Ragesha's shoulder, threw his foot behind his leg and pushed him down.

A deep rumbling shook the ground beneath them and rolled across the sky like thunder. Birds the size of small trucks took to the air, flew over the children and banked away, darkening the sky as they passed.

Dorothy yelped and covered her mouth. Charlie and Ragesha sat up, wide eyed.

Ragesha looked to Charlie, who exclaimed, "It wasn't me!"

Dark clouds formed to the left, and another bellowing roar sounded below.

Dorothy ran to Ragesha, spun him around, and in a burst of adrenaline, pulled the keys from his pants. She tumbled to the ground under their weight, pinning her left hand. She roared in pain. "The keys! Get them off me!"

Charlie rolled the keys out of Dorothy's hand—didn't even try to lift them—then pulled Dorothy upright. A burn raced along the ridge of her thumb to her pinky, and Dorothy displayed the wound to Charlie, before cupping her fist to her chest.

Dorothy looked over Charlie's shoulder, toward the building storm. The clouds suddenly dissipated, as if never there. The rumbling stopped. The pain in her hand all but disappeared. Far in the distance and above the second range of trees, the birds settled into a nest of panicked conversation.

Ragesha looked at the fruit dangling on the thorn tree and licked his lips. Charlie smacked him across the back of the head. He reared, then turned to Dorothy. "Are you all right?" Ragesha asked.

Dorothy nodded. The pain had subsided, allowing her to think clearly, again. She turned to face the boys and said, "I don't like it here anymore. We should go."

Charlie agreed. Maybe the key fall did some good, other than banging up her hand and giving her a screaming headache. Ragesha sank, and peeked backwards over his shoulder. He bit his bottom lip.

"We need to go, Rags!" Dorothy repeated.

"What was that rumble? An earthquake?"

"Sounded almost like an animal," Charlie replied, mounting nervousness written all over his face. "A really huge animal."

Ragesha protested. "I don't think so, no animal I know of sounds that big. Not even a lion."

"Everything's bigger here." Dorothy reminded him. "And the storm? The one that just appeared and disappeared, like that?" She pointed toward the clear sky to the left and snapped her fingers. "Care to explain it?"

"I can't," Ragesha admitted, and he bounced on his heels. He took another longing look at the fruit.

"I think she's right, Rags. We should go," Charlie affirmed. Ragesha turned back toward Charlie, and reluctantly nodded.

"All right." He gripped Charlie's shoulder, and Dorothy did the same. She nodded, and Charlie presented the three keys, turning Ragesha's so he could grip the bit. He started counting to three, but Ragesha stopped him.

"Before we go…we are coming back, right? Tell me that this doesn't end here."

Charlie smiled at Dorothy, and pressed his hand against her waist. She blushed, and sank contentedly into his touch. "Three Key Children, right?" Dorothy whispered, the words catching a little in her throat. Ragesha smiled, and separated his key from the pile. Charlie held his and Dorothy's keys. In an instant, the two of them were standing in Charlie's camp and Ragesha was gone. Dorothy let out an enormous sigh.

She perched on the edge of a chair, and he pulled the trunk over closer to her, straddled it, and took both her hands in his. They recapped all the strange happenings in the new world they'd found. After a long silence, Charlie said, "We're totally going back, aren't we Dorothy?"

"I don't know, Charlie. I mean, should we? I feel like we're pushing it, our luck, I mean. Don't you?"

He looked to the ground. "Maybe, but is it any worse than our world? Or Ragsy's? I mean, it's different. Bigger. But we haven't explored any of it really. What if that world is the center of the key-worlds?"

"Key-worlds?" Dorothy mused. The question had merited some thought, musing aside. She pulled the paper from her pocket. Charlie's World, Ragesha's, the desert, Windex Land…they all shared a feeling, as if she were standing in a bowl. Like each little world was a snow-globe, and the Three Key Children stood as a centerpiece. All but one…

"Best I could come up with." Charlie dropped his shoulders, and sighed. "This really isn't going to be where the Three Key kids end it, is it?"

"No, I guess not," Dorothy replied after some consideration. "I guess, we cannot. We've got to be careful this time. Charlie, you have to promise me!"

"Of course, my lady!" he teased, then lifted her hands to his lips, and gently kissed her knuckle. "Anything for you, Dorothy."

She sighed, and did her best to acknowledge Charlie's sweet attempt at comfort.

She supposed another trip wouldn't be the end of the world, not as long as they were careful. Maybe…maybe treat it like one of Dad's hunting trips? Stop, listen, evaluate, and either approach or run for the hills—run for home.

Dorothy turned as a gentle breeze brushed across the wildflower fields, jostling the tiny perennials toward the frilly-tuft trees, then fading amongst a dim haze of gray just beyond the tree line.

Within, a shadowy figure stood. The children would return, and this pleased it, and it thinned to a wisp of black smoke, and quietly waited for their return.

.

Chapter 9
The Ocala Conundrum

Dorothy said her goodbyes, hugged Charlie—and oh, was that heaven on a stick after the day they've had—and returned to her home in Ocala. The sun had disappeared behind the trees, casting a stunning mix of purple, orange, and red in the late afternoon sky. She guessed it was around 8:00 p.m., and she'd most likely missed dinner. Not a big worry—her body was still a bit shaken up, probably wouldn't acknowledge hunger for some time.

Had it not been for Charlie's touch or his gentle words after they returned to his world, she would have ditched this whole gig lickety-split. She'd sulk alone, lost in memory, mostly of her mother, forcing her to grow-up—again—when she wasn't ready to. She enjoyed her return to childhood adventures and antics, no matter how brief. The Key-Worlds, as Charlie put it, was like running through depths of her manifested imagination. She felt like Alice stepping through the looking glass.

Lost in these thoughts, she didn't notice where she landed when returning home. She stood just outside the back porch—a stark, black semi-circle cut into the bottom step. She must have sheered the wood clean when she left this morning.

Dorothy knelt to examine the porch and felt a stiffness roll up her legs to lower back, lingering aches from the day's activities. She stretched, groaned, then turned her attention to the lower step and ran a finger along the cut wood. What happened when she jumped away to Charlie's world? Was it like a bubble? A swirling cylinder? A big ball of fire? Sheesh, she wished she had a camera.

The porch door opened, and her father and uncle stepped outside. She fought the urge to leap to her feet and stand at attention, her natural reactive posture before the inevitable pre-deny, deny, lie, and more deny. Typical reactions when she'd done something wrong. She thought curiosity would be a better play here.

"What did you guys do?" Dorothy asked, and rubbed an itch above her collarbone.

She continued to inspect the scarred wood.

"We were going to ask you the same question," her father replied. He twitched, waggled his mustache, and leaned against the handrail. Uncle Al crossed his arms but remained silent.

Dorothy met his eyes and shuddered. Did he know? He must, right? And this is what? Day one of his sobriety, and suddenly he has the right to interrogate her? Over this?

Her lip quivered, and she began to sweat. Her eyes felt like they might swell shut at any moment, and her mouth turned to cotton.

In the following heartbeat, something absolutely miraculous occurred. Her body loosened. Skin cooled. The nerves which typically pressed against her temples, turning her into the stiff cone of culpable, uncensored nonsensical blabbering machine which always landed her in the hot-seat, expanded into a panorama of calm. Her mind cleared. The gooseflesh chasing along her arms and into her shoulders, raising the tiny hairs on the back of her neck—all but disappeared.

She's got this.

Dorothy shook her head, peeked under the stairs and blurted without a lick of hesitation, "Nope, not me. Maybe it was the storm or something?" She turned to him with earnest curiosity, then to her uncle.

Al frowned and rubbed his chin.

"Could be, there was a pretty good storm last night."

"What, like lighting?" her father asked and ran a finger through his hair. "I would have thought we'd have heard that."

"Stranger things happen in the sticks, Pete."

"Lightnin' though? Lightnin'? Look at that, Al, I can't remember ever seeing lightnin' do that."

"Well, Christ, Peter, it's a fair better theory than a 14-year-old with a lighter," Al replied.

Dorothy reddened as anger welled within her. Yes, she was responsible, but how in the hell would he know? He saw something wrong and amped himself up thinking she was responsible. The nerve of this guy!

"Wait. You thought I did this?" Dorothy stood, putting a hand on her hip. "How, Dad? It's freaking round, I mean, look at it. How could I have done that? With what?"

His mustache twitched, and he scratched his nose. Uncle Al lifted his hands, palms forward, and turned to go inside.

"Dorothy, I didn't say you did it. It just seems odd." He glided his fingers around the shape. "Doesn't smell burnt, like it should. Looks cut out, like a big core drill. It's just dang odd..."

"Well, of course it's odd!" she thrust both her hands to the ground. "It's round!" She spun her hand in a circle. "Round! I mean a core drill? I don't even know what the hell that is! God, Dad, quit buggin' on me!"

He took a breath and frowned. "I...Dorothy, dammit, I don't know what that means." He slapped his hands to his trousers and sat on the step beside the burnt wood. "Ah hell, kid. I don't know what I'm sayin' anymore. That was your mother's job, tryin' to figure out what in tarnation you're talking about. Now I can't even do that." He sucked in his breath, leaned into the rail, and cried.

Dorothy stepped toward him, and knelt. He shivered, choked, and balled his fists. He punched the base of the railing, each strike slowing as each sob strengthened.

"God, I miss her, Dorothy. I miss her, I can't get her out of my head, I just want to be with her one more time. One last time," he sobbed.

Her uncle reappeared behind the closed screen door. She turned and spotted Isais at the barn. Her father reached for her, and she pulled her hand away. She stood, took a step and shook her head.

"No," she whispered. "You don't get to do that." She stepped away, still shaking her head, hands raised in steady defiance. "You did this, all of it!" Dorothy sneered, and as her father rose, Dorothy raised a finger and slowly waggled her rejection. "You don't get to comfort me, you don't get to say you're sorry. I won't hear you!" Her voice trembled. "She-can't-hear-you!"

She stormed around the house, slipped into the barn, and pressed her back against Alice's stall. She slapped the gate, looked to the ceiling, and pushed all of her anger into one long, horrifying shriek. She slid to the floor and dropped her head to her knees, wishing she could just let it all go. She wished she could cry.

"Little miss? Are you all right?" Isais asked, slowly emerging from Ulysses' stall.

Dorothy stood, dried her eyes, and stepped to the center of the stable. She pulled the handkerchief from her front pocket, spun the key bit-side up, and tucked it in her back pocket, sneering at Isais before closing her eyes.

Night had fallen in Charlie's World, and she recalled his stern warning, "You don't want to be here at night." Oh well, a little late, not at all, sorry. You're here—make the best of it. She lit the lamp hanging from the tree above the tent and felt instantly better.

The clackety-clack monkey-creatures grunted and stomped seemingly everywhere around her. It sounded like they might be in the open field outside the camp, though she had little desire to go wandering out into the darkness to find out. Another sounded just beyond the tent, no more than 20 or 30 feet away, but this one soothed rather than frightened her. She wanted to see it, touch it, offer it an apple like she did with Ulysses and the foal. Why not? Why the heck not!

She spun as the sound of wings whirred over her head. A purple light pulsed briefly, the sound faded, and the light pulsed again a ways off. First purple, then pink, red, and yellow danced about the open field, and the sound of her father crying faded in the enchantment of it. She smiled, and walked toward the closest light.

It strobed green, then red as she neared. She could hear the beating of its wings and feel a gentle brush of air on her cheek. The creature zipped past her toward the camp, and she caught a glimpse of its body, which she thought resembled a dragonfly, if dragonflies were a couple of feet long. She gave chase, slowing as she approached. She sang to it, hoping the soft tones of her voice might calm the creature. "Hush little baby, don't say a word. Mama's gonna buy you a mockingbird…"

The insect slowed, and Dorothy inched closer. She was only a few feet from the camp now, and the creature hovered at the tree line.

"If that mockingbird don't sing," Dorothy continued. The wings whipped and danced in the light of the lantern, and she could see its abdomen arching under a spiny, iridescent thorax. Three sets of eyes—one left, one right, and a smaller one below—shifted curiously about, and it mimicked the angle of Dorothy's head. She giggled and the insect danced, as if it was laughing along with her. The red light of its abdomen faded, lit orange, faded again, and turned yellow.

"Mama's gonna buy you a diamond ring," Dorothy finished, and slowly dropped to her knees. "There, isn't that nice?" she asked, and the insect dropped a foot to meet her eye. Its abdomen flickered, and slowly brightened. It drew closer. Dorothy stretched out her hand, then retracted it with a jolt, when she spotted something in the trees. At first, she thought it was the flicker of another light-dragon, but these lights didn't fade—they blinked.

A large claw extended from the shadows, wrapped around the thorax of the light-dragon, and squeezed until it snapped. Yellow liquid oozed over shiny black knuckles. Thick wisps of hair dangled from the hand, which wobbled, then shot back into the darkness, sounding as if it slammed into one of the frilly-tufts, pulling the insect along with it. She heard the crunch of carapace and bone.

The glinting eyes vanished.

"Wow," she proclaimed. "That's one wacked out monkey!" She had wished Charlie were here to see it. Maybe not the eating part which was a bit gross, but the bug, the light-dragon bug…the creature was simply incredible. It responded to her! It copied her movement, and even changed color! Like a mood ring, only, well on its butt. How righteous was that?

The last memory of her crying father slipped away within the sound of her carefree laughter. She curled herself into a ball, looked deep into the starless sky, smiled, and fell asleep.

Part II

Chapter 1
The Spintwister

A smile stretched across his face. It felt so foreign, so uncomfortable, he thought something must be wrong. It stirred something within, a feeling he supposed, or a memory. A dream?

He recollected the day he'd returned to the no-lands with his no-things, standing atop his no-hill, looking upon the vast amounts of nothing he'd accumulated through non-existent time. He couldn't remember why he had left or why he had returned. He only remembered the sweet poisons he drank, and the blurred faces of those who drank with him. He had smiled then, or thought he must have smiled. The vagueness of the memory was agonizing. He wanted to remember, *must* remember, yet, when he tried to focus, the vision bled from his mind like a teardrop in water.

His thoughts were thin. Words foreign. All hazy and wispy, here one moment, gone the next. It was all so confusing, and so very tiring. He wanted to sleep. Lay back, stretch, thin himself into a fine, comfortable mist. He found this form made it possible to think.

"Who am I?" he mused. "Or what? I know why. They are why," he whispered. "The children." The thought, one balanced on the cusp of consciousness, slipped away like leaves on a river.

He turned his gaze toward a very large mountain and peered through the clouds blanketing the peak like a warm pillow. A mountain, he realized, he had created. He thought these lands must be his...children? This was the word which came to mind. That didn't seem right. Not the word, but the objects he charged with its name. The word seemed right and true. Children indeed.

He pondered the correlation, and wondered, what use were they to him? Now, here, in the fogs of his life, they seemed so pointless...But the word had crossed his mind, as if he'd bitten into fruit and sprayed sweet juice across his tongue. Quick, savored, forgotten.

He drifted, hovered, then expanded, again, clearing his mind. As far back as he could recall, he hadn't needed a reason to grow beyond the mists of thought. He enjoyed ebbing and flowing in and out of an ocean of consciousness, so far from perceivable matter it was as if he was not only above…he was—all.

He understood for the first time, all that lay before him, belonged to him. The sky—his. The plains that served the sky, the waters that served his plains—his. The air, fragrant and musky with flowers, dung, and sweat, called to him. Beckoned him lower.

"Come Spintwister," sang the wind. So, he had.

The Spintwister hovered over the land—his land—as a dark splotch on a paper-thin sky. His world appeared small from here, like a view through a kaleidoscope. Dots and specs spinning about in endless circles of glorious light. Yet, all he beheld, the lands, grasses, trees, seemed so far away. As if giant, invisible hands cupped his creation with the sole purpose of keeping it from him. Could this be all he opened his eyes for? To look down upon a world moving on without him? He wouldn't believe it; it would mean he had no purpose.

"The Spintwister always has purpose," his voice rippled softly. Of course he had purpose. All things had purpose, even the dead. He considered this and wondered: was he living? He could see, or so he thought, but had he the eyes to do so? He could hear, but had he the ears?

The Spintwister focused, condensed, and the speck solidified into a mottled form that adhered to no true shape. A breeze touched him for the briefest of moments, then passed through him. He panicked, fearing he might lose himself to the wind. He focused all of his energy into one central point in his vast sky, consolidating himself into a pinprick. At first, he felt nothing. Then, a voice, a sweet, young voice sang below, in, and through him.

"Scaredy cat!"

The Spintwister couldn't identify what it was it at first, had no idea what he would even call this…thing. The walleyed sphere grew. Expanded. Odd tendrils appeared and disappeared in his wide, new vision, and soon he found he could control them.

Wiggle them, like tiny snakes. All inspired and realized from what he now knew were words, spoken by children playing below.

"Watch your back!"

He stretched and pulled at skin so blissfully taught, not even the strongest of breezes would scatter him. The Spintwister found he could move and turn in all sorts of directions: up, down, left and right, at will. He could squint and cut his vision, or widen his eyes to his world and all of its splendor.

Now he closed them. Here, in his own familiar darkness, he recalled a sliver of his past. A taste of sweet, sweet poison, which—made him. Like a birthing of both light and darkness. Like a key, poised to open a door.

"The big bag man will snatch you back!"

This wave of succulence beckoned him, and he drifted toward the haunting, delightful cadence of the young. He would drink their sweet tunes like wine, and he would remember.

The blurred faces of those infected souls appeared once again. They raised cups, fell to their knees, and begged for deliverance. "Yes, yes. Poisoned the lot, fine, I've established this," he said with a grimace, and discarded the vision.

He focused on a single thought. *A key, poised to open a door.* He turned his attention below. He could see children, two specks of black on a field of green. He closed his eyes and the picture inverted. Fields of silver, with a single hazy speck at the center. A thousand keys sprang up around the field in this new form of clairsentient vision, displaying a single vacant soul amongst a forest of glowing keys. He opened his eyes.

The Spintwister slipped closer and settled above a plot of fruit trees, humming with birds and bees.

"Oh, scaredy-cat wants us to stop, Charlie Brown. What do you say, shall we drag her there? I get the feet, you get her hair!"

The Spintwister turned ever so slightly, ever so cautiously, and there they were. Two children, ripe with pain. He could sense it. Was this important? Why? Should he help them, could he help them? Rid their pain, take it from them, rip it from them? What would he do with it, this suffering? And they did suffer, oh my how they ached!

"I make it my own." Yes, this felt correct. "My purpose," he amended, and felt satisfied.

"I said, don't call me that!" echoed below. The shrillness, the exquisite, awkward shame and anger enveloped him. Oh, how he wanted this. No, needed it! As if nothing in this assimilated world held meaning, nothing he created held purpose. Only pain and suffering had purpose. These pained and stricken children were his. Helping them would feed him, empower him.

"I," he thundered, "have purpose!" The Spintwister exploded into a thick, ominous black cloud, raged, and grew with each bellowing laugh. "I call the children! I call their pain! And I REMEMBER!"

"No, that's not quite it." He suddenly receded, then thinned to a withered wisp of smoke. The revelation was close, yes, but inaccurate. He didn't remember—but he could. His purpose, it seemed, was symbiosis. They, the suffering, needed him, so they could forget. He needed them, so he could remember. In this revision, he found solace. "Not a thief, but a saint." The Spintwister turned to the children and noticed something odd among them.

Two children stood together, looking at him, but not seeing. Another thing peered in his direction. It didn't resonate like the boys beside it; didn't tease his pallet. His fingers did not twitch nor did his mind wander to the shores of his lost memories. Quite the opposite. This creature turned his stomach. Its shrilly voice scratched needles down the base of his back and burrowed itself deep in his spine. It was a she, or so he thought, yet the creature hadn't the soul like the tasty boys it stood beside. The thing moved as they moved, even spoke as they spoke.

"So curious, this no-thing." Was it his creation? Certainly not, it looked far too feeble to exist here. No, this no-girl is not of his mind. He wasn't quite sure she was of any mind at all, not one that belonged to her, anyway.

"We need to go, Rags!" the screechy little no-thing shouted. He needed to see it, touch it if he could. He had to know what it was and why it was here. Or, why it was not here. These lands of the no were his to create—and destroy at whim. Was this no-girl sent here to challenge him? Steal from him? Is she suddenly his purpose?

He slipped closer.

The no-girl and two boys raised their keys to separate them. He thinned once again, and settled at their feet, and listened. The strident no-girl huffed orders to her two delectable companions, and they compliantly agreed to her every demand.

"Oh no, this will not do at all," the Spintwister hissed, and he slithered up the no-girl's leg, determined to wrap his claws around her throat and strip the arrogant boldness straight off her stolen bones. Yet, before he could lay hands on the creature, his lands vanished, his mind whisked into a whirlwind of stabbing needles and he released the no-girl, settling upon the ground like fog on a cold winter's day. He could hear the no-thing and the boy, smiled, until these too faded, and his mind unfolded.

When the Spintwister solidified into coherent thought, he found himself alone. The land had thinned. His vast flowers and trees shrank to thumbnail facsimiles, a shade of his former creation. This place constricted him.

His mind sank into a horrible dark pit. Memories, so recently reacquired, steamed away.

A song came to mind, and he hummed along with it, despite the mousy-like pitch grating against his ears. Never the less, he found it soothing, and thought he recognized it.

"A memory," he whispered, raised his ghostly fingers, and conducted himself into a deep, dreamless sleep.

Hush little baby, don't say a word. Mama's gonna buy you a mockingbird...

Chapter 2
Dad Day Plus One

The fragrant air reminded Dorothy where she was before she even opened her eyes. She'd spent a full night in Charlie's World. In her own world, this would have consequences. Her father would search for her. He would find the burn circles on the east side of the property where Dorothy normally jumped from there, to here. He would correlate these with the cored section of the front porch, and the mark she'd left in the stables. They would confirm what her father had suspected, and she had so avidly denied. She was responsible.

And then there was Isais, who had witnessed her crossing at the center walkway of the stable. What would he say? "She was here, then gone." Something told her she wasn't going to get out of this one so easily.

She stretched out her aches, and, despite the feelings of guilt topping an incredible stiffness from sleeping on rock-hard dirt, felt energized by this new morning. She shook the feeling back into her right arm, and inhaled the clean, crisp air.

She had her backpack, so she had breakfast. She felt her key stretching the denim of her right pants pocket. She had a camp, toilet paper and a field of flowers tall enough to conceal her womanly business. What else did she need?

Dorothy stood and brushed herself off. She sniffed her t-shirt—a little rank. Thankfully, she'd considered this possibility when packing and had brought a stick of deodorant and a change of clothes.

Pulling the knots from her hair, she surveyed the punchbowl of wildflowers and frilly-tuft trees. Everything looked bigger somehow, and brighter. The sky seemed impossibly deep. Did this place grow at night and dwindle during the day? Or maybe her presence fed into these lands, as if she were its gardener in a strange perpetual cycle.

Dorothy walked behind the tent and examined the ground where she figured the light-dragon had met its untimely demise. If it had bled, she couldn't tell. No discoloration on the ground. No body parts either—thankfully. Keeping the bugs in the air and out of her hair, well, that was just fine with her. Her little night time visitor cleaned up its dinner. Well, kudos to you, clackety-clack.

After finally seeing one of the tree-monsters, she wasn't convinced 'monkey' was the best way to describe it. Shiny black skin and glinting yellow eyes did not a monkey make. And what's with those crazy snake-hairs anyway? Did everything out here have those? Milk-bugs, scaly monkeys, geez, what else?

Dorothy inspected the tree bark above the tent, and sure enough, a hole presented itself where it hadn't been the day before. She stretched and tried to touch the edge, maybe stick her finger in and see how deep it went, but gave up. She simply wasn't tall enough. No biggie. Charlie would be here soon, and she was getting hungry.

Dorothy sifted through her pack, changed into a white tee-shirt—praying that Charlie wouldn't pop in while she was dressing—then wrapped her old tee into a ball and tossed it beside the tent.

She grabbed one of Charlie's blankets and laid out the food stored in her backpack. Two cans of soup, three apples, a pear, few bits of hard-candy, and a half-empty bottle of water. Charlie might have a stockpile buried inside his trunk, but she guessed it wouldn't amount to much, maybe sweets and a few chocolate bars.

"This isn't going to last," she commented and sank a bit. She had two-day's worth of food at best, and only if she rationed it. A half a day's water.

The reality of returning home to resupply hit hard. Her father wouldn't be sympathetic, nor could she expect his grief to distract him again, not this time. Out in the woods all night? No, he was going to be mad, and she knew he had the right. Sheesh, what would happen after he talked to Isais? Cat's out of the bag then; no secrets, no lies.

Setting her worries aside, Dorothy decided breakfast would have to be the first order of the day. She hadn't worn a watch, not since her friends told her the Swatch she wore was 'so five years ago'. Still, the yellow face with the lightning bolt streaking down the plastic band held great appeal to her, so she kept it, until the fire claimed everything she owned.

Since then, time didn't seem to matter so much, and Charlie's World was no exception. There was something rugged about her internal clock dictating her schedule. She growled at the prospect and giggled afterward. Hungry? Dorothy eat. Thirsty? Dorothy drink! What's next? Dorothy hunt? Fish?

She did wonder when Charlie snuck away in his natural world before porting here. She knew there was a time difference between England and the US, any post third grade kid would, but was it a couple hours? Ten? Did this affect when he arrived here? Charlie always landed before her, and she'd never bothered to ask how much time had passed when she arrived.

She shrugged—he'd show up eventually—and took a pocket knife from her pack and began to peel and slice the fruit.

After polishing off two of the three apples, Dorothy kicked back, closed her eyes, and enjoyed the scent of flora dancing about the air. She sighed, and her mind drifted into various explanations she could give to justify her failure to come home the night before. She'd slipped into a light doze when she heard Charlie calling her name.

She spotted him out in the middle of the field and waved. He waved back, ran to the camp, glancing occasionally over his shoulder, then took a seat at her side and scarfed down a few apple slices.

He continued to scan the area, the field and perimeter frilly-tuft trees, as if he couldn't quite decide if something was out of place.

"What's up?" Dorothy finally asked, curiosity getting the better of her.

"I don't know. Does this place seem bigger to you? Or brighter, maybe?"

Dorothy looked about and shrugged. "I don't know, maybe? I thought it was just me—after I woke up." She smirked.

Charlie's eyes widened. "You slept here? Overnight?" Dorothy nodded. He turned to face her. "Wow! What was it like? Did the clackety-clacks come out?"

"I saw one, and one of the fireflies came really close! It looked like a huge dragonfly! So wicked-cool. I don't think those things are monkeys," she added excitedly, motioning toward the woods.

"What did it look like?"

"It's bigger than you and me together. And I think it has those thorns like the milk-bugs, like huge snake-tube…things." She pointed to the hole in the tree above the tent. "That's the mark it left. Oh! And they eat the light-dragons!" she added, then amended, "light-dragonflies."

Charlie listened as she told him how she sang to the insect and its response to her voice. She guessed the clackety-clack monkey had also heard her singing, because it appeared above the tent, black scaly skin and all. She said she hadn't thought it was dangerous, at least not while she was in the camp, and even felt comfortable enough to sleep afterwards. When she finished, Charlie asked, "Why'd you come back after we left?" Dorothy reluctantly told the story.

"What will you say when you go home?" Charlie asked after a long, uncomfortable pause. Dorothy lowered her head. What could she say? *I found a magical key and it transported me to a world outside their own? Hey, forget about crossing the street, Dad, I cross continents…universes! Oh, and in case you were wondering, I made some friends, heck yea! Two of them. Two fourteen-year-old boys born 40 years apart.* He'd ground her for all their lives combined.

"I don't think I can, Charlie." She said this soberly, and her heart raced to hear it aloud. Ever since the fire, Dorothy thought a lot about what life would be like without her in it. She'd imagined her father's unbridled sorrow would carry him to the brink of insanity. She'd imagined standing next to her own grave, right beside her mother's, laughing at all the people grieving over her untimely death.

Then she'd imagined the same, dark scenario, but with no one, not a single person standing at her grave. No one cried for her. Typical mumbo-jumbo she fantasized about when in trouble.

Charlie stared at the ground. He was rifling through his own thoughts, she supposed, maybe looking for the right words to magically cheer her up. She loved him for it; friggen' kid always found the bright side of anything. He turned his head and ran his wrist under his nose. "He'd take your key, wouldn't he?"

"Yeah, probably. I mean, assuming he found out about it. He wouldn't let me out of his sight, that much I'm sure of." Charlie nodded again, crossed his legs, and leaned forward.

"I thought about running away. Then, I thought I didn't have to. Mum's always drinking, and last year I only went to school a day or two a week. No teachers, and not enough places to teach, even if there were. I heard they opened a new school at the church around the corner from Mrs. Caldwane's place, and they have three volunteers who are supposed to catch all of us up to the grades we missed."

"Missed?" Dorothy asked.

"It's because of the war. When I was nine, Mum and Dad sent me with a whole mess of kids to a farm, far outside of town. It was supposed to be safer there, I guess. So many of us, and all ages, from my age to little kids who could barely walk, to big kids who wanted to join the fight and 'teach those Krauts a lesson!'" He triumphantly thrust his arm across his chest as he said this. "They tried to make life normal, I guess. But we didn't have many books. I had to share mine with four others. I learned a little, but I barely remember any of it. I could never get home out of my mind. My dad volunteered with the fire brigade, after the first Blitz. He said, 'The bloody German's are bombing London!'"

"You were there for that?" Dorothy asked.

"Yeah, I was. Least for the first one. I spent a week in the shelter while dad tended to the city. I remember the ground shaking, but not like an earthquake. It was like a thumping that pushed you around, all around your chest. Never been so scared. Me and Mum just cried and held each other. Boom, thump! Boom, thump! The shelter shook, and it rained dirt and dust. Mum made me leave soon after. I was ten when I returned home. Dad died at the docks. Mum said he was beneath a building when it came down on him. Ever since then, she's drank everything he had in the house, and when that ran out, she used our ration tickets to trade, even though she promised I'd never go hungry," he said, then made a prim and mocking face. "Don't be silly, Charles, food will come when it comes. I wouldn't trade your breakfast for a cocktail, what kind of mother do you think I am?"

"I have to wear a tag with my name and age on it whenever I go out. I carry a booklet and it says in big, black letters, 'You will be told how and when to use it.' We're told when and what kind of food to buy!

"All my friends are gone. Some maybe even dead, I guess. Mum's barely alive at all, anyway. So, I don't have to run away. I am already alone." His eyes were wet. "Just like you," he looked up while wiping away the tears. He continued after composing himself. "What was your mum like?"

Dorothy slumped. Describing her mother was never easy. There had been good times, of course. But to describe them, to put her emotions to words after her mom's death…"I hate her," Dorothy blurted, gasping at the crass tone of her voice. Charlie looked startled as well, but recovered quickly, and offered her his unyielding attention. "She left me, Charlie. She left me when I needed her to stay. I don't know why I hate her for that. But I do."

"It doesn't sound that way to me," he replied. "I don't hate my dad for leaving."

"What about your mom? Don't you hate her for what she's done?" Charlie shook his head. "I would," she snapped. "And I do. Not your mother, but my dad. He drinks too. Sometimes a whole lot."

"Well your mom did pass, right? Maybe that's why he drinks."

"So did your father." Her tone was cold. She hadn't considered the similarities between their surviving members of family and how they each coped with the unusual circumstances of their deaths. Booze, the timeless remedy.

"That's why I *don't* hate Mum for her drinking." He sat across from her in silence, running his finger in a circle against the rough wool they sat upon. He drew a line, then two more, creating an imaginary bit at its base. "The key calls when it wants to be found," he whispered. He looked up at her. "You know, we aren't so different."

"I know, your dad, my mom…"

"No, that's not what I meant. I mean we aren't so different from them." He pointed to the drawing of the keys. "Different drink is all."

Dorothy frowned and avoided meeting his eye. She wasn't sure where Charlie was going with this, but his words echoed back at her. *The key calls when it wants to be found.* He's talking about these fish-bowl worlds. About three kids running.

"My mom was beautiful. She had this long, flowing hair. Blonde, like mine, with so many curls. She used to sit me in her lap and read to me. Sometimes she'd read a book she'd recently finished. There was one," she chuckled thoughtfully. "I think I was around nine when she read it to me. She told me it was scary, but I didn't find it scary at all. It was about a couple who lost their little boy in a car wreck and buried him in a pet cemetery. Was like a day later or something when the kid came back to life. Stephen King wrote it. He's like the class A spook writer of my time."

"That does sound scary; your mum read that to you?"

"She did, but she'd always follow the chapter with the truth. It was kinda neat. She'd say the boy was a zombie, and asked me if zombies existed. I'd tell her no of course, and then she'd ask me how I knew? God, I'd say. Cause he wouldn't allow that to happen. I've never had a bad dream after she explained what she'd read to me. She always knew what to say to make me feel better."

"Doesn't sound like you hate your mum at all."

Dorothy smiled. A chill raced up her back, and she settled into her memories. She laughed, and tears streaked down her face.

"I bet you have some good memories of your dad, too."

"I suppose. We did go hunting a lot in Georgia. I remember some of the lessons he taught me. He showed me how to track animals, light fires, stuff like that. He showed me what I could eat and what I couldn't eat if I ever got lost. When it was just us, yeah, I kinda liked it."

Charlie nodded. He brushed the back of his hand over both eyes, and looked away again, choking back a sob. Dorothy wrapped her arms around his neck and kissed him on the back of his head. She embraced him, he let loose and cried in her arms.

She wept too, allowing the idea she might never see her father again settle deep into the pit of her stomach.

"What should we do, Dorothy? I mean, can't we stay together? Maybe I could come with you to your home," Charlie suggested. She considered this, and shook her head.

"My father wouldn't want to keep you. He'd probably send you to a foster home, if the police didn't send us both to a loony bin first. No," she continued, and scanned around the wildflowers and tuft trees. "I think I have to stay here, somehow."

Charlie turned, and his face brightened. "We don't have to stay here, not in this place I mean. We can go anywhere we want to," he said, and displayed his key.

The air turned sweeter, and Dorothy found herself almost laughing at the notion.

"How, Charlie?"

"Well, we'd have to get Rags in on it, but I think if we sneak into the same place we were yesterday," he said, and Dorothy frowned. "No wait! Yes, it's about the fruit, and maybe other things to eat. Look, if you can't go home, and I can't go home, well, what other choice do we have? We must eat something…and find some water. We'll definitely need to find that." He considered this for a time, then added, "So let's explore and take what these worlds offer us." He held out his hand.

For a moment, the trees, even the punchbowl flowers seemed to widen, as if the land around her opened expectantly. For a heartbeat, the world became exponentially larger.

They'd have to be careful, but they could do it. She nodded, pulled Charlie into her arms, and held him tight.

Together, just like always.

They cleaned up breakfast, stuffed a blanket in Dorothy's pack along with three chocolate bars and the Luger, despite Dorothy's objections. Her mood darkened, and she attributed this to the potential bloodshed that a gun might bring. Odd for her, considering where she was raised. Guns had always been in her life, heck she owned a .22 caliber rifle—before it, too, burned in the fire. Something told her keeping this thing was wrong, and it should not exist here. Or, after some thought, she should not exist here, not with it.

She shook the notion from her mind, deciding it to be nothing more than paranoia—it may destroy ya, as the song goes—and turned so Charlie could retrieve the key from her pants pocket. She laid both hands over his shoulder and closed her eyes.

Ragesha was waiting when they arrived. He greeted them by waving a pair of long tools with serrated hooks over his head. Wire wrapped around the discolored wood near the bases, securing the makeshift blades in place.

"Look! I thought about our little problem yesterday, and I stole these from my brother. They won't reach the top of the trees, but I think we can pluck the lower fruit!" he proclaimed. "Maybe if we are quick enough, we can nab one of those super birds, too. Have what you Americans call Thanksgiving." Charlie nodded agreeably.

Dorothy said nothing, only marched to the edge of his camp, and sat down to his left. Ragesha glanced at her for a moment, then peered over her shoulder, and grunted. Charlie looked in the same direction and said, "Something wrong?" He picked up the pruning stick and proceeded to wave it about as if holding a spear.

"No, nothing I guess. Just seemed like this place got…"

"Bigger?" Dorothy asked, then turned to see what had caught his eye. The field did seem bigger, like Charlie's. She looked up, and the sky felt deeper. The chameleon grass beneath seemed thick, lush, and bright.

"You know, my place seemed kind of…wider too, I guess. I jumped in quite a few meters away from where I normally land when coming here. Thought Dorothy had something to do with that, but now I'm not so sure. She spent the night, you know."

Ragesha raised his eyebrows. "You did?" Dorothy nodded. "Why? I mean, I like this place too, but to spend the night here?"

"Afraid of the milk-bugs?" Charlie teased, but cut it short when he saw Ragesha's eyes widen.

"What if they crawl around the ground at night? What if more than one stings you? One sting is bad enough. And besides, there could be other things sneaking about after dark."

Something just plain felt rotten in Denmark. It had something to do with the growing landscape, but she couldn't pinpoint it. The only thing different between yesterday and today was the night she'd spent in Charlie's camp.

"Say, wouldn't it be rad, if, by me staying the whole night, the land grew?" Dorothy asked. She turned back to the boys.

"What's 'rad'?" Ragesha asked. Charlie raised a hand, as if to say, "I got this," and told him Dorothy meant it would be cool. Ragesha still looked blank, Charlie tried again: "Neat?"

"Oh. What made you spend the night?"

Charlie and Dorothy relayed her tale and finished with their decision to make a permanent camp in either Charlie's World or the new one. He listened intently, and by the end, she noticed he'd become a bit antsy.

"My brother joined the 'resistance'," he blurted at length. Dorothy and Charlie turned to each other, shrugged, and gave Ragesha their undivided attention. "I don't even know what that means! He told me I had to tend the farm, and he would return when he could. He picked up a leaflet, said it was a 'call to arms', and ran off to join the war. I didn't even know we were at war." He looked to Dorothy for confirmation. She shrugged and shook her head. "No idea, *amigo.*"

He continued. "There wasn't much to farm before, even less now." He raised his hands in defeat. "I spend all of my time here. How can I farm there? And I think some of my neighbors have taken our land, though I can't be sure."

Dorothy moved over and took a seat beside Ragesha.

"I don't think there will be much for my brother to return home to. And I don't want to be there when he does come home. He will be very angry."

"Well," Charlie proclaimed. "Sounds to me like the Three Key Children are about to undertake a new and exciting adventure!" He slapped Ragesha on the back. The boys looked at Dorothy. She shivered, a feeling of uneasiness coursed through her then, and she looked around apprehensively. She felt suddenly dirty, as if she had stolen a candy bar and waved to the cashier on the way out of the store. She couldn't explain why.

She suggested they head for the fruit-lands of yesterday, and do it quickly. They joined hands as Charlie combined their keys.

Chapter 3
What Do I Know?

Ellen stood and stretched. Mr. Dutta had excused himself to use the bathroom. Afternoon turned to evening and the perimeter lights snapped on, casting a white-yellow light into the neighboring forest. She had seen the same cluster of trees through many of the rear-facing windows and had never thought they looked as ominous as they appeared tonight.

The box sitting at the foot of Mr. Dutta's chair caught her eye. That box held the stone key he'd shown her this morning. She turned her attention to Dorothy, then back to the key. What was the goal here? Keys unlock doors sure enough, but she suspected this particular key was symbolic for something far greater. Unlocking Dorothy's mind, perhaps? Opening the door to her subconscious?

Mr. Dutta didn't project the paranoia typical of so many schizophrenic patients, though she'd be the first to admit she was far from an expert. He obviously had his details straight, twenty years of story crafting would do that she supposed. He wasn't self-obsessed, which would have been a stronger indicator of schizophrenia. His care for Dorothy was obvious. The entire story revolved around her and—if anything he said could be trusted—his entire life, post whatever trauma landed her like this. That's a lot of guilt he's atoning for.

She supposed, given enough time lost in the recesses of one's mind, even the most reasonable person could believe their own fabrications and build a semi-normal life around them. If this was the case, then why did she want to believe him? Seriously, keys that unlocked lands beyond time? Giant birds, milk-bugs, and tree faring monsters? Heck, all she'd have to do was drop the rock key in her back pocket to disprove the whole thing.

But something within, call it intuition or a voice of reason, something told her to wait and hear him out. Disproving—and she wasn't so sure she could—or overtly proving his story, might be detrimental to her health. No, the oversized wall decoration can stay right where it is, in a box, on a floor. This didn't ease her mind nor sway the little voice within from screaming, "Danger!"

She didn't know why, Ragesha's demeanor has been nothing short of downright likeable over these past few hours, but still, looking down at his box seized her insides up. Damned thing gave her the heebie-jeebies, and there was no escaping it.

She turned her attention to the window. The wind was gusting. She glimpsed a shadow dancing between two of the larger trees near the edge of the property and she jumped, then shuddered. "Jesus, my mind is playing tricks on me," she whispered. Mr. Dutta exited the restroom and joined her at the window.

His eyes had a strangely knowing look. "I have been running from shadows for 30 years. It becomes a normal state of being."

"Ragesha, how do you stand it?" she asked and covered her chest with her hands.

"The eyes tell the truth, Ellen. The mind, however, interprets emotion. I could tell you everything you have heard today is a lie, and you would be relieved. The shadows you see would simply be trees swaying in the wind. On the other hand, I could say all my words are true, and that the phantasms you observed have been following Dorothy all her life. What do you think you would see then?" Ellen took a seat and closed her eyes. The pulse in her neck throbbed.

Occam's razor, she reminded herself. He's crazy, she's a vegetable, and he's fishing in a barren lake if he thinks she can rehabilitate Dorothy back to consciousness. *The mind interprets emotion.* His words. He wants this to be true, and that's how he's made it. The simplest explanation.

"Did she ever meet…the creature?" Ellen asked. Just saying the words, *the creature*, not *the manifestation*, not even *the man*…the creature. The monster.

Ellen shuddered.

She could argue it was a slip of the tongue, a tired mind adhering to a tall tale, but it wasn't. She believed it, heart and soul, blood to bone.

Ragesha nodded. "Yes, and unfortunately sooner rather than later. Are you tired, Ellen? I have kept you well beyond our scheduled time."

"I think I'm fine. Right now, I couldn't sleep even if I wanted to."

He smiled wide and slapped his armrest. "Good," he nodded, "this is very good. Now, where were we?

"Dorothy, unlike myself and Charlie, sensed something had been out of sorts. I don't know if it was a result of having spent the night in Charlie's World, or the brush with the Spintwister the previous day. I think she was just special. One step ahead of the rest of us. She was hoping her fears and reservations would diminish when we arrived in the land of fruit. They did not."

Chapter 4
Birds, Bees, Fruits, and Trees

"All this traveling must be getting to me. Now this place seems smaller," Ragesha said. "And look at our circles," he pointed behind them. Dorothy turned, and sure enough, a large black patch of dark earth stood approximately fifty feet from the one they currently stood in. Yesterday's entry point.

"Yeah, I don't know," Dorothy shrugged distractedly. Something had been troubling her. Was it guilt? Over running away? Over taking Charlie and Ragesha from their worlds and running away with her?

The commitment she made with Ragesha and Charlie warmed her. Made her feel hopeful. Having both at her side, exploring new lands and potential campsites, heck, maybe even a new home, should luck have a hand in it, and she believed it might. This commitment was as solid as the ground she stood upon, and it didn't trouble her at all.

Perhaps the idea she might never see her home again tugged at her heartstrings. She'd forget her father's face. The farm. The foal. This bothered her, but not as much as it probably should have. Maybe that's all it was. Dorothy simply not caring one way or the other. She wanted to believe this. If only she could.

Dorothy turned to the closest batch of trees, shook her head, and began walking. "It doesn't matter. Just means everything's closer and we don't have to walk so dang far. Let's do what we came to do."

Charlie shrugged, grabbed one of two pruning sticks, and paced behind Dorothy. Ragesha picked up the other stick and fell in line. A thin stream of mist appeared and trailed behind them.

They plodded toward the oasis in relative silence. Charlie had refilled his canteens before returning, as had Ragesha, so water was in good supply. Dorothy could hear their heavy breathing behind her, in sync with her own.

As they approached the oasis, the growing caws of giant birds drowned out all other sounds. After about an hour of hard walking, they could make out hints of orange in the silhouetted black canopies. Soon, they would see the cobalt veins running along the giant leaves, and then be able to retrieve the long-awaited fruit. Maybe find a pond or two feeding the vegetation. The place had to get water from somewhere, right? Certainly wouldn't feed from storms that disappeared before they produced any rain. Still, it couldn't hurt to be careful, so she turned to ask Charlie if he might take her canteen home with him, should this trip prove dry.

She stopped in her tracks. A ripple of smoke had stretched around Charlie's midsection, split into five smaller strands, and was hovering around the center of his tweed vest. In a heartbeat, it dissipated. She shook her head to make sure she wasn't dreaming, and boy, did the feeling of not-quite-right return with a vengeance.

The boys assumed that her stopping meant break time, so they dropped their belongings and fell to the ground. Charlie stretched, coughed, and untied the canteen from his belt, drawing a long swig before handing the bottle to Ragesha. Dorothy remained frozen, contemplating whether what she witnessed had been real, where it had come from, where it went.

Ragesha was the first to notice her odd expression. He tapped Charlie on the shoulder, and they eyed Dorothy warily. She ignored them, and continued to observe the area around them. She stiffened, lowered to the ground, then pressed her thumb to her finger and wiggled her hand. Charlie nodded and pulled the bonded keys from his pocket.

"What is it?" Ragesha asked.

"I saw something," Dorothy replied. She cocked her head and closed her eyes.

"What?" Charlie whispered.

"Smoke," she replied.

"Is that all?" Charlie blurted and both boys laughed.

Dorothy stepped over to Charlie. "Open your shirt," she demanded, and pointed at the three buttons near the center of his chest, where she saw, what? Fingers? It sure looked like a hand, or the shadow of one. He looked at her askance but pulled his shirt apart anyway, displaying the milk-bug wound which had all but healed. It appeared agitated and slightly discolored, with a thin red ring around the scabbed puncture wound. The cut from Ragesha's knife looked darker, as if Charlie had been scratching at it. Four greenish-blue bruises surrounded the wound, each the size of a dime. These looked fresh.

"You should put some ointment on that," Ragesha commented. Charlie brushed a finger along the scab and shrugged. Dorothy spread her fingers and matched the four bruises. She pulled her hand to her chin and frowned.

Charlie's amusement turned sour. "Dorothy, what's going on?"

Dorothy waited, considered, then shook her head. She turned to the oasis, still a ways from where they stood. She sighed. "Let's just get the fruit and bolt."

They pressed on, silent but for their footfalls. When they arrived at the first cluster of fruit trees, Dorothy kept a watchful eye on the boys, making sure neither of them turned into the gob-head, looney-toon dorks of the previous day. Apart from wielding their mighty sticks of pruning, they showed little sign of idiocy. If she hadn't known better, she might say they were erring on the side of caution. A pleasant change for once.

The boys searched the branches of the large trees and the sky above them. Satisfied they were freak-bird free—you never know what's going to lunge at you out here, giant birds included—Charlie lifted his pruning stick and jumped to tap the nearest branch. The fruit hung at least four feet above it.

Ragesha suggested they attempt a climb, but they couldn't find any footing. The trunk had to be the size of a small house, and the bark was smooth all the way around.

"They didn't seem this tall yesterday," Ragesha said, took a step back and sighed.

"You'd think they would have shrunk, like everything else did."

Charlie hoisted the pruning stick over his shoulder, stepped back, and hurled it, striking the lower branch. The stick wobbled and fell to the ground. Ragesha laughed and raised his spear, which flew just under the branch and disappeared in the woods.

"Rags," Dorothy protested. "Now we have to go in and get it."

They approached the edge of the woods and listened. She couldn't see anything through the canopy of oversized leaves, and there wasn't much sunlight. Come to think of it, there hadn't been much of any sun in any of the worlds they had visited. It was dang dark in there, and almost black beyond the first few sets of trees. It didn't feel right, just like this whole bugged-out place didn't feel right.

"I wouldn't go in there." A deep, hollow voice sounded behind them.

The three children gasped and spun around. A freakishly tall man—or…creature?—hovered before the children and seemed to fade in and out of view. He had no feet, as far as Dorothy could tell, and she could see the outline of grass through his knees. His chest—coated in a thick, steaming skin, trailed into thin smoking tendrils which popped as they broke free from the dark cloak covering his body. His face was pale white, with dark sunken eyes—or at any rate, patches of black which blurred the skin where eyes should be. A smoky, flat-brimmed hat covered his head, shadowing a smile that stretched from pointed ear to pointed ear. He moved with his hands clasped behind his back. The children pressed together. Dorothy fumbled about for Charlie's hand, hoping he would get the hint, get the keys.

The creature stretched from the waist, thinned, and sped alongside Ragesha within a heartbeat's time—his legs trailing after. Each movement erupted into a chorus of crackling and popping, like the sound of bacon on a skillet.

Dorothy leaped to the right, away from the boys, and toward the camp, hoping to make a run for it. Charlie and Ragesha were frozen. The creature rubbed his chin, and clucked as if calling a chicken to roost, and commented solemnly, "Nasty things in there."

"Charlie!" Dorothy hissed, and motioned quickly with her hand. The creature cocked his head, snapped, stretched, and appeared an inch from her face.

"Now, now, little no-girl, not so fast," he grumbled. She turned her head, closed her eyes and wished it away, the putrid breath, dead skin, all of it…gone.

She cringed, and he bared a set of sharp, crooked teeth, as if to confirm her obedience. He receded, and returned his attention to the pruning stick and the fruit above.

He tapped the base of his long, pointy chin.

"You weren't going to eat that, were you?" he asked with a touch of amusement. Dorothy turned to the boys—now a good 30-feet away—chivalry ain't dead here—and sank. She watched as Ragesha lifted the keys, and Charlie blindly groped for his hand.

The creature crackled, turned, and glanced at Dorothy. He stretched to Ragesha's side and wrapped a pale claw around his shoulders, three bony fingers covering the entirety of the boy's chest. Ragesha stood rigid, eyes wide. The creature calmly took the keys from his hand and smiled.

"No need to rush away," he said. A thin pincer extended from one of his claws and ran through the bow of the glass key. He swept sideways, trailing his cloak in a stream of smoke behind him, as if a breeze brushed over a wet fire. The eerie crackling sound followed, then slowed when he turned. He twirled the keys around his massive finger. "I see you have found my keys, and they brought my children home." He perked, turned, and smiled his horrible, yellow smile. "A reward!" he said, and his arm stretched past Dorothy in a fury of snaps. It plucked an orange fruit from the tree and dropped it at Ragesha's feet. It slapped its tremendous clawed fingers together and a horrible clattering echoed in their ears, like bricks falling against concrete.

"Now we're all happy," he mused.

Dorothy's mind was screaming for her to run, hide—anything. But her body was rooted to the ground. She forced herself to keep breathing.

His jagged-toothed face, dark eyes, and white claws were solid and bright now, but the clothing he wore distorted their shape, trailing and popping in tiny puffs. He was never fully still, like a figure on the highway during a blistering afternoon, wavering into translucent steam. Dorothy's mind danced with the undulating lines. She reeled, suddenly faint.

The creature placed himself between the two boys and curled his vile head around to look at Ragesha, evidently wanting him to retrieve the gift in front of him.

Ragesha, though, was still as a stone. Charlie crept from Ragesha's side.

The creature snorted, spun, and placed himself at the center of the triangle the three children formed. It looked Ragesha and Charlie over, then sighed, as if insulted by their lack of appreciation over its gift. "Oh, come now, children, it can't be all bad, can it?" he asked, and drifted in a circle, as if pacing. "Is it these?" he asked, and displayed the cluster of keys to the boys. He looked at Dorothy and gripped them tight. "Don't worry, I won't keep them." He snapped next to Dorothy, and leaned in to whisper, raising a claw so the boys wouldn't see him speak. "Kids these days, eh no-girl?" he mused, and ran a claw under her chin. She sucked in her breath, as if to scream, but choked as he pressed his claw into her skin. Blood trickled down the length of his finger. "I wouldn't," he hissed, then snapped back to the center of the children.

"I don't want your keys. Not today!" he shouted, as if this should have been obvious from the start. "You two children have done me a favor, and I return a favor for a favor!"

"Then give them back," Charlie blurted. His voice pitched, and he jumped upon hearing it. The creature raised his eyebrows as though amused.

"Don't fret, dear boy. All in time, all in good time." He pointed to Ragesha. "You there! Little brown boy, pick up that fruit."

Ragesha yelped, and ran to the fallen orange. He strained, lifted the fruit, and held it out, barely able to keep it steady. The creature nodded, extended a claw, and cut a slice along its side. The rind bulged and parted, and two milk-bugs slipped from its center.

Ragesha released the fruit and leaped backward.

"You see my dears, your friend, the Spintwister, is here to serve you," he said passionately, then zipped in front of Ragesha. He raised a claw, smiled, and smashed the fruit into the ground, then turned to Charlie. "Never hurt you."

"So, we'll get our keys?" Ragesha asked while stepping away.

"Of course!" He raised his claws innocently. "What must you take me for?"

"You're—a bad man! A monster!" Dorothy exclaimed, relieved she could find any words at all.

"Me? Nonsense, no-girl, I'm not a bad man. I'm no man at all!"

"Then what are you?" Charlie whimpered. "I'm sorry, but you're really scaring us!"

Dorothy gathered her courage while the creature's attention was on Charlie, and circled around him to the right, meeting up with Ragesha. She nodded to the keys, and he shrugged helplessly.

"I am like you, little boy. Lost, scared, and alone. Why," he looked to the sky in a flare of melodrama, holding a smoldering hand against his chest, "it was only a few days ago—if that means anything here—that I didn't even know who I was. I was this," he said, displayed his hand, and smiled as it popped into a wisp of smoke. "And now you two are here, and I am this!" The creature's hand reappeared, solid.

"But there are three of us," Ragesha replied.

"What? Her?" he asked, snapped behind Dorothy and inhaled her. She winced, then shivered as its breath trailed down her neck like a serpent. "Oh no, dear boy. I know children, and this is no child at all."

Dorothy's defenses snapped on. In a single moment, her fears bled from her and she turned to the Spintwister, as if he were her father accusing her of wrongdoing. The familiar sense of shame heated her up. She spun and the creature lurched backward. She shouted, "What do you mean, I'm not a child? I'm fourteen, same as those two!" The boys nodded. The creature clapped and knelt. Dorothy still had to crane her head to meet his vacant eyes.

"No," he whispered menacingly. "Children who visit me, emit pain and suffering. What do you think those keys are for? Fun?" He snapped between Ragesha and Charlie and placed its tremendous claws on their shoulders. "Look at these two," it said, drew in a breath, and tussled Charlie's hair. "Fruit, ripe for the picking. What is it boys? Parents, brothers, sisters perhaps? Society got you down?" Both nodded compliantly. The creature sighed, almost sympathetically. "It always is, isn't it? Some grown-up drags you down the paths of sorrow. Life becomes unbearable. You run and hide and when you do, my keys find you and bring you here."

"Why?" Ragesha asked.

"Why? To take the pain from you! To make it...my own. Isn't that why you've come?"

Both boys looked at each other, to Dorothy, and back to the creature. She didn't like the sense of understanding in their eyes, the sense of acceptance. She didn't like how the creature was playing them against her. Why were they falling for it?

"I've been through—" Dorothy began, and the creature erupted in a crackle of smoke and bubbles. It rematerialized inches from her face, and snarled.

"You have been through nothing! You have seen—nothing!" it said, and inhaled her. "Your pain is not your pain." He sniffed at her. "It is stolen!" He vanished, and snapped back to the boys.

"My children, I have been through this before, and I can guide you. One step to the next, creating a paradise for you. I will take your woes, your troubles, your worries and doubts, and pull them within me. A thousand children I have saved, and a thousand more I crave."

Dorothy stomped her foot, hoping to pull their attention away from the creature, but they stared stupidly at his bewitching face.

"Now, your nights are calling. Your parents will worry. You must go. Return to me in the morning, and we will begin to take away your pain." The Spintwister displayed his hands to the boys, as if it were their humble servant. Darned if those two idiots didn't nod like a couple of hungry puppy-dogs. Boy, she'd give them a proper tongue-lashing when they got out of here.

The Spintwister presented the keys to Ragesha, who retrieved them, as if in a trance, then stepped over to Charlie. They looked at Dorothy expectantly. The creature's arm extended between Dorothy and the two boys, and he shook his head.

"The no-girl stays."

"The hell, I will!" Dorothy exclaimed, and darted under his arm. The creature bubbled, snapped, and reappeared in her path. Giant claws wrapped around Dorothy's body and pressed her into the ground. The Spintwister craned his head to meet hers.

He did not look at the two boys when he spoke. "Leave now or never again."

"No!" Dorothy screamed, and wiggled to break free. His claws dug into the ground, pressing around and against her chest until she struggled to breath. Ragesha mouthed, "I'm sorry," and pulled the keys apart.

Just like that, they were gone.

The Spintwister released her and stood. "Why!" Dorothy shrieked, leaping to her feet, and scanning the trees and the horizon toward their camp. They couldn't, wouldn't leave her there, not with him—it.

"Relax, little no-girl. I'm not going to hurt you. I don't even know what you are."

He turned away from her.

Dorothy brushed herself off and glared. "Stop calling me that." The Spintwister flapped his white claws at her, as if sweeping her under a rug.

"What do you want me to call you? 'Dorothy' perhaps?" He laughed at her.

"That's my name, isn't it?"

"No, no, little no-girl, you've worn that one out. And it's not even yours," he mused, his back still toward her. He looked to the sky, and rubbed his chin. "No, I think I'll stick with a no-name, at least until I figure out what you are, instead of what you are not."

She slumped to the ground and crossed her arms defiantly. He had a lot of nerve calling her no-anything, when he didn't resemble anything either. At least he didn't want to eat her—not yet, anyway. But his words troubled her. Not so much the name-calling—well, maybe a little, telling her she wasn't a girl, when clearly, she was, and by God, she had the parts to prove it. That was annoying, but not ground shattering. What bothered her more was that he viewed her as separate from Charlie and Ragesha, as if she hadn't made the same trips they had. Each of them had a key, and each had traveled from there to here. They were the *Three* Key Children.

The creature popped and fizzled as he shifted about her. "You're trying to figure out what I mean by all of this, aren't you?" he mused. Again, Dorothy glared.

"You don't see it?"

"See what?" She crossed her arms defiantly. He erupted a few feet away from her, then slowly drifted to the ground and stretched prone, so he could meet Dorothy's eye.

The Spintwister ran a claw into the ground near Dorothy's knee, and scraped a small line in the blackened earth. He tapped the dirt, never breaking eye contact. He extended two fingers and walked them along her leg.

His voice was hoarse. "Fear, no-girl. Your boys have it. Every child who has crossed into my realm has it." He stopped below the knee, and met her eye. "You do not. You have nothing. Only borrowed emotion, and when you are here," he snarled, and suddenly pressed his claw through her skin and muscle and into the ground beneath.

"You lose all connection!"

Dorothy roared in agony, and she struck at the creature, grabbing at his arm and writhing.

"Your pain is false! I cannot take it from you!" he howled. "You are a thief! You steal emotion! You steal identity, you steal everything!" He dragged her by the leg, along the edge of the trees. She thrashed, begging him to stop, but soon her mind grayed, and she lost control of her limbs.

The Spintwister extracted his claw and stood over her, hands behind his back, watching her intently. Dorothy curled, and cried. She gripped her calf, thigh, and knee, expecting the warm stickiness of her blood to ooze around her fingers. She wondered how she would survive such a gaping wound without medical treatment, or even so much as a band-aid. She could lose every single drop of her blood, and who would know?

"You cannot steal here, no-girl. Nor can you lose what you do not possess." When Dorothy didn't move, he wrapped a claw around the top of her head and yanked her upright.

She cried out and shifted to her left leg, fearing she'd fall if she didn't. The creature snarled, and swung a claw across her face. The pain was jarring, but then gone. Not even a lasting sting or tingle of nerves. Dorothy looked into his vacant eyes, and he raised a brow. She shifted her weight, and pressed both feet firmly against the ground.

She bounced on her heels, hopped a little, and when she was satisfied there were no wounds, bolted into the forest. She moved quickly, darting between trees while scanning for the missing pruning stick. The Spintwister's laughter thundered behind her and faded with each pounding step.

"You cannot run from me! I am the birds, the bees, the fruit, and the trees!"

Dorothy slid alongside the pruning stick, snatched it up and heaved it toward the field, striking only air. She scanned about, expecting the creature to appear alongside her, and she readied herself. Leaves rustled above her. Milk-bugs lurched from tree to tree. She closed her eyes and forced away the burning stains of daylight that flashed each time she blinked—and then, listened.

She recalled her father's advice given to her on one of their hunting trips. "You'll hear the critters long before you see them. Trust your senses, close your eyes, and listen. Know what each animal sounds like," he had said. He'd scattered some leaves at her feet and mimicked the footfalls of the different animals with his hands. "Deer tend to pause when grazing. Step-step-step, then silence. Boar have a rhythm when they walk. Smaller critters move around in spurts."

She wasn't sure this applied here, hell the dang thing didn't have feet as far as she could tell, but it was worth a shot. *Close your eyes, hold still, listen.* Dorothy's breathing slowed, and the white shades bouncing off her lids—faded. She opened her eyes.

The canopy of giant leaves blocked out the sky, but hadn't darkened the floor completely. Iridescent leaves littered the ground around her. Light bled dimly from the edge of the forest.

Snaps echoed behind her, and the deep crows of the birds thundered overhead, drowning the rattle of the clackety-clack monkeys.

She backed against a tree and sighed. What could she do? She couldn't leave, and there wasn't anywhere to run to. The woods offered a feeling of cover and gave her a moment to catch her breath. But could she hide here? Could a person even hide from…it?

What troubled her, maybe even more than the creature, was the boys. Why had they so readily abandoned her? Weren't they the Three Key Children? Was that all just a stupid game? She wouldn't have done same if the situation were reversed. She didn't think they were cowards, so how could they do this to her?

"Because they had to," she whispered. The first jump would be to Ragesha's World, and she thought the trip might stop there. Or she hoped.

Three taps, like a woodpecker chipping away at an old oak tree, sang overhead. Behind this, and lower, a thin cracking rolled from the ground toward the canopy. Dorothy drew in her breath and pushed her back against the bark. She held the pruning stick to her chest.

More tapping, this time to her right. Another round to her left. She peeked over her shoulder. Just trees. She rolled her eyes upward, and the Spintwister's white claws scraped the bark above her head. Dorothy whirled, side-stepped, and pushed the stick around the side of the tree. It pressed into what felt like a sack of sand. She heard a moan and a grunt, released the stick, and ran towards the open field.

The blue sky had grown so bright it was blinding, and the grass seemed to twist and knot around her ankles. Dorothy found herself leaping between thick patches, zigzagging toward the black scars of land marking their entry-point.

She hoped, God she hoped…

The Spintwister's voice thundered across the plain. The cracking and popping drew near, then shot off to the right. She jumped, and poured on the speed. Her legs burned and she struggled to maintain pace. Each step diminished her breath and chipped away what little energy she had.

Not much left, and so long to go. She wouldn't make it. Had she expected to?

The Spintwister snapped on her left and drifted alongside Dorothy. She dared not look at him, but pumped all she had into one final push.

The Spintwister laughed manically.

"Birds, bees, flowers and trees!" he shouted. Grass thickened in front of her; flowers bloomed to her left and right. Blades scraped her knees and twisted around her ankles. Her run slowed to a walk, then to a crawl.

She struggled for a time, then fell to her knees and sobbed. The Spintwister hovered, then gently sank to the ground beside her.

"I am all, little no-girl. I am all."

Dorothy collapsed. The grass loosened, and without warning Dorothy stumbled forward, launching into a full run once she found her footing.

"Where are you going?" His voice trailed after her, sounding genuinely confused.

She didn't answer, but plowed forward.

"Stop running. There is nowhere to go!" he shouted. His deep, hollow voice grew distant, falling further with each pressing, painful step. There was no way to tell how far she had run. She thought she'd passed several of the entry circles they had made, but couldn't be sure. Somewhere ahead, she thought, lay her only hope.

Another patch of grass emerged in her path. She leaped in a wild effort to clear it, then felt a weight against her chest and the breath was snatched from her. The sky darkened, and the air grew thick as soup.

Dorothy landed on her back. She blinked. Charlie and Ragesha were staring down at her—holding the keys. The boys were wide-eyed and trembling, and she had never been so happy to see them. She pulled them to her and cried.

"Go," Ragesha said, extracting himself from the hug and adding, "and good luck to you, brother."

Dorothy rolled her head toward him, but Ragesha was gone.

Charlie turned the glass key, bit down, and held it above Dorothy's torn pants. He kissed her on the forehead, smiled, and whispered, "I love you. Don't come back."

She felt the world dissolving, and a second later, was kneeling in the center of a large hole in the concrete at the center of the stables.

Chapter 5
Officer, I Cannot Tell a Lie

Dorothy's father and uncle ran to her side, her cries echoing throughout the ranch. A half a dozen police officers swarmed out of the house. Dorothy, still on her hands and knees, knelt in the center of a hole cut in the stable's concrete floor. She locked eyes with her father and curled her knees to her chest. He slid alongside her, there in the dirt, and embraced her.

The next few hours were a blur of questions, answers, and half-truths. She was honest, as much as she could be, when telling her story. The detective, a burly man nearing his retirement, met with Dorothy in the kitchen, accompanied by her uncle and father. The once pristine living room featuring her uncle's masterful woodwork, now housed bulky, blinking boxes on every flat surface. The machines were manned by men in suits, some with headphones, others with pen and paper. Red and blue lights reflected off the walls of the living room. Dorothy found herself sinking into her chair, feeling oppressed by the cacophony. They were here for answers, but they would find nothing.

The burly man introduced himself as Detective Hodges, the lead investigator in her missing child case. He spoke softly, often brushing his mop of peppered hair away from his brow, or biting his lip. More than once, he excused himself to slip outside for a smoke.

"Are you hurt?" This was the first question everyone asked. She wished she could answer yes. It would be so much easier to explain, even understand her own experience.

Dorothy assured everyone she was unharmed. It couldn't be, *shouldn't* be true, not with the memory of a claw piercing her leg through and to the ground, but there she was all the same: fine.

The detective apologized for the next series of questions, but he had to ask them.

"Who did this to you?" he asked. She answered this honestly. "I don't know. A man, I think?"

"Do you remember when you were abducted?" he followed while scribbling on a small, ring-bound notepad.

"Abducted?" Then it dawned on her: Isais hadn't told anyone how she'd disappeared. They didn't know.

"I wasn't, I don't think. He just wouldn't let me leave." Again, truth above the lie. She was getting good at this. "After we argued, me and my dad, I ran into the woods. I got lost, turned around. I guess he found me then."

The detective asked about familiar landscapes. "Did you recognize where you were? Could you find your way back? Can you point in the general direction? How long were you walking before finding her way back?"

Again, she answered honestly. "No, I have no idea how to find my way back." Without the boys, she'd never see the fruit-land again, so, truth. When asked about direction, she pointed toward the stables. A dozen men and two hound dogs raced past the paddocks toward the woods. As for the last question, she figured it had been only a few hours since the crossing.

Hodges asked if she was alone during that time, and she told him no, two boys were with her. They escaped before she did and returned to help her. Dorothy told the detective their names, feigned ignorance on details, save for their physical appearances and age. It didn't matter, he'd turn up a goose egg no matter where he dug. She described the Spintwister as a tall, pale man, thin at the waist and dressed in black. No facial hair. She wasn't sure if he had hair on his head because he wore a hat. She omitted details about him having claws and a tendency to bubble-pop-smoke everywhere he moved.

He asked what kind of hat, and Dorothy shrugged. "Sort of like Richie Sambora, just bigger, maybe flatter."

"Richie who?" he asked, and Dorothy rolled her eyes.

"Bon Jovi's lead guitarist, hello?" How could anyone not know that? Dorothy scanned the room. A few officers smirked, others shrugged, and her father sighed and looked embarrassed, but maybe also a little relieved.

The detective cited his age as an excuse, then asked if Dorothy could help by retracing her steps home, hoping to clue in on where in the mighty Ocala forest he might have imprisoned her. Here she had to lie outright. She told how the boys led her out of the woods, though when and where was a blur. She wasn't even sure how she wound up in the stables, nor how long she had been there when her father found her. No, she didn't recall any structures, just lots of trees. Hodges nodded, and asked his associates to join him outside.

Dorothy's father and uncle took seats to either side of her. She turned away, embarrassed about lying, sad at having no other choice. It was during this awkward silence that Dorothy—trying to avoid eye contact—happened to notice her clothing for the first time. Her pants were ragged from the knee down where the Spintwister had clawed and dragged her. Black soot mixed with iridescent flakes darkened her skin from her thighs up to her shoulders. Sweat and dirt stained her tee-shirt. She couldn't see her hair, but imagined it was as nasty as the rest of her.

"How…how long was I gone?" she asked. She guessed two days tops, but who knew how time rolled over there.

"Four days," her father replied. He hugged her again and when he pulled away she noticed how bloodshot and weary his eyes were.

"I'm sorry I ran off."

"We'll worry about that another day," he said, twitched, and wiped his eyes. He asked again if she was okay, did the man do anything to her, did he have a name, did he…touch her.

She wanted to tell him yes—all of the above, but couldn't. She wanted to tell him about the key…

The key!

She flipped her hand around her hip and pressed against her rump, brushed the key, and cringed when the pocket of her jeans tore as her fingers brushed the glass. The wooden chair creaked beneath her. She withdrew her hand, relieved. The key was there, safe and sound. She didn't figure anyone was going to frisk her, so she'd have time to hide it later.

The detective continued his questioning upon return, often repeating inquiries, and since Dorothy hadn't—mostly—lied about her encounter, her story remained relatively consistent. When it seemed he was running out of questions, she requested the chance to shower and eat, saying she hadn't had much other than fruit over the course of the *four* days. No lies there. She wouldn't mind sleeping either. Hella-truth on that. What a craptacular day.

"You're back, safe and sound. That's the most important thing," the detective said, then addressed her father. "I think it's best if Dorothy sees a doctor, Mr. Alston. Now, there's a mess of reporters at the gate. I'll issue a statement, but as soon as our boys start to thin, or as soon as they see the flashlights in the back woods, they're going to know something's up. They'll sneak about like a pack of hungry vultures. I'll do my best to keep them out of your hair. In light of that, perhaps we can get someone to come do an in-house visit? I know a good doctor in town."

As he suggested this, she heard the Spintwister's voice as clearly as if he were standing next to her, pasty white lips curled in a snarl. *Bring the doctor, little no-girl. Let him see what you are not.*

"I'm fine, really," Dorothy blurted.

"Are you sure, honey?" her father asked.

"Yes, for real. I really just want to take a shower."

"I'll keep an eye on her, take her down to the doc's office in the morning, once this settles down. Can you leave anyone here?"

The detective nodded. "We'll be combing the woods most of the night, myself included. I'll make sure someone is always here, if for nothing else than to keep the reporters at bay. You'll get your sleep, miss, don't you worry. If you're up for it, I'd like to continue our little conversation in the morning." She suspected this wasn't an actual choice, and agreed.

"Good, until tomorrow then. Al, could we speak a minute?" Al nodded, and the two men stepped out the back door.

"Come on sweetheart, let's get you cleaned up."

Dorothy sank into her father's arms, and he led her to the bathroom. She brushed her teeth while her father picked out a pair of pajamas. She inspected the stranger staring back at her in the mirror.

Her hair had frizzed into a mess of dirt and oil. Grime streaked down her left cheek, under her chin and along her neck. Dark rings settled under her puffed eyes, and her lips seemed to droop into a permanent frown.

"You steal everything," she whispered. "Identity, emotion…everything."

"What's that, sweetheart?" her father asked. He entered the bathroom and set a pair of yellow pajamas on the toilet seat next to the sink. She shook off the memory and picked up the pajamas. "Thanks."

Her father kissed her on the head and gently closed the door. Dorothy leaned against the panels, placed her hand on the lock, and let her hand slide down the door to her side.

"Dad?"

"I'll be right outside the door. You go on now, get cleaned up. I'm here if you need me." His voice was steady. When she'd hugged him earlier, there had been no hint of whiskey, only the musk of man drenched in worry and fear. He would sit outside the door all day and night if he had to, and she wanted him to. She turned the nozzles in the shower, undressed, and sank into the heat.

Dorothy washed her body, hair, and face, and still felt she wasn't clean. She reached for the scrub brush, and scraped every inch of her body, pressing with all her remaining strength. That didn't feel right either, so Dorothy turned off the cold water. She sank to her knees as steam filled the bathroom, watched as her skin reddened and puffed, and curled into a ball when she realized she felt nothing.

Following the scalding shower, Dorothy ate. Uncle Al had whipped up three scrambled eggs and a ham-steak, then added toast and grits when she polished off the first two helpings. She didn't smile, but she thanked him, thanked them both. She kept her replies short, and diverted any inquires by saying she just wanted to feel like a kid, even if only for a night. Again, not a lie, and not quite the truth either. She wanted to feel like a 14-year-old, wanted to drift into an LP playing at a volume so high her father would beat down the door trying turn off the music. She wanted to slip into the dreamy eyes of the pop star poster she might hang on her wall. She wanted to lie in bed, curl the phone cord around her finger and talk the night away with one of her friends. Nothing heavy, nothing meaningful. Just a boy or a band. She wanted a date, or to tease the boys smoking butts behind the school, flexing their muscles as she strode past them.

On the flipside, she wanted to see Charlie and Ragesha. Throw her arms around them and thank them. Tell them she would never doubt them again, never doubt they loved her. Shower Charlie with kisses.

She wanted to toss the key hiding under her mattress into the garbage. She wanted the hot shower to burn her skin. She wanted to sink into her mother's arms one last time. Normal. She wanted things to be normal.

Dorothy excused herself after dinner and asked her father to walk her to her room. His mustache arched over his smile, and he pulled her into his arms. He folded back the covers, tucked her in, and pulled a chair to her door. He didn't ask, and she didn't protest. He sat, reached over his shoulder, and flipped the switch.

She smiled, nestled, and closed her eyes. She began to drift, and as her mind slipped into sleep, she whispered, "I love you, Daddy."

Dorothy woke in a panic and rolled onto the dimly-lit floor of her bedroom. An all too familiar crackly, sizzling wisp filled the room, and she frantically searched about for the source. She screamed for her father, kicked herself into a corner and gripped her temples.

I am the birds, the bees, the flowers and trees! You cannot run from me little no-girl! You cannot hide!

It was as if he was above and all around her, his voice echoing in stereo and that horrid crackling pervading her inner thoughts. "You are a thief, little no-girl. What are you? What made you? Whom did you steal it from? I will know; I will find out!"

She cried out for her father again, even as he slammed into the doorframe, calling her name. He dropped to his knees alongside her. He pulled her close, and she clawed at him. "Get away from me! Don't touch me! Daddy, HELP!"

"I'm here, sweetie! I'm here, I'm here!" He cried over her in a mad panic, patting her shoulders, pulling her into an embrace, gripping her tightly until her hysteria subsided, and she met his eyes. She broke, and fell into his arms.

"I'm sorry, I'm so sorry!" she sobbed, and softly pressed the ball of her wrist against his shoulder. "He's coming, and I'm sorry."

"Who's coming? Who, sweetheart?" he begged. Al burst into the room, ran to the window, then looked inquiringly at Peter, who merely shook his head.

"You've got guns, right?" her father asked, and Dorothy mind slipped into dizzying images of the key-worlds, and then nothing at all.

"I was cooking, few clanks of the pans and such, I don't know, would that set her off?" she had heard her uncle say as the black turned gray. She sat up quickly, searched, called her father, and nearly climbed the back of the couch before he could sit at her side and take her in his arms.

"I'm here, so is Uncle Al. Everything is all right. We brought you out here to keep an eye on you, is all. You're on the couch," he whispered, and she nodded. Al stood in the kitchen, and Detective Hodges sat at the bar. He dropped a half-eaten piece of bacon onto his plate, washed a mouthful of food down with a slurp of coffee, and took a seat across from Dorothy. She sat up and pushed her clammy bangs to the left side of her forehead. Her arms glistened, and her pajamas stuck to her body.

The detective glanced at Peter, then Al, then leaned toward Dorothy, resting his elbows on his knees. "Do you remember me?" he asked. She nodded. "Good, that's good. A good start, right?" he continued, and patted his knee a few times. "Dorothy, your dad called me in here and asked me to talk with you. He's worried about you; so is your uncle. Frankly, so am I."

Dorothy said nothing, and had nothing to say even if she could. She guessed the crackling sound she heard was breakfast cooking, and felt a little stupid about the scene she'd caused. But the fear of it, of him, still haunted her. He was here, even if only in her mind. She hadn't the means to fight him before, and now he had planted himself within—*birds, bees, flowers and trees*—she didn't have a chance. A no-girl with no tools, and no hope.

"Honey, you said he is coming. Is the man who abducted you, after you? Do you know who he is?"

"I wasn't abducted," she reiterated, and Mr. Hodges amended, "Is your captor, the man who held you in the woods, do you think he is coming after you?" she nodded.

138

"Do you think we should put her in some kind of protective custody?" her uncle asked.

The detective scratched his head, "Well, let's not get too far ahead of ourselves, though the option is available, should the need arise. But I don't think this guy—the one who held you—I don't think he's the aggressive sort."

"Not aggressive?" Dorothy's father jerked forward. "Are you freaking kidding me?"

The detective raised a meaty hand, and clarified, "I didn't mean he wasn't abusive. That's a given. Most men like Dorothy's captor, these types of scum, kidnap for one of three reasons. First is sexual, and we've established he didn't touch her, though I'd still like a doctor to look her over to be sure. Second is trafficking, which we can't rule out. But trafficking children is a business of sorts, and the big picture is worth more than a single kid. If that's the case, it's likely he'll cut his losses and get as far away from this town as he possibly can."

"And the third?" her father asked.

"The third is a bit more complex. From what your daughter tells us, he hit her, dragged her, pushed her around a bit," he looked to Dorothy again, and she nodded. "That's a man who wants to assert power. Power over the children, over the system, maybe over you." He pointed to Dorothy's father.

"Guys like this get off on..." he glanced sideways at Dorothy, "obedience. In Dorothy's case, the three kids defied his rule. If he's one of these types, that'll make him mad. Sloppy mad. Good for us, because most of those types aren't assertive, meaning they're cowards when confronted by authority," he said.

"What he put the kids through, is probably what he's gone through himself. Abusive father, mother, whatever the case may be. We'll start our research there. Check some of the older town records, see what kind of history we can dig up. It's a longshot, mind you, but worth a look.

"We're going to expand the search," he continued. Yeah, good luck with that, el detective-o. "He might even be wandering in the woods, hiding until things cool down. Who knows, maybe we'll get lucky and nab the bastard. But my guess is, he's holed up somewhere, like a basement, or some shack outside of town. Don't worry, kiddo. We'll find him, and we'll lock his a—" he

139

paused, "lock him up for good." He turned to her father. "It might help if we get a sketch artist in here, get his face out into the public. My guess is that he's done with Dorothy, but there are a lot of other children out there and I don't think we've seen the last of him, not yet. Not after he lost three of them."

Lots of kids, and lots of keys, Dorothy thought. Lot of kids who need their pain taken from them so it could make it his own, whatever that meant. Lots of kids whose keys would end up at the bottom of a box somewhere. Lots of kids who won't be kids anymore.

In the end, Dorothy agreed to a doctor's visit and the sketch artist. The doctor confirmed she'd suffered no physical damage, and all her girly parts were still intact and daisy fresh. Mom would have been proud. He recommended a therapist, pulled her father aside, and whispered for a good five minutes before wishing them both a good day.

Dorothy had described the Spintwister as best she could, even down to the detail of his massive claws, something she'd kick herself for later. The detectives and caseworkers must have guessed this was how she perceived them and not a true representation of his physical appearance, as neither questioned her on the odd detail she gave. They kept to the long-faced depiction of a pale man in a brimmed hat, and a few without. One bald, which was creepy, one with a full head of hair, and one with a buzz-cut.

Only the first rendering seemed right to her.

Dorothy's picture—one displayed nightly during her disappearance—along with the Spintwister's sketch, appeared on the news, over the course of the next few days.

"The manhunt continues," the nightly anchors intoned, followed by a brief report on the status of the search, and Dorothy's alleged condition. The story's prominence tapered off by the end of the week.

The detectives hit all the surrounding counties in search of the two boys held with her, and naturally came up empty. Wrong town, wrong time, pilgrim.

Life settled in a haze of placid normality when the police presence lessened, and soon, she found herself back in the stables caring for Alice, once Al cemented the hole in the center of the stable. Isais had not appeared once.

On Wednesday, Pete decided it was time to register Dorothy in her new school. He asked her if she wanted to tag along, maybe get a 'lay of the land', and she declined. "Seen one, seen 'em all," Dorothy replied, and said she wanted to relax before the first bell rang. He understood.

Dorothy, assisted by her uncle, led Alice to the round yard. He hooked a long lead to Alice's new bridle, directed Dorothy to the center of the yard, and handed her a lunge whip—leather-on-a-stick, if Dorothy had to name it. The idea was to flip the leather behind the horse to make it run around in a circle. Go here, go there, run little horsey, run. Oh, how the process seemed eerily familiar.

Alice nervously cantered along the perimeter fence when Dorothy and Al stepped into the center. Al stood by Dorothy's side and showed her how to point the lunge whip toward the ground, in whichever hand was facing away from Alice. She swapped hands, right to left.

"Normally this is Isais's job, so I might be a bit rusty," he began. "Now, stand firm, you have to be confident. Shoulders parallel to the horse, like this." Dorothy obeyed, and he called this her 'neutral' position. "It's all about your body movement, and how you encourage the horse to move. You have to gain her trust, and identify yourself as the leader at the same time."

"What's the whip for?" she asked.

"Just reinforcement to keep Alice focused. You don't hit her with it…" he warned, and she nodded. "Now turn your shoulder toward the left, where you want Alice to go. If she doesn't move, take a step in toward her hip. Cluck, when you want her to go, kiss to trot, and say 'whoa' to stop."

Dorothy turned, then stepped in toward Alice's hip. The animal lurched forward, nodding furiously. Dorothy stepped back, and her Uncle held her by the back of her arms, gently guiding her as Alice circled the pen.

"She's a little nervous, just like you. You gotta keep the body language simple, so she'll understand what you want her to do. Now get her to trot!"

Dorothy smacked her lips, turned her shoulder further to the right, and flicked the lunge whip into the dirt at her side. Alice began to trot.

"Good! Remember, it's not about domination. It's about trust. All you're doing is applying a little pressure, just like the herd leader would in the wild. Now get her to stop by taking a step or two toward her neck and saying, 'whoa'." She did, and Alice turned, trotting in the opposite direction. "That's okay, just do it again. Switch hands, step in…"

Dorothy repeated with a soothing "whoa", and Alice slid to a halt. Dorothy moved to her side, stroked her neck, and offered her a carrot. Al beamed.

"Where is Isais anyway? I haven't seen him since…" she paused. *Since she'd vanished in front of him and cut a hole into the concrete floor.* "Since I left."

Uncle Al nodded. "Well, I think he took your disappearance a bit hard. Might even blame himself for it. I called him yesterday, he said he'd swing by today. Which is good, because I'm getting tired, and your father isn't much of a farm hand."

She considered what she'd say to Isais, what he might say to her. He hadn't told anyone what he witnessed, she was certain of that. If he had, someone would've questioned her on the mysterious hole in the concrete, the back porch, and of course the many burnt patches of grass near the surrounding woods.

Oddly, no one had mentioned them at all, as if they hadn't existed. Not her father, Uncle Al, or even the police. If she were to guess, they might have assumed these were the Spintwister's campsites, from when he was stalking Dorothy…something like that. She could understand why they wouldn't mention it to her. Maybe they didn't want to freak her out, knowing he was so close to home. Well, what they didn't know, right?

She decided if Isais accepted what he had seen as fact, she would be forthcoming with the details. The decision brought relief, and she felt the weight on her shoulders lighten exponentially. If he didn't believe what he saw, well, she could play that game, too.

Her father returned mid-afternoon, acceptance documents in hand. She was a proud Callaway Bobcat, whatever that was worth. He offered to take her shopping for some new clothes, and she agreed. They decided on Saturday. She was actually looking forward to it.

Isais showed up at the farm at around 3:00 p.m. and kept to himself, clearly avoiding Dorothy. He kept looking at her, and quickly turned away if their eyes met. When Dorothy tried to approach him, Isais switched tasks and huffed away. If she'd been wondering whether he believed what he'd seen, she had the answer.

After an hour of cat-and-mouse, she decided that it would be better to let him approach her. She led Alice from her stall and into the round yard, setting the bait. Dorothy practiced leading, turning, and stopping Alice, offering the horse treats for jobs well done. She smiled and found the company pleasant. It seemed Alice had become her only friend in the entire state of Florida.

Isais rambled in and out of the stables, penned Ulysses and the other horses, and puttered about until the sun slipped behind the tree line. He approached round yard and stood a good ten-feet from the fence opposite Dorothy.

"Miss, she needs to go in," he said. Dorothy's shoulder fell, and she stomped to the fence. Isais backed away.

"Isais, come on!" she complained, and he turned and stalked away from her. Dorothy vaulted the fence and ran after him. The big man covered half the distance between the yard and stable before Dorothy caught him, grabbed his arm, and spun him around.

"Please, Isais. You're supposed to be my friend."

Sweat beaded along his brow and traced down his cheeks.

"At least, let me explain. If you want me to leave you alone after that, I will. I promise."

Isais was quiet for a moment, then nodded. He led Alice to her pen, then pulled two white buckets from the washroom, placing both upside-down near the fresh concrete at the center of the stable.

"Okay," he sat and gestured to the floor. "Explain this. Because what I saw you do…I can't. And I've tried. Believe you me, I've tried. You know what my grandmother calls you? She says you're *la novia del diablo.* The bride of the devil."

"That's a bit harsh," Dorothy said.

"Is she right?"

Dorothy's eyebrows shot up. "No. My God, Isais!"

"No, Dorothy. I know what I saw! You fizzled and popped like piece of hamburger meat. I watched you dissolve," he said, extending the word so it hummed, "and you vanished into smoke! And the floor, right here." He stomped his foot for emphasis. "Melted. Just plain disappeared. Tell me I'm crazy and I was dreaming. Me being crazy would make more sense than...than..." he shouted, and threw a finger towards Dorothy.

"You're not crazy," Dorothy replied somberly. "I'm sorry that you had to see it. I honestly wish I had never left."

"What happened? How did you do that? Where did you go?"

Dorothy sighed and searched his face. She wanted to tell him. She needed to tell him. So, she began her story from the moment she found the glass key. She told him about its weight when she touched it, where it took her when she tucked it in her pocket. She admitted she didn't know how or why it worked. She told him about Charlie and Ragesha, and how she missed them. She told him of the Spintwister, and what he had done to her leg, and how it didn't hurt her. How the boys helped her escape.

Isais listened intently, fingers interlocked. He nodded, leaned forward when his interest sparked, and his face grew fierce when she described the Spintwister. When she finished, he raised his eyebrows and released a long, exasperated breath.

"That sure is a story," he commented, and Dorothy thought she detected a twinge of disbelief. Even after what he had seen, he doubted her.

"So, you're saying all I have to do is put a key in my pocket, and boom, I'm outta here like last year, huh?"

"I guess. I'm really not sure how it works."

Isais raised a hand to his shirt and pressed his fingers against a necklace beneath. Dorothy imagined a slim cross hung from the chain. She wasn't sure if he was cognizant of this gesture.

"Maybe you're not supposed to. Maybe it's like that creepy guy says, you know? A place for children to escape. God has done stranger things, I suppose."

"You think God has a hand in this?" she asked, incredulous.

"I don't know, little miss. I would like to see this key of yours."

"You shouldn't try going. I mean, it didn't sound like he was a fan of adults."

"So, he only lets kids in? That's kinda creepy."

"I get the feeling he wasn't always like this. I don't know if he was nice, or maybe...understanding, of what kids go through."

"How does he do it? The pain thing?"

Dorothy shook her head. She'd guessed, putting the puzzle pieces together—dead world, abandoned keys—that when the Spintwister took kids' pain—making it his own—he gradually took their life from them. A thousand keys, down to only a few.

"A thousand?" Isais asked, emptied his lungs, and slapped his knee. "Lucky you got out when you did."

Dorothy agreed.

Isais asked if she planned to return, and she told him no, because she didn't think the boys were going to either. There would be no sense in it. Isais asked if she planned to discuss this with her father, and she wasn't sure she should. She had two methods of proving her tale, and she thought the risks of both methods—impaling herself or crossing over—were too high. Besides, he might just go bat-crap crazy and lose what little sanity he had left. Something she didn't want to take responsibility for, no way, no how.

Isais nodded, saying he understood her logic. He stood and pulled Dorothy to her feet, and embraced her. "I'm glad you're not the devil's wife."

Dorothy attempted a little laugh, and nudged him with her elbow. "Me too. So, are we friends again?"

"Yeah, we're still friends. No more of the snap-crackle-pop business. And tomorrow, you show me the key."

Chapter 6
School in a Daze

The following day, as promised, Dorothy presented the glass key to Isais. She explained its weight effect, and when Isais doubted her, she asked him to hold the key.

She pressed her finger to the barrel, and he didn't doubt anything she told him afterward.

They agreed that mum was the word, and that a little normalcy might do Dorothy some good. She promised to stash the key in her closet, instead of under the mattress. And she did, for two days. The key returned to her mattress on the third day, and by the Sunday before school started, it was under her pillow.

Monday morning, first day of school, Dorothy rose, showered, and put on a touch of make-up—a very light touch, per her father's instructions—consisting of a peach lipstick, blue-black eye shadow, and a little blush. She pulled her hair up in a banana-clip, slipped into a pair of white capris, and opted for the CHOOSE LIFE t-shirt. She stocked her purse with the necessities: brush, lipstick, lip-liner, hairspray—extra hold cause, hella-yes—mirror, two packs of Hubba-Bubba bubble gum, and, of course, her key.

She was sitting at the kitchen table before the sun was up, and soon her father, uncle, and Isais joined her for breakfast. They were staring at her, awkwardly silent.

"Did I miss something?" she asked. Al slid her a plate of eggs, grits, bacon, and toast. Isais poured her a glass of orange juice, and her father buttered her toast. His mustache twitched up, and the laugh lines around his eyes deepened.

She noted the men dressed in button-down shirts, unstained jeans, and—she leaned back to check under the table—their good boots. Three Stetsons waited on the counter nearest the door. She peeked out the window, and noted four of the five paddocks occupied by horses.

"Nope, we're just excited for you, honey," her father replied. Isais and Al smiled.

Dorothy slumped in her chair.

"You're all taking me to school, aren't you?" she asked. They nodded, a bit sheepishly, and Dorothy closed her eyes. She supposed it could be worse...but not much.

There was nothing so embarrassing as a cavalcade of adults trekking to school with you. Classmates would part like the Red Sea, eyes would widen, and oh the whispers would begin. She should know—once upon a time, she had been one of those judging voices.

"Now, Dorothy..." her father began, but she quickly cut him off.

"It's all right, Dad. I understand. I'm kinda glad that y'all are coming. It's only been a couple weeks...I bet I am the talk of the town by now." She shoveled down her eggs after mixing in the grits, then sipped her orange juice.

"You think I should pack the ol' iron? Might be trouble brewin'," her uncle said mischievously, and when Dorothy choked on her juice, the three men laughed.

"I'm just joshing ya, Dorothy. Your teacher thought it best we drop you off today, is all. She said our farm, being as far out of the way as it is, would be the first stop along the route. It'd pick you up at 6:10 in the morning."

Dorothy's eyes widened, and she shot a glare at her father.

"I get off at five, and I don't mind staying up for a couple hours. I'll drive you as often as I can." He leaned in, and added, "Are you sure you're okay with this? We can hold off on school, if you like. I met with your teachers and they understand if you don't want to go."

"All the teachers know?"

"They knew before I showed up," her father said.

"You were all over the news. Heck, I just saw a clip this morning about it. Lady says it's the first day of school for the victim of the Calhoun Captor. They called you the Calhoun Kid."

"Oh, my God..." she felt a piece of food jump to the back of her throat. "You've got to be kidding me. I have a nickname?"

Her father winced sympathetically.

"The principal called this morning. News crews are camped out front," Al stated, and her father added, "behind police barricades, if you can believe it."

Isais rubbed his chin, and she noticed he had shaved a few days of scruff into a goatee. He demonstrated his fiercest snarl. "We're gonna put the big Mexican out front." He pounded his chest. "Nobody gets around The Fluff!"

The other men turned to him, eyebrows raised, and he scrunched his shoulders defensively. "Term of endearment," he declared, and ran a hand over his belly.

"I cased the school last week. We can park around back by Shunt's Creek and walk through a break in the fence. It's a dirt road, and I know Jethro's boy has been playin' on the scraper tryin' to smooth it out," Al considered. "It'll be a bumpy ride, but I bet there won't be anyone snoopin' around back there."

Dorothy's father nodded.

"This is an awful lot of trouble for a little no—" Dorothy began, and felt the blood rush to her cheeks over the unintentional slip. "For me," she amended. She glanced at Isais and looked away when she saw how wide his eyes had become.

"Is it an actual gate, or a hole in the fence?" her father asked after some thought.

"It's a hole, looks like it's been there a while."

"It's okay, Dad, let's go in the front," Dorothy suggested, and the men fell silent. She ran a finger over her collarbone, then added, "Really, I don't want the other kids bugging over this. It'll be hard enough getting along. We can just go a little later, I guess? Maybe after the first bell rings?"

Her father twitched and ran his index and thumb over his mustache. "Could work. Hey, Al, why don't you call that Hodges fella and ask him if he minds clearing out the gawkers. Tell him we'll drop Dorothy off afterwards."

"Well, sure, Pete, do you think he'll do it? Might be a bit below his pay grade."

"Yeah, I think he will. He's not too keen on Dorothy going in to school yet, anyway, not with the two kids she was with still missing. I'm bettin' he's already been down there a few times today."

Dorothy glanced at Isais. He lowered his head and looked at her out of the tops of his eyes. *Nothing to do but keep your big mouth shut.* She read him, clear as day, and she swallowed hard.

Her uncle picked up the phone hanging against the wall, opposite the refrigerator, along with a business card pinched behind the base, and dialed Detective Hodges. He stretched the cord around the entryway, and after a quick greeting, his voice dropped. She didn't hear the rest.

"You sure you're good with this? You know how kids can be," her father asked.

"I guess," Dorothy replied. She assumed those *kids*, ones who normally liked to tease, pick, and prod—as she so often used to—might be awkward around her. Dorothy was new, so she wouldn't have the impact of, say, classmates who grew up together, but she was still a kid. Someone who has lived a nightmare, and if you were to believe the news, one so very close to home. Their homes. Thinking back to the Spintwister, they were right to feel awkward. These kids should be downright terrified.

Building on her day with the Spintwister, Dorothy considered how she could turn a bad situation in her favor. She wondered what the Spintwister might do, since the boys had awakened his memory, then absconded with his dinner. He had no pain to feed on.

The notion of its hunger had troubled Dorothy since her return. She couldn't decide if what he did—taking pain—was all bad. If the Spintwister took away Charlie's painful memories— bombs dropping like snowflakes, hiding in his shelter while his father perished in a fire…wouldn't that be a blessing?

In a sense, she felt a bit gypped when it came to her own haunted past. He could take the night of her mother's death from her and swallow the pain like a pill. Her mother's face would no longer haunt her. Fire wouldn't send ice crackling down her spine. She wouldn't look at her father with resentment. She could be a kid again.

But what would be the cost? Would she think of her mother at all, and if she did, what memories would remain? Could she— would she—retain the fond memories they shared if the painful memories had been taken from her? Can one side exist without the other?

Dorothy decided she didn't want to find out. Painful though it was, she owed her mother this, and the grief of her mother's absence should fuel her memories, both good and bad. It's what makes up Mom as a whole and complete person, right? In an odd way, Dorothy felt a deeper connection to her now than when she was alive. So, some good might come from her lies, concerning her imprisonment.

As Charlie said, the children hurt, and the keys called. They want to be found. As far as she knew, there had only been the three. Two of them she could do nothing about—Charlie's and Ragesha's—but the third was hers to control. And she was intent on letting the Spintwister starve.

"Hodges will clear out the reporters. He's also going to have a few uniformed officers parked outside the school, front and back. The principal told me to have her there by 8:30 a.m."

"At the front?" Dorothy asked her uncle, and he nodded.

"All right amigos, we've got an hour to kill. Let's say we finish this breakfast, and get this girl off to school."

Dorothy began tapping the side of her eggs, lost in thought. She mouthed "the keys call" repeatedly, and tried to ascertain precisely how this had all happened. She didn't think the key had called to her. "*You are a thief, you are a liar.*" His odious voice echoed in her memory. If the key hadn't called her, had she stolen it? Finders-keepers may not apply in this situation; that made sense, if each key belonged to a specific kid. So, the one great question remained. If the key wasn't hers…whose was it?

Dorothy hustled through the rest of her breakfast and ran to her room. She closed the door, knelt beside her bed, and retrieved the glass key from her purse, using a washcloth as a buffer between her skin and the glass. She placed it on her comforter, and rested her head on her hands.

The floral pattern was obscured through the cylinder of the key. No lights or auras emanated from it; she had no mystical feeling in its presence. It looked like some bizarre decoration, at least until she pressed her finger against the glass. The floor creaked, and the mattress sank under the weight. Would it keep getting heavier, the longer she kept it?

"This key is not for you," she dictated. "But if not me, then who?" She decided it was time to find out, and guessed if the key was near its intended child, then it would call to them like a fish to water. She considered hiding the key, and guessed it would be pointless. The key would call, and eventually, someone would hear it. Then she could warn them, steer them away from the key. Save a life. She felt comforted in her new mission. If the key was not hers, it didn't matter. Nobody would have it, she could at least make sure of that.

At five past eight, Dorothy, her father, uncle, and Isais left the ranch. They turned down Country Road 35, toward Callahan Middle School, where a hundred or so potential key candidates would bustle or shuffle from one room to another.

Like most homes and buildings in Florida, Callahan Middle School was a single-story building, but it was expansive. The school split into two elongated sections, with a connecting canopy over the main sidewalk, leading to the administration building at the rear. The drive looped around the front, and exited at the other end of the campus.

She climbed out of the vehicle with her escorts, and glanced across the street, beyond the school's fence. Police barricades stretched across the perimeter. The area was otherwise blissfully devoid of people, except a few elderly people walking their equally aged dogs. She could make out the husky form of a man in a tan suit, leaning against a car. Hodges, she guessed, and he confirmed this with a wave. Her father took off his Stetson, raised it high, and slipped it back on.

"Not much of a show, eh Dorothy?" Isais said, frowning at the empty walkway.

"Oh, don't worry, Fluffy, they'll see you," her father teased, and pointed toward the windows on either side. Isais slapped his belly, pointed to her father, and offered a thumbs-up approval of the nickname. Her father tilted his head toward the rear building, and said, "Head honcho's in there, best get a move on. Last chance, kiddo. You're sure you're ready?"

Dorothy smiled, and stepped onto the sidewalk. Isais pulled her back, opened a pair of mirrored sunglasses, and pushed out his chest. He contorted his lower lip into a snarl, snapped his finger, and marched toward the office at the front of the pack.

As they trekked down the main drag of the school, parading past rows of open windows, most of the classes droned on, unaware of her presence. But she could see the sidelong glances of the kids sitting nearest the windows, and occasionally someone would lean in, and whisper, compelling others to look.

The principal met the group at the door. He turned to Peter, and shook his hand, then Al, followed by Isais. The portly, balding little fellow brushed a few strands of gray hair over his scalp and smiled. He wore a brownish-orange suit with strands of thread flailing along the lower edge of the coat. "Isais, you're about as menacing as a titmouse. Suck in that gut, straighten your back. Haven't I always told you…"

"Posture is everything. Yes, I remember, Mr. Morgan," Isais sulked. Al chuckled.

The principal turned to Dorothy and extended a hand. "You must be Dorothy. We're all glad to have you here. I'm going to guess you're about ready to put this mess behind you and get on with your life." She considered the idea for a moment, then admitted that she was. More than ready, truth be told. "Very good. You'll find our little clan of Calla-nooks—that's my pet name for the kids here—very welcoming. You'll fit right in." He lifted his hand and signaled to a woman standing by the glass door to the office, a woman Dorothy hadn't spotted on the way in. She was tall, the bee-hive hair adding a good foot to her already impressive height, and thin-legged, with a stern face and piercing eyes. She smiled and marched to his side, placed a folder over her cleavage as she bent to introduce herself to Dorothy.

"Ms. Coraline Sweetwater, guidance counselor. If you have a moment, I'd like to have a chat before escorting you to second period."

Dorothy slumped, and turned to her father. He cocked his head and motioned toward the door. She reluctantly agreed, and followed the woman inside.

So much for the nice, easy day.

Chapter 7
The Candy Shop

He knew the no-girl was unusual. Now he'd discovered her to be equally unpredictable. Her behavior—her courage—in the face of hopelessness, baffled the Spintwister, and now he wanted to play.

When the little no-girl ran to the woods, he followed. He slipped into the shades of the trees, danced up and about the great canopies among the song-siren birds.

The no-girl picked up a pointed stick and ducked in and about his forest. She stopped, she listened, and she waited. For him? He glided across and away, dancing between the trees. He rustled the leaves, then twisted a torn branch into several sticks and tossed them around the no-girl. She didn't move, only turned her head.

"Who did you steal that fearlessness from, I wonder," the Spintwister teased in a whisper. He slipped behind her tree, and tapped his fingers against the bark.

She ran; he gave chase. He called for the grass beneath her feet to cut her, entangle her, but she pressed through.

"My, what a persistent little creature." He wavered at her side when she finally fell to her knees and gave up. Or did she? This no-girl was full of surprises, and had at least one more in her. When he lessened the grip on her legs, she sprang to life—marvelous!

The Spintwister watched with delight, not unaware that the two boys had reentered his domain. Rather than chase them down, he contented himself to observe.

The no-girl veered off and ran straight for them. How did she know they were there? She couldn't have seen them. Did she feel their presence, perhaps their pain? For him, those two were beacons. He could find them anywhere and in any time. Did she know this, or just react instinctively? He had to know. The Spintwister erupted into mist and slipped through the grass. He landed at their feet, and wrapped himself around the two children and the no-girl.

Darkness…swift and cold, like nothing he felt before, and hoped never again. No pause, no warning. There was light, his lands; the children among them. And then, a gloom so deep, it seemed an endless chasm of nothingness. The no-girl vanished. His boys—gone. Their voices chirped, then fell silent. All was silent. Until it wasn't.

An unfamiliar buzz, not unlike the insects around his home, though remarkably smooth and stagnant, as if fixed, jumbled his typically keen sense of perception. He turned, then again, slowly centering his head until the sound echoed equally in both his ears.

A pinprick of white appeared, and split to another, then a third. The images blurred for a moment, widened, and the Spintwister pressed his eyes tight before a sudden dizziness returned him to the chasm of black.

Cold raced along his spine, and in the same instant, heat boiled along his left arm and shoulder. A heartbeat later and his body began to shiver uncontrollably without any reason as to why.

The odd buzzing drifted to his left, then centered. He caught the faintest notion of a breeze before his body dissipated into wisp of smoke. He solidified a moment later.

Still, the icy cold chill coupled with a lingering burn remained throughout, as if he parted not once, but thrice. He opened his eyes, and quickly turned away. The specs of white grew, floating like three great doorways above an oil-slick sea.

Another breeze pressed through the center of his body and he again felt separated, split even. Looking back toward the doorways—now two instead of three—the Spintwister fought the urge to turn away. A moment passed, his muscles hardened, and the third lighted door appeared.

He couldn't perceive what caused this. Vision in this misted form was by touch, and typically fed through the millions of tiny, twisting tendrils. Never had he split in such an odd fashion, not unless he willed it of course, and never had he the impression of three from one, as if he were three parts of a singular whole. He forced himself to focus.

A kind of pain slid into his memory, familiar but ambiguous. He turned his attention on it. The sensation was whimsical, as if it beckoned him. A growing wind scattered the smoke and haze of his body—he receded, and returned.

He reached for the strewn memories, and they began to congeal. At first, they were nothing more than faint landscapes, faceless faces, white noise. He reached toward the chilled air furthest from him, possibly the left door, though he wasn't entirely sure of this, and converged all of his energy on the clearest image within. A tree. He stood by a tree and—

He couldn't finish the thought, not quite. His body thickened, and the image blurred. He felt the odd presence near him, and slipped silently toward it.

Another memory struck him. He tried to speak and found that he could not. No-voice, like a no-girl, who he felt nearby; he could feel her nothingness. But the no-girl also meant two boys, and two boys meant two keys, and two keys meant two doors in a mind waiting to be unlocked. Doors, like the three before him. He pushed himself forward, towards the no-girl, as this seemed the easiest route to take.

Dim light replaced the darkness, and he found himself hovering over the sleeping no-girl, the stolen key hidden beneath her. To his left, a small round object thing moved, stopped, and turned, and he again felt a chill as its air brushed past him. Curious and familiar.

He closed his eyes, returned to the lighted doors, and pushed through another. When he opened them again, he found himself in a small room with mud walls. The dark-skinned boy slept on a rug. He too, kept his key close—beneath his bedding. The Spintwister found it hard to hold his shape in this place; the sticky-hot air weighed him down.

He closed his eyes again, and entered the final suspended door. The small, pale boy slept fitfully. The only light danced from a lantern resting on a small table outside his room. He was shivering, and jerked constantly. The Spintwister drifted to the side of Charlie's bed, and brushed the matted hair from his eyes, so he could look at and through them. He could take the child's pain here and now, he supposed. A simple flick of the wrist, straight across his throat. He would bleed all the impurities of his tortured life into a sweet, deep cup, and the Spintwister would drink and remember.

But should he, without the understanding of how this transference of himself to his key-children, took place? The glowing, floating doors, he surmised, were parts of himself.

Three parts: two for his boys, and one for the no-girl.

The Spintwister returned to the doorway. He ran mental fingers along his arms and legs, across his cheek and chest. A void, slight to be sure, but present none-the-less, split his body into three sections. One for each child, and one for the no-girl.

Again, he closed his eyes and returned to the no-girl. She slept peacefully and dreamlessly, as he suspected she might. In the realm of dreams, thieves are silent. Where there is no self, there is no voice. So many clues; so many hints. He wondered why she didn't understand this. Surely, by now, she must see and feel how nothing encompasses her being. Can a creature, such as this exist with nothing but a lie to guide her? He had been her only truth. She rejected him.

He solidified further, and found he could stand. He could do many things using the same adherent focus. But he could not drink her stolen pain, nor could he sever her tie with the key hidden beneath her bed. "There is truth somewhere in this," he whispered, and his voice crackled, popped, and echoed off the wooden walls surrounding him.

He blinked and found the travel between doors easier, and stood over the little brown-skinned boy. He awakened, and gawked at the Spintwister. Blinked again, and so was the Charlie-boy. He smiled, and spread until the darkness returned. He didn't need to see the children any longer, he was whole enough, and they could not run from him. Not here, and not this time.

The no-girl had moved from her room, and in this new space, he could sense the presence of elders. Two or three, he wasn't sure, and surmised this must be the effect of the mist. He wanted to firm his smoked form enough to see, and decided against it. She needn't worry herself about him, not just yet. Knowing where she is—he wasn't able to hear her voice in this state—is more than enough for now. He felt her stolen emotions, and oh, how troubled they were. She retrieved her key, and her relief so overwhelming, he almost laughed himself solid!

In this joining of thief-to-key, he realized what should have been obvious the moment he encountered the no-girl. The key did not call to her, but she to it. The key rejects her, but she refuses to let it go, so its weight becomes unbearable as it fights to relinquish itself to the true owner.

He sensed her worry, and this transcended from fear, to acceptance, to ambition.

She moved, recovered her key, and her presence drifted away.

He followed and found that he could barely keep up. Why didn't the no-girl move this fast when she was alongside him in the woods? Truly fascinating! When she slowed, he solidified slightly, and could hear and feel aching cries all about him. Deep, sorrowful cups called to him like chimes in the wind. The cry so fierce, he could no longer maintain focus on the no-girl and found himself drifting among the sorrowful voices like a rock falling through water. When he struck bottom, sand, water, and air coiled around his body. Within this grip of elements, the Spintwister transformed himself into two beady red eyes.

He could see them now, dozens of children. Some were of little taste, others were so viciously beautiful, he couldn't find the words to describe them. A boy sat a foot from him, cradling his arm, rubbing a blackened bruise above the base of his elbow. Beside him, a young girl wondered if her mother would return home, and she worried what she would eat, should she not.

Rage from one, fear from another. Pain and more pain! He drew a breath, and found his body quaking with excitement.

A child caught glimpse of him and screamed. The Spintwister shut his eyes, and returned to the no-girl. What a waste that she should have this key, a key belonging to another. And perhaps another still, if his suspicions played true.

Chapter 8
The Return to Innocence

After a somewhat congenial meeting with the guidance counselor, Dorothy was determined to settle into a routine and find some level of normalcy. She'd missed her first class—math, no great loss there—and after an embarrassing escort down the hallway through a crowd of gawking peers, she parked herself in room 123, Mrs. Ambrose's Social Studies class. She was the third person to enter the room.

Dorothy took a seat behind a dark-haired girl wearing jean cut-offs and an Ozzy Osbourne concert shirt. She set her bag on the floor, and the dark-haired girl turned, and introduced herself as Mary. Dorothy commented on her *Ultimate Sin* tour t-shirt and how she thought the succubus, a demonic girl clad in sinners' white, was 'aces'. Mary lit up and launched into an animated description of the show. "Man, it was gnarly, I mean, Jake E. Lee was no Randy Rhodes, but he's the absolute sh—"

"Mary, language." Mrs. Ambrose commanded, without turning from the blackboard. Mary rolled her eyes, Dorothy stifled a laugh, and the girls agreed to discuss the fine details sometime later.

The bell rang and children poured into the room. The class grew from three to full in under a minute. There was a time where Dorothy might have been among those who barely crossed the finish line before the hell-bell, hastily scanning the room for familiar faces; or if she were first among her friends, snatching a cluster of desks she marked as *ocupado*. She'd offer up seats based on the popularity of the friend requesting it, reserving the left and right to those most highly esteemed in her current social network.

She wondered how in the flipping freaked-out world had she fallen into such a clichéd social trap, and why any of it mattered.

She wouldn't go as far as the kumbaya hand holding, peace and love, and all that…there's just so much more to worry about outside of those tiny little circles. Sheesh, it's like watching ants scramble to a piece of discarded candy. It was ugly, just damned ugly.

A few arguments erupted, and were quashed just as quickly, and soon the social hierarchy played through its natural course. Jocks and burnouts vied for the back of the room. The dweebs naturally flocked to the front, and anybody without a social group to latch onto picked any empty desk they could.

Mary's circle of misfits consisted of three boys. They surrounded her, and thus Dorothy by proximity. Mary slapped the first, a long-haired runt wearing a denim vest over an Iron Maiden tee—they all had the hair, including the mountain high-top spray job on Mary—and flipped him the bird. The boy nodded, and Dorothy thought she saw a pair of ice-blue eyes beneath the oiled mat of bangs. He replied with a quick tug of his privates, and Dorothy suddenly felt like Molly Ringwald in a bad re-make of *The Breakfast Club*, minus the red hair and dreamy lips, of course.

Mrs. Ambrose, who looked about 80 to Dorothy—so, probably around 50 in reality—stood behind her desk, running through introductions, what the year would cover, and what books she would assign. Should any student not return the book in the same pristine condition, his or her report card would be held as ransom. *Civilizations: Eighth Grade Social Studies*.

A girl named Amber distributed the books, perkily suggesting the recipient wrap their book in a brown paper shopping bag. Dorothy snorted. Book covers were a given, no advice needed here. How else do you deco-up your class-wares? Stickers, album covers, drawings and band-names were a must if you planned to survive beyond the first week. She didn't have the usual mess of stickers, but she had a freaking pen, and she wasn't afraid to use it.

The dweebs in the front thanked her; the boys around Dorothy nodded and snatched the books from Amber's hand, earning a sneer and thumbed nose. Dorothy offered an impartial smirk. Seemed the best play, until she decided what social class would best represent her, here in the grand town of Ocala.

She could be anybody now, all it would take is a different shade of make-up and a few choice t-shirts. A little hairspray and black eyeliner, and she'd be a shoe-in for Mary's crowd. A little peach and pink on the eyes, and she's in with the jocks. Just that quick; just that easy.

By lunch, Dorothy classified her day as fricking-A normal. She felt like a teen again. There were a few questioning eyes shifting in her direction—she was the local celebrity after all, the great survivor of men and their despicable deeds. In school, that meant either pity or jealousy, and she ignored both with equal vigor.

Dorothy took her lunch to the courtyard between the gymnasium and main office, parked her rump on a concrete bench, bit into the hyper-salted pizza-bagel, and chewed as if it were a nasty stick of gum.

"Yo, Alston," Mary called, and offered a seat amongst her burnouts. One girl, four boys, and not a sleeve among them. Not her typical crowd, but whatever; new school, new day. She joined them.

The boys offered her a downturned nod, and she returned with an upward nod. Sort of like a burnout secret handshake, or the dweebs Vulcan—live long and prosper—parting of the middle and ring finger.

One squinty eyed, pale-faced boy, on her left, slapped the pimply kid next to him.

He looked up from his meal and flipped the bangs from his eyes with a jerk of his head. He introduced himself as Charlie. Orange top afro-kid was Mike. Steve was all elbows and hair, and was taking lunch as an opportunity to nap, using his forearm as a pillow.

Freckled-face introduced himself as 'Rock'. Not Rocky just…Rock. Wow.

"Rock?" Dorothy asked.

"'Cause I'm hard-freaking-core!" the boy responded, and high-fived the one called Charlie.

The name filled her head with images of her Charlie. His sweet smile. His lust for oranges, and the goofy face he made after stuffing the rind in mouth. The soft and beautiful tones of his voice, which were a sharp contrast to the pitched tones of these crass dolts here.

I love you, don't come back. She stifled her thoughts. Not a good time to start crying.

"Yo, Alston? You deaf or something?" the Charlie boy asked, and she stared at him blankly.

"Rock asked you what that guy was like. The one who swiped you."

"Swiped me?" she asked. When had the conversation switch from introductions to interrogation?

"Yeah, come on, tell us. What's it like?" Mary asked.

"How did it feel?" the Rock added.

"Feel?" Dorothy asked. Her mind swam, and she began to sway in her chair. The group nodded, and the bustling courtyard turned silent.

"Yeah, Alston. How did it feel, ya know?" His voice dropped. "Did he touch you up here, play down there? You still a fresh little girl? Inquiring minds want to know!"

The table leaned in for the answer. Mary tapped the top of the table. The boys joined in. The table to her left stomped their feet. Children near the doors slapped their hands against the wall. Mary tapped, then the boys, the feet, then the wall. The pace quickened and rolled. The wall beat and Mary's tapping overlapped. Children opened windows in nearby classrooms and slapped the windowsill.

She scanned their faces, all of their faces, from the kids standing against the lunchroom door, to others sitting on the stairs. They panted and grunted in time with a snapping and crackling beat. More children exited the cafeteria doors, snapped, turned toward Dorothy, and stomped the ground.

"Did he hurt you?" Mary asked. The courtyard repeated the question in unison, and the echo sent a shiver up Dorothy's spine.

"Did he play? Did he touch you and you told him no way?"

She grabbed her backpack, and ran through the hallway doors, then peeked through the vertical, wired slit window. Every kid, maybe 30 of them in all, huddled together for a last, longing look. Dorothy grimaced, held her pack to her chest and backed away.

A hallway filled with silent, motionless children faced Dorothy. She turned, met their eyes and her heart leaped into her throat. She jumped, and three children parted and stepped away from her. Their brows were furrowed and their lips curled. One hissed as she strode past, then filled in the gap behind her.

"What are you doing here?" a small blonde girl asked. She shoved Dorothy and stepped into her path. Dorothy gasped, and ducked around her.

"You don't belong here," another said. She quickened her pace.

"You can't be here!" another shouted. Children filed and crowded in. "You don't exist, little girl! You don't exist!" they screamed, and then fell suddenly silent. A boy, possibly her age, dirty-blond hair, stepped to her and looked her dead in the eye. He smirked, sniffled, and grinned wide. The boy parted his lips, and touched his tongue to the roof of his mouth. He annunciated a phrase, one Dorothy had hoped she'd never hear again.

"No…girl…"

Dorothy stumbled. The boy smirked, turned, and gestured toward the crowding children. They quickly parted and Dorothy ran. They shouted as she passed, "No girl! No girl!" and lurched toward her, as if to tackle or trip her, stopping just short of the open path that the blue-eyed boy had cleared for her. She ran into the bathroom and locked herself in a stall. Outside, the children returned to the mass of intelligible conversation.

"Oh, my God! What is going on?" She had to be dreaming. This was just her mind, just tricks. Like in Uncle Al's living room. It had to be! Man, she felt ill, like someone was tugging at her in two different directions.

Dorothy ran to the sink and splashed cold water on her face, and the dizziness subsided. She fell to her knees. "He's here. Somehow, he has followed me here," she whispered. But what about the boys? Had he followed Charlie, too? Ragesha? He needed them. He didn't want her or need her; what was he doing here? Could he not get to them without her? She pulled her pack open and wrapped her hands around the wooden box.

"Oh, you don't want to do that." Dorothy whipped around. The blond boy with the blue eyes stood between her and the door.

"What are you doing here?" she asked, and stepped away. "This is the girl's bathroom. You can't be in here."

"Are we really going to play like this, little no-girl? Have you lost your stolen wits?" the boy asked. He walked to the sink

162

and sat on the edge of the basin. "Relax, no-girl. I'm not here to hurt you. I'm here to talk, just like old times."

"You don't talk, you play games!" she said in a fit of fury. "What do you want?"

"Aww, no-girl's *fee-wings* got *huwt,*" he laughed.

"That's a real boy you're in, isn't it?" she asked.

He shrugged. "Just borrowing him for a bit. Seems to work for you." He pinched the skin under his arm. "Had to test the fit. See how I looked, and all. He does remind me of a boy whom I poisoned once," he paused, and looked to the ceiling. "Many years from now," he amended, and offered her a cold smile.

"You're a monster!" Dorothy growled. She dropped her backpack and displayed the box with her glass key inside. "If you want this so bad, take it! Just leave me alone!"

The boy perked, jumped off the sink, and snatched the key. He bounced it about his hand, then placed it on the floor, at her feet. He frowned, and she thought he shook his head, as if disappointed. He returned to the sink.

"I don't want the key, not given by you, not that you could. And if you haven't figured it out, you cannot simply lose it or toss it away. It will understand soon enough that you are not who it was intended for, and then it can be taken from you." He placed a hand to his chest, and added, "You know this already, don't you, no-girl? Can you feel the weight of its disappointment in those borrowed hands of yours?"

"I don't understand," Dorothy replied. She retrieved the box off the floor and cupped it to her chest.

"I doubt you would. Steal a better brain next go-around."

"I didn't steal this one!"

"You don't know what you did or didn't do. You don't know what you are, no-girl."

Dorothy grimaced, and dropped her hands to her sides. She stomped over to the boy, then backed away when he cut her a burning, wicked glance. She saw the Spintwister then, and gooseflesh chased up her arms.

"You don't know what I am either," she muttered. The boy smiled wide.

"So, you admit you are not who you claim to be?"

She lowered her head. "No, just not who I should be."

The boy clapped, and pushed off the sink. He stood before Dorothy, gripped her shoulders, and beamed. "It is a start, no-girl. You are correct, I do not know what you are, only what you are not. I cannot take your pain from you, nor can I simply kill you and take the key," he leaned in, and whispered, "But oh, how I want to," he pressed his fingers into her shoulders. "How I want to rip the flesh from your stolen bones. When that day comes, no-girl, oh, how you'll burn." He tapped her arms and shook her gently, "I'll just have to settle for your friends. Two more keys and I'll have all the answers I need. Then I'll take you, and all these little boys and girls around you. Until nothing is left but bone."

He leaned and kissed her before she could object. She shoved him and when his back hit the wall, the boy's face transformed—eyes wide and mouth agape. He searched blindly around the room, until his frightened, confused gaze met hers, and he nearly fell over his own feet.

Dorothy took a step away. The boy, obviously himself again, looked like he was about to vomit. She raised her hands, palms forward, but before she could speak a word, he turned tail and ran through the door.

Dorothy opened the box, and held two fingers, an inch over the glass.

"Don't come back," she whispered. "But I have to warn you, Charlie." She slapped the box shut and looked in the mirror with ferocity. She exited the bathroom and ran to the double doors at the end of the hallway, burst into the afternoon sun, and raced toward home, hoping she remembered the way.

Chapter 9

The Sum of Her Fears

Ragesha extended his hand and brushed a single finger over Dorothy's limp arm. Ellen sat in silence and watched. What could she say? Wherever this story began and whatever theories she'd developed had taken a left turn beyond the surreal. All she could do was sit back, enjoy the ride, and hope there was a drink hiding somewhere in the bar-car. Oh, a drink would be grand, just downright superb. Anything to cut through the edge of this tale.

Somewhere, and she couldn't quite place the shift, but somewhere, she not only wanted to, but started to believe. She could feel Dorothy's agony at school, and this Spintwister, oh my lord, did he ever give her the creeps.

She rubbed the sleep from her eyes and discovered that 2:00 a.m. had snuck past nearly 15 minutes ago. In another hour and 45 minutes, the alarm clock would go off in her apartment, and no one would be there to silence it.

"She was correct in assuming that the Spintwister had visited Charlie and myself, though I cannot say what transpired between him and Charlie. I never had the chance to ask."

"It must have been scary for you."

"No, quite the opposite, actually. He was charming, sympathetic even…" He looked thoughtful, then resumed the story. "When I returned from our last visit, I decided to build up what remained of our farm. My neighbors, people my family had called friends, saw fit to educate me—not in proper horticulture techniques, but my place in the social hierarchy.

"The farmers who remained in my village saw the land we owned as wasted opportunity—for them. The soil had been too dry, the season was very bad, and no help came from the government. All one could do was amass as much land as possible, and harvest what meager scraps grew. What could I do, other than get in their way?

"My neighbors—and remember, these were people who raised me alongside my mother and father—had taken it upon themselves to liberate what remained of my home while I was away. They caved the roof and punched holes in cemented walls with their sledgehammers. Our beds were burned, and tools stolen." He chuckled, "You know what I did? I walked into my fields, stood alongside my neighbors, and plowed." His smile faded.

"They thought it amusing at first, and annoying soon after. They chased me away with words, then with fists and sticks. When this didn't work, they put me in a closet with no food or water. I spent two days in complete darkness. Had it not been for the Spintwister, I am not sure I would have survived at all."

"The same Spintwister who told Dorothy that he would take the lives of the children in her school?"

Ragesha nodded and said, "The very same."

"Why would he do that?" she asked. Ragesha smiled, and tapped the box containing his stone key.

"I knew what he wanted. Dorothy knew what he wanted. He used what I needed against me."

"Which was what? Freedom?" Ellen asked, leaned toward Ragesha, aches all but forgotten.

"Not quite, Ms. Ellen. I needed a friend. I needed to not be alone in this big and scary world. You see," he continued, and adjusted his posture so he could look Ellen squarely in the eye, "even though these worlds we traversed were dangerous, possibly more so than the events that led to the uprising in my village, they had one thing my home did not. They had Dorothy, and they had Charlie. So, no matter what the Spintwister might have thrown in our paths, we tackled it as a group."

"The Three Key Children," Ellen reiterated.

He nodded, and widened his eyes. "Precisely. It became an odd reversal of reality for me, where one was a dream, and the other a nightmare. The dream was being with Dorothy and Charlie. The nightmare was coming home to a closet where I had no family, no friends, and a village who saw me as nothing more than a nuisance—another mouth to feed."

"And so he fed on that pain?"

"Not in a physical way, not there. I don't think he could have at the time. I think his feeding took place only in the key-worlds. He certainly fed on my emotions, though." Ragesha looked at his lap. "I believe I lost that game. If I had won, Dorothy might still be with us."

"What did he say, and do to you?" Ellen asked.

"He said all the things which a child wants to hear. He said that he was my friend. That he would never leave me. He said he could take my pain and make it his own. 'Just use the key, Ragesha, and all your troubles become my troubles.' For a child, there are no stronger words."

"You didn't!" Ellen found herself aghast, at the notion of succumbing to such a monster.

Ragesha nodded. "By the second night, I had grown so hungry, so thirsty, so tired of the darkness that I would have done anything to escape. So, I took my key, placed it in my pocket, and closed my eyes. He joined me in my camp that night, and did as he promised." Ragesha stood, turned his back toward Ellen, and pulled his shirt over his head. Dozens of scars lined his back, shoulder to hip, crisscrossing white over his mocha-brown skin. He lowered his shirt and sat down. "I don't recall ever feeling his cut," he said. "His claws were sharp, and his touch, gentle. He would cut my back, and draw the blood from me. What he did with it I couldn't see, and I don't think I wanted to. When I finished, I felt better. I couldn't remember the names of my neighbors, and by the end of the second session, I didn't remember what they had done to me."

"But you do now?" Ellen asked.

He nodded. "Yes. But most are not true memories, you understand. Only what I have extracted through interrogation. I've recovered bits and pieces of my memory as time has passed, it seems his methods of theft are only on the surface. A mask, if you will. To this day, however, I cannot put a face to my mother or father. I have pictures, many pictures, but the faces that look back are of strangers. As for my brother…" he lowered his head, and sighed, unable to finish.

"The Spintwister stopped after 20 sessions and said he would do no more. Not without Charlie and, as he put it, the no-girl. He asked if I would help return them to his worlds."

"Oh my God," Ellen breathed, absently placing a hand on Dorothy's wrist.

"You see, what the Spintwister had done by taking the hurt and the pain of my life—up to that point in time—was everything I had ever wanted. Between sessions, I could be a child again; play again. He played with me." He laughed, then, caught up in the memory for a moment. "Imagine if you can, a dark creature, part solid and part mist, with gleaming white claws that can wrap and squeeze the life out of you, imagine this thing hiding in the woods, counting to twenty. 'Ready or not, here I come!' He was soothing, forgiving. Those few days, he was my best and only friend. There was no choice for me. I said yes."

Chapter 10
What You Are Is What You Are Not

It had taken two days for Dorothy to muster the courage to approach Isais, during which she avoided her classmates as if they had the plague. He listened intently as she told of the encounter with the blue-eyed boy. She concluded her tale by stating nothing like that had happened since, and she'd crossed paths with the blue-eyed boy on more than one occasion. He avoided her, as if she were the disease carrier, but otherwise there was nothing out of the ordinary.

This was Wednesday afternoon. Isais asked for some time to consider her story, and Dorothy agreed. She spent all of Wednesday and most of Thursday locked in her schoolwork. Her nights were filled with worrisome thoughts of Charlie and Ragesha, and what the Spintwister might do to them. His absence had been a relief, but it was troublesome, too. If he was busy tormenting her, then they were okay…right?

Isais was waiting when Dorothy stepped off the bus on Thursday afternoon, two horses in tow—Ulysses, and a mare named Starlight, a Morgan with a shiny chocolate coat.

"Hey," she greeted, then ducked her head when she noticed Isais's grim expression.

"Hey, little miss. Come on, hop on this old girl here, and let's go for a ride."

She took the reins. "Please, don't call me that. Reminds me too much of him." She pursed her lips. Isais nodded. He offered to carry Dorothy's backpack. When she refused, Isais shot her a stern glance.

"Key?" he asked. She nodded. "Right." He mounted, and led Dorothy down the trail surrounding her uncle's property.

They traveled along the west path, keeping the blazing sun hidden behind the tree line. Not enough to keep them cool, but enough to keep their skin from melting off. It was nearing four in the afternoon, peak hour of the Floridian hell called summer, and Dorothy was feeling the burn. Sweat streamed down her cheeks, and her t-shirt pasted against her chest and underarms. She could see Isais was faring no better.

The trip to the southern edge of the property took 15 minutes at the slow pace Isais set and seemed even slower with his deliberate silence. She opened her mouth to ask why he had brought her out here, but he raised a hand and shook his head.

"Just a little further. I want to show you something." They continued down the trail in stony silence, finally veering left into a cut amongst the thick forest of palm fronds, pines, and bushes, down a path, barely wide enough to fit Ulysses' mass of body and muscle.

Isais pulled a large machete from a sheath strapped to his saddle and swatted the occasional orb-weaver—or Florida banana spider—from his path. A few minutes later, they emerged at the edge of a lake where he had built a large camp, hitching posts and a small shed for equipment. He helped Dorothy dismount, tied both horses, and crawled inside the shed to retrieve two lawn chairs, which he placed around the brick fire-pit, facing the water. He pulled two water bottles from his saddlebag and handed one to Dorothy. He sat and smiled up at her, invitingly.

She took the other chair, leaned back and peered across the lake. Water striders danced along the surface like tiny ships. Dragonflies hovered above them, zipping curiously in and around Dorothy and Isais, then back out over the water. Bird-song carried for what seemed like miles, and mixed with the sloshing of bass surfacing for a quick meal. "It's nice here," Dorothy commented. Isais nodded, and sipped his water.

"I've been building this camp for a few years now. Got a wood-pile set up on the other side of the shed. I come here a lot when I need to think, or just want a night to myself."

"Aren't you worried about alligators?" Dorothy asked.

He released a whooshing, sarcastic sigh. "What do you think I eat?" he teased, and the two of them relaxed into a laugh. "There were," he began, then cocked his head and reiterated, "were, a couple of 12-footers that came to visit a year back. I popped both with a .30-06, right here." He placed a finger between his eyes. "Still got a bit of the meat left, too. Not here, in the freezer back at the barn. You see a few of the small ones drift by now and again, nothing too big, maybe seven-feet, tops." He slapped her arm, "Hey, you know what I did see?" She shook her head. "Black bear," Isais nodded boastfully. Dorothy felt he could have kept this information to himself.

"Tiny little guy, maybe hip height. I had a .45 pointed at his head, you know, just in case. Never know what a bear's gonna do. He sniffed my feet, walked to the lake, took a drink, and wandered off. I thought that was pretty darn neat. You see deer, armadillos, 'possum…hardly ever see bear, unless one wanders into town."

Isais rambled on about his various wildlife encounters, and she couldn't sustain her attention. She enjoyed the view, though. The lake was wide enough to take a boat out, and she could see the opposite shoreline, but anyone standing on the beach might go unnoticed through the heat waves drifting off the water.

"You want to fish? I got some nice lures; made 'em myself," he asked. She shook her head. He shrugged, pulled a pouch of Redman chewing tobacco from his pocket and stuffed a large wad between his cheek and gums. He chewed for a moment, then spat a river of black tar onto the sand and wiped spittle from his chin.

Dorothy stuck her finger in her mouth, pretending to gag.

"Hey, don't knock it sister. A buzz is a buzz," he replied in jest, then settled. He fixated on the water, kicked out his feet and grunted, then spat again.

"You told me about your friend's camp. Charlie, was it?" he asked, and she nodded. "Similar to this?"

"Sort of. No fire pit, and no lake. He's got a trunk rather than a shed, and a tent roped off to the trees. We don't really spend the night."

"Smart kid. I like him already," Isais mused. "And the Indian boy? Same thing, right?" She confirmed that Ragesha had a similar camp as well, though there were certainly differences. "Of course, 'bout 30 years of differences, I'd think. Newer stuff, right?"

She wasn't really sure, but humored him in order to push his train of thought along. "I guess. Ragesha's stuff is kind of, well, raggedy. You can't tell how old it is."

"Camps can certainly age belongings, that's for sure. You know, places like this used to be everywhere. When my family moved here from Mexico, there were more forests than towns. Heck, you couldn't take a step around here without slipping in some kinda poop," he looked like he was talking to himself at this point, but suddenly had her interest. "Seems like every time you turn around, someone is out there trying to take away everything you love."

"Yeah, I know what you mean."

"You know, I believe you do. I'd never say that to a kid, I mean, what do they know? They know how to play, and they know how to whine. But you sister, I bet you do know, don't you?"

"I'm a little scared, Isais. I got mad at my dad, and I ran. Then when things turned bad, you know, when the Spintwister came after me, I ran right back...but, I brought it with me." Dorothy said earnestly.

"Well," he began after a long sigh, "if what you said was true, you probably should be scared. There's a lot of kids out there who hurt, Dorothy. A lot of kids who need a friend, to—"

"Take their pain away," she finished.

"Mm-hmm. I bet it won't stop there, you know? Kids are small, like little jalapeño poppers. Imagine what that thing will do when he discovers the pain most adults carry with them? Like your dad, you know?" Isais raised his hand to stave off Dorothy's objections, and continued his explanation, "I know, I know. He probably deserves every bit of suffering God's placed on his guilty shoulders. But that's not what I'm saying." He spat and wiped his chin. "Imagine the regret he feels. You losing your mom, having to move you here, watching his daughter suffer the way you've suffered. Now multiply that by a hundred. A thousand. Millions...people carry that crap with them, in here," he said and patted his chest above his heart. "That little kid buffet just turned into an appetizer, you know?"

Dorothy lowered her head, and this time, let her tears fall. Isais leaned over and patted her back.

"So, what do I do?" she asked.

"Well, I thought about that. And that's why I brought you out here," Isais said. He walked to Ulysses and reached into the

172

saddlebag. He handed Dorothy a small satchel. She nearly dropped it after miscalculating the weight.

Inside were two items. A claw hammer, and an old buck knife. She cocked her head at Isais.

"I'm going to ask you to do two things, and if I am correct, neither is going to work. Take out the key Dorothy, and set it on the rock in front of you."

She looked toward her feet and noticed a large, flat rock partly buried between her legs. Isais tossed the backpack and she pulled the key box out, wrapped the key in her handkerchief, and placed it on the stone. It glinted in the afternoon sun, casting white sparkling strobes across the surface of the stone.

"Take out the hammer."

"No!" Dorothy protested vehemently and plucked at the key. Her fingers slipped at each attempt, the weight preventing her from gripping it.

"Dorothy!" Isais thundered. She jumped, sank into her seat, and covered her eyes. "Take out the hammer, Dorothy. You said he wants your key, so the thing to do is break that dang thing before he can get it."

"You do it! I can't. I just can't!"

"You know it has to be you," Isais calmly replied.

"Why does it have to be me? I didn't ask for this. I didn't want this."

Isais wrapped his hand around her wrist and yanked her close. She broke from her panic and fearfully turned to him, hoping beyond hope he'd make this whole mess go away. He loosened his grip.

"You didn't? Wasn't it you who told me that you wanted an escape? You told me the key called to you. It wanted you to find it. But it didn't, did it?"

She thought on this, and decided it had not. If anything, she had called it.

"Even now, you still want a way out, right?" He motioned to the bag. "It's right there, Dorothy. Pick it up." He nudged the bag closer with his toe.

Dorothy took a deep breath, wrapped her hand around the wooden handle, and pulled the hammer to her. Her muscles loosened, and the head fell to her feet, and she dropped to her knees. She pulled the hammer up, using both hands.

"Remember, Charlie and your friend, Rags. He didn't want their keys, just yours. Because you are the no-girl. No key means no reason to hurt you anymore. He can't hurt anyone here without that key. Do you believe that?" Isais asked.

"And then I will have you, and all the children in this world," she recalled in a low, thoughtful tone. "One key at a time…"

She brought the hammer down hard, striking the key along the shaft just below the base. The impact echoed across the lake, and birds took to the air, while small animals scurried away. The key bounced into the dirt beside the rock, without even so much as a scratch. Dorothy grimaced and raised the hammer again.

Isais raised his hand and motioned for her to stop. "Listen," he whispered.

The lake had turned calm and expectant. She could hear nothing, only the beating of her heart and Isais's breathing. They looked at each other. His eyes widened and he parted his lips, then licked them.

She heard a familiar crackling behind her, and she spun toward it. Isais turned with her. Another echoed to their left, then across the lake.

"He's here, isn't he?" Isais asked. Dorothy nodded, and slowly rose to her feet.

"Don't, Dorothy. I don't think he can do anything to you, at least not yet."

"How would you know?" she whispered.

"Because he would have by now." Isais cupped his hands over his mouth, and shouted, "You got nothing, *espectro*! Nothing! I got more pain than all of these *niños pequeños* put together!" His voice roared across the lake, and the snapping grew eerily close, with each rising word.

"I don't think you should say those things," Dorothy warned, tugging his arm. Isais pulled himself away, and screamed into the sky while slapping his chest, "Take my pain, *pendejo*! I got miles of it for you!"

"Isais, don't!" she panicked and backed away from him. He turned, grinned, and pointed to the ground.

"Don't forget your key." He took a seat, and mused, "You think he heard me?"

"Kansas heard you!" She wrapped the key and returned it to the box, then stuffed the box into her pack. "We have to go."

174

"Relax, sweetie. If it's still here, it's just trying to scare you away from me. I'm like your fluffy little wall, and he ain't gonna touch you. I can prove that too!" Isais proclaimed and kicked the satchel toward her. "Pick up the knife, and slice open your hand, or wrist. Hell, it don't matter to me, just cut something."

"What?" Dorothy asked. She shook her head, and slowly backed away from him.

Isais pulled the knife from the bag, opened the blade, and tossed it to her. She jumped clear as the blade buried into the ground. He shook his head, retrieved the knife, and walked it over to her. "What are you afraid of? Didn't you say he put a claw through your leg? Do it. Show that beast you know he can't hurt you."

"Please Isais, you're scaring me!" Dorothy cried. He cursed, grabbed her arm, and led her to the side of the shed, then pressed her wrist against the rickety wood.

"Do you believe he can hurt you?" Isais screamed. She shook her head. "Do you believe what he tells you, little no-girl?" Dorothy thought on this, dropped her eyes, and nodded.

"Then if you are nothing, nothing can hurt you. Not even me." Isais slammed the knife into the palm of Dorothy's hand. She screamed, more over the shock of the action than any pain she felt, and found herself scolding Isais with a great many, choice, colorful words she rarely used. When she was done, she pulled the knife from the wood, and threw the blade into the water.

"You could have killed me!"

He shook his head, grabbed her, and pulled her close. "I…I didn't think that for a second." She felt a droplet of water strike her shoulder, and wrapped her hands around him when he began sobbing.

He pulled away, wiped his eyes, and sat down. Sweat beaded along his brow, and his breathing turned heavy, and rapid.

"So, now what?" Dorothy asked.

Isais raised a hand, and worked in a few, deep breaths. "Well, we know what you aren't. That puts us on even ground. I got one thing that *espíritu malvado* doesn't have," he stated, proudly. "I got ancestors, and I got culture. You think a ghost gonna scare this Mexican off? No way, *amiga.* You and me, we're in this for the long run. We're gonna find out what you are before he does," he leaned in, and whispered, "and we'll use it against him."

Isais woke early the following morning and hastened through the daily chores he performed before turning the ranch over to Dorothy's uncle. She had packed and loaded a cooler full of drinks and lunch into his truck.

Dorothy sat at the breakfast table, now an hour past the first bell. Her father slid a coffee in front of her. She thanked him, sipped gingerly, then added three teaspoons of sugar.

"Add any more and you'll turn it into Jell-O," her father said.

"Coffee blows on its own. Sugar and spice, right?" She took a long swallow.

"No school today?"

"There is, I don't think I can go in," Dorothy replied.

"Right. Guess that's got something to do with the phone call I received from the principal. Says you had an episode the other day; scared the bejesus out of some boy. He also said you pulled it together over the past couple of days. So what's this all about?" Dorothy sagged in her seat, and drank from her mug. "Everything still hitting you pretty hard?"

"I keep dreaming about Charlie and Rags. I feel like he's still got them in some way," she began cautiously, adding, "Last night, for instance. I dreamed about Charlie, and he was running away from him, but couldn't get away. He cut him, Daddy, the monster cut him up and down his back. Charlie couldn't do a thing about it, he just laid there, looking at me…I think he wanted me to help him, and I didn't do a thing!"

"That's one heck of a dream, sweetheart. Is this why you and Isais are driving to Orlando?" he asked.

"He says his grandmother can help. I'm sorry, I didn't ask."

"No worries, sugarplum. I've known Isais for years, and his grandparents even longer. They were good friends with your grandma, and helped raise your mother after your grandpa passed."

"They knew Mom?" she asked. He nodded.

"Treated us all like her own grandchildren. Even helped build this place before they grew too old to work. They moved, five or six years ago, to some new-fangled retirement community, east of the city. She's as spiritual as people go. If Isais thinks she can help you, I say go for it."

"Why don't you come? Sounds like you haven't seen her in a while."

He thought for a moment, and his mustache twitched. "I better not. Bills to pay, and all. Besides, Al will need a hand around here with Isais gone. You go on, get your mind right."

Isais and Dorothy were on the road before noon. They sat in relative silence until they entered Wildwood, exited off I-75, and circled onto the Sunshine's State Parkway, where a pleasant woman in a tan pants suit handed Isais a ticket, which he passed to Dorothy. The ticket looked like it was cut from a manila folder. The entry number, along with the date and time stamped above large brown text depicting its name, read, *Florida's Turnpike.*

She ran her finger along the left side, and found their exit— 70-Orlando South, then down to 90-Wildwood. The whole trip would cost a buck-fifteen total. Not a bad price for a journey of the soul.

They exited into Orlando an hour later, then skirted along various country roads lined with palm fronds and thick brush. The scenery was insufficient to distract Dorothy's increasingly worried mind. She had been fidgeting ever since they left the expressway. She bit her nails, shifted in her seat, rolled down the window, and peeked outside. Isais stared at the road ahead and said nothing.

Dorothy had an unsettled feeling that the Spintwister was following them. But why? Isais was right; she didn't feel he was out to get her. "He's just playing games with me," she whispered, and turned to look behind them. She saw nothing, only the road stretching to a hazy pinpoint in the distance, and yet, a ripple up her spine told her different. He was out there; he was just keeping his distance.

She considered what Isais's grandmother might say. Isais insisted she was a spiritual woman—but who isn't at her age? Isais had to be in his upper thirties to mid-forties by now, so...what, she's double, maybe triple that? Getting close to the Almighty is sort of a prerequisite to retirement. It'd be like her special ticket, her key to get into heaven. In this sense, maybe she would understand, even believe.

Isais depressed the clutch and the truck angrily chugged into to second gear as he turned into a small trailer park. Dorothy turned in time to see the name welded on a wrought iron gate overhead. *Solace Key.*

A few months ago, Dorothy would have said something like, "Welcome to redneck's paradise!" She would have certainly played the good little teenager with all the 'yes ma'ams' and 'no ma'ams' any grandmother would want to hear, all while quietly scoffing at the lower level of lifestyle, then relaying the details to her schoolmates upon return. Now, though, the sign stood like a beacon of hope.

She had expected to see the typical drab graveyard that these retirement parks often became, full of forgotten souls, marching their way toward a slow, lonely death.

Instead, Dorothy saw comradery between neighbors as they scuffled to and from doorsteps. Hands raised in greeting as they passed, and she returned the gesture with an accompanying smile. When she scanned the road behind her, she could no longer feel the Spintwister. No, traveling within Solace Key, down a narrow road called Memory Bay, hanging left around a small oval pool-yard and onto a cul-de-sac named Rally Road, she felt at ease.

Isais turned to her and smiled. "You feel it, don't you?" he asked. What *it* was, she couldn't exactly say, but agreed she certainly did. It grew steadily as they neared the end of the road, and she was jumping in her seat when they pulled into a small driveway alongside a white doublewide, trimmed in pastel blue. A narrow slate walkway led from the center of the drive to a canopy covering the front door and extended outward by about ten-feet. An old woman rocked in her chair, gray hair pulled in a bun. She was knitting. She sat next to a small table with a jar of iced tea at its center. Three glasses filled with fresh ice surrounded the pitcher, and two chairs rested beside the table, each facing the old woman.

"She's expecting us?" Dorothy asked, and Isais nodded. "What did you tell her?"

Isais shook his head and turned off the engine. "Nothing. I haven't been here, and she doesn't have a phone."

Dorothy eyed the glasses and turned back to Isais, who tapped a finger to his head. He slapped her shoulder, and exited the truck.

The old woman dropped her knitting as they approached. She hugged Isais when he bent over to kiss her. They talked for a moment, and Dorothy could hear the faint hints of Spanish over the warm breeze poking at her cheek. They turned to her, and she shrank, feeling suddenly exposed.

The old woman seemed to wear a permanent frown, and looked at her with what she viewed as contempt. She leaned toward Dorothy, fluffed out the skirt of her yellow paisley dress, and rested her elbows in her lap. She picked up something from the table, a string of beads maybe, and cupped both her hands around it, then turned to Isais, and spoke in a whisper.

"Yo, Dee! Come meet Nana!" Isais waved her over. She sighed, gathered her courage, and walked over to the porch. The old woman turned, and poured tea into the three glasses, handing Dorothy a cup. She knelt, not sure what else to do. The old woman patted Isais on the arm and pointed to Dorothy while speaking. Isais nodded.

"She said she's not a queen, and to tell the small white girl to please get off the dirt."

"Sit," the old woman said in accent, parting her lips and revealing a sparse set of yellowed teeth. Dorothy took the seat to her right, and nervously sipped her tea.

"Does she speak English?" she asked Isais.

The old woman hooted, pointed, and commented to Isais, then turned to Dorothy. "For more years than you." She motioned for Dorothy's hand, and dropped a set of rosary beads into her palm and closed her fingers around them. "This is for your dreams."

The beads shone in the afternoon sun, and though they appeared plastic, Dorothy noted carvings beneath the sheen. Judging by the cross and cut jewels, she guessed this was no dime store knock-off. Dorothy wrapped the beads around her hand, and rubbed the cross with her thumb. The old woman smiled.

"Now let me see it," she asked, and stretched out a shaking, liver-spotted hand.

Dorothy raised a brow.

"The key," Isais nudged her.

"She knows what I mean, don't you *mi hija*?"

179

Dorothy un-slung her pack and placed the key-box on the table. Isais moved the pitcher to the floor, the old woman opened the lid and lifted the glass key. She leaned in for a closer look, turned the key in her hand, and whispered something indecipherable before dropping the key back in the box. Isais returned the lid and slipped the box back into Dorothy's pack.

The old woman shook her hands, blew against her fingertips, clasped them together, and muttered to herself. Isais lowered his eyes.

Dorothy looked between them with a mounting sense of panic. She opened her mouth to ask a question, but the old woman grabbed her wrist and shook her head, shushing her.

"The key is not yours," she said sternly, before slapping her hand. Dorothy rubbed her wrist. It was as if struck by a brick. She leaned into her chair, and sulked.

"Where did you get that abomination?" the old woman croaked, sounding out the syllables, struggling with the words. She seemed irritated with Dorothy and judging by looks thrown at Isais, she was angry with him, too. But for what? Bringing Dorothy here? The woman knew they were coming—old lady's iced-tea trick—so why the sudden mood swing?

Isais must have sensed this as well, and began to soothe his grandmother, speaking gently, often motioning to Dorothy. She swatted him across the cheek and scolded him, "In English, fat-boy. You brought it here." She pointed at Dorothy. "At least let it understand you."

"It?" Dorothy asked. This wasn't the first time someone or something had referred to her in such a manner. It was starting to piss her off.

Isais began to explain, "I said, 'Nana, she's a girl who is in trouble. She found the key, and now—'" The old woman interrupted with an angry torrent of—well, it might have been Spanish. She was talking so damned fast that Dorothy couldn't really tell. Isais nodded, shook his head, nodded again, tried to counter, and finally bowed his head like a scolded schoolboy. The old woman turned back to Dorothy and glared.

"I'm sorry, Mrs...." Dorothy began, and paused, realizing she hadn't been properly introduced. "My name is Dorothy," she said, and extended her hand. The old woman scoffed, sat back, and turned her head. She continued her rant, and Isais began to translate.

"My grandmother says she doesn't want to talk to you, so she's going to talk through me."

"What? Why! What did I do?" Dorothy asked Isais, then turned to the old woman and repeated the final question. The old woman responded to Isais, though she kept a stern eye on Dorothy.

"Nana says she is sorry, but she only speaks to people and spirits," he paused as his grandmother elaborated. "She says you are neither, so she cannot talk to you."

Dorothy felt a pang of shame swell within and explode into anger. "You know, I'm getting real tired of everybody telling me that I am not a person!" Tears welled and Dorothy pressed her hands into fists while trying to maintain her composure. She settled, turned to Isais and asked, "Please ask your Nana what she means?"

Isais pointed to his grandmother, "She's right there, Dee, you can…"

"ASK her." Dorothy demanded. By God, if Nana wasn't going to acknowledge Dorothy as a person and speak with her, then she'd shoot the same discourtesy right back at her. Take that, grams.

Isais turned wearily to his grandmother. "What she said."

The old woman shifted glares between Dorothy and Isais. She nodded, motioned Isais closer, then slapped him across the back of the head.

She continued in Spanish, sighed, then looked Dorothy in the eye, and clapped.

"Dorothy. If that is what you call yourself, then that is what I call you, too." She turned to Isais, who nodded, and egged her to continue. "Isais is trying to tell me what you do with two boys. I don't want to know."

She sat back, and Isais dropped into his chair. He and his grandmother resumed their rapid-fire Spanish argument. All the language swapping was irking Dorothy, and she was beginning to wonder why exactly he drove her out here in the first place.

"Hey!" Dorothy shouted, and the two of them stopped and stared at her. Dorothy sighed and asked, "Why did you bring me here, Isais?"

"I thought Nana could help you," he replied.

"With what?" Dorothy asked, and at this point, Isais's grandmother turned to him as well.

"You know, with the thing," he said, then puckered his lips, and made a buzzing sound while flapping his arms. His grandmother whapped him again, and the two continued bickering.

"Oh, my freaking God, will you two knock it off!" Dorothy shouted. They turned to her again, and she calmly continued. "Use your English words," she said, modifying her mother's mantra from so many years ago.

Isais sighed, and she could see him struggling with how to explain what he thought he knew. "With the key, the other world, the two boys, and the monster."

"*Que?*" the old woman asked, shaking her head. "What monster?"

"It's a demon," Isais replied.

"Oh, what do you know of demons, fat boy? All you know is horse dung. Let the no-girl explain."

Dorothy's jaw dropped, and Isais glowered at his grandmother. "Why did you call her that?" he demanded.

"Call her what?" the woman replied.

"No-girl. You said 'let the no-girl answer'."

The old woman sat up, and parted her lips as if to speak, then reclined again. "I don't know." She looked sideways at Dorothy. "Does that mean something to you?"

Finally, the old woman was ready to listen, and she did, for nearly three hours.

Dorothy told the story of her mother's death, the trip to the ranch, where she found the glass key and what it did. She told the story of the Spintwister and his promise to her. She told her of the young boy he possessed in school, and the dreams of Charlie and Ragesha.

Shadows stretched, the sky turned to marmalade, and Dorothy continued. She ended the story with the drive here, and the feelings of being followed, and its amusement when nearing the old woman's home. Isais's grandmother pulled Dorothy's backpack to her, and opened the key box.

"Nana, do you know what that is?" Isais asked. She pursed her lips and nodded.

"Sure, it's a key made of glass."

"That's it?"

"That's all it is to me, *mijo.* To you, it might be something more. To Dorothy, it is an escape. To its owner? I can't clearly see it. But to your Spintwister, it is something far more valuable," she said. The old woman closed her eyes and ran her fingers along the barrel. "I feel him dancing on its edge. He wants to take it from me and…" She opened her eyes in surprise. "And give it back to you."

"You see him?" Dorothy asked excitedly.

She shook her head and looked past Dorothy. "No, I don't see him. I don't want to see him, and I tell you child, he doesn't want me to see him either. You should destroy this thing," she said, and offered the key to Dorothy. She didn't take it. "It's your key to keep, little one. I cannot hold it for you."

"It's not that," Dorothy explained, "it weighs too much if I touch the glass. It has to be wrapped."

"Really?" Isais's grandmother gripped the key again and rubbed the barrel with both thumbs and index fingers. She cocked her head, raised a brow, and frowned.

"The key calls when it wants to be found. It didn't call to you, it didn't want you to find it. It's not your key," she repeated.

"So you've said. Any idea whose key it is?"

"No names come to mind, though it knows the owner is close. Perhaps someone at your school?"

"Nana, what about the demon?" Isais interrupted.

"That thing is no demon. It is not human, either, from what I can tell. Give me your hand, Dorothy," she asked, and Dorothy slipped her hand into the woman's cold, dry fingers.

"Close your eyes and walk with me," she said, and Dorothy stood, then sat back down when she saw Isais's face. Apparently, not that kind of walk. She closed her eyes, sighed, and waited.

An image of Ragesha flitted before her eyes. He sat inside a closet, curled into a ball on the floor. He was trembling, as if cold, though she felt as if the closet was hot as an oven. She could hear whispers in a language she didn't recognize, and then the sound of a rock or fist striking the door. Ragesha twitched for a moment, then settled again. His chest rattled, and he wheezed as he struggled for breath.

She heard a pop to the left, and the Spintwister's claw stretched toward Ragesha's back, from the shadows. It drew a line from his neck to his waist. Blood trickled from the wound and chased down the creature's claw as it slowly pulled away.

Ragesha's breathing slowed, and he smiled. The vision blackened, and Dorothy was looking upon the old woman once again.

"He's killing the boy," she said empathetically. "He'll do the same to the other one."

"But not me?" Dorothy asked.

The old woman shook her head. "No. I don't think he can hurt you, little..." She paused, and forced, "girl. You have a history with this creature that reaches far beyond any vision I can summon. What you are, Dorothy, is what you are not. You are not alive, and you are not dead, either. You are neither daughter nor friend. You are not a sibling, a student, or a niece."

"Nana, what does that leave?" Isais asked.

"It leaves nothing, *mijo.* It leaves nothing at all. Come on, let's go inside before the mosquitoes start to eat us for dinner. I'll get a brew going and see what my spirits say, as long as Dorothy will listen."

Dorothy agreed, eager to press on. Seeing Ragesha, even if only in a vision, offered her hope. Knowing the old woman saw the same, comforted her. Perhaps something could be done to stop the Spintwister before he harmed him further. Perhaps the old woman knew how.

The three stepped inside.

The old woman's home was filled with a variety of smells Dorothy couldn't place at first. Cinnamon mixed with vanilla struck her, then blended into something resembling nutmeg. They moved through a small living room cluttered with books; figurines of Mary, Jesus, the reaper; each inspected with a passing glance. She noticed the feel of the room changed from welcoming to an easy, peaceful calm with the different fragrances.

They entered the kitchen and Dorothy took a chair next to Isais's grandmother, who instructed Isais to boil some water. She set out three small cups and opened a container, handed to her by Isais. As the water boiled in a kettle twice the age of Dorothy, the old woman whispered to herself, and scooped dark leaves into the bottom of a floral ceramic pot. A grim reaper clad in white robes with jewels along its robe and scythe was painted on one side of the pot. The more familiar black reaper painted on the other, also decorated with many colorful jewels. Both reapers held glowing orbs in their right hands.

Dorothy turned to Isais.

"It's *Nuestra Señora de la Santa Muerte.* Our Lady of the Holy Death," he informed her, and quickly followed with, "Don't worry, she's only scary on the outside. All good things, I promise."

"Is Nana going to read the leaves? Tell me my future?"

"Yes," the old woman agreed, and nodded. "The leaves tell me you are about to drink tea."

Isais and Dorothy smiled. "So, what is all this? A ritual to ward off the Spintwister? Can I go back to school? Can things just go back to normal? What about Charlie and Rags?"

The old woman pushed the teapot aside. Her expression was softer now. She reached for her hand and Dorothy accepted it, as if placing her entire future in this woman's premonitions. Her words, whatever they might be, will be her new path. She just knew this…believed it. She sighed expectantly, and the old woman sadly shook her head.

"Dorothy, Isais brought you here because he thought your spirit needed healing. If that were true, then I would be able to help you. He thought you may have angered a demon. If you had, then yes, I could help you. He thought your key might have been possessed, and if it had been, then yes, I could help you."

"But you can't help, can you?"

She shook her head, then asked for the key. Dorothy set the box on the table, removed the lid, and the two stared at the simple glass glinting in the dim light of her kitchen.

"Do you know what it is?" Dorothy asked. She brushed her finger along the smooth edges of the bit, and quickly pulled her hand away, when the table beneath moaned under the increased weight of the key.

"Well, I cannot say what the key is, but there are stories. Always a story eh, *mijo?*" she chuckled, and Isais agreed. "One such story is *La Llorona.*"

"The Weeping Woman," Isais translated. He poured the hot water into the teapot, and sat beside his grandmother. She tapped his hand.

"Here, she is called Maria. Greeks call her Madea. Germans, Lorelei. They all speak of a wailing woman, who lure the unsuspecting through weakness. What is weaker than children in pain, eh *mijo*?"

"Yes, Nana."

"We will talk of *La Llorona.* Maria," she clarified, "because of the children. Maria was a beautiful *senorita* with long, elegant, dark hair. She was born a peasant, but believed she would marry the most handsome man in the world."

"Because she was so pretty," Isais added.

"Do you want to tell the story, dung herder?" Isais cowered behind raised hands, and gave an amused chuckle when his grandmother looked away.

"Maria decided she would marry the most handsome man. Every night she slipped into a white gown, to entice the many men who admired her. One day, she met a man riding into the village. Maria knew right away that this ranchero was the one for her, and she knew how she would seduce him. She ignored the ranchero, ignored the many gifts he tried to woo her with. This made the ranchero want her desperately, so madly that he asked for her hand in marriage. She accepted, and together, they had two children.

"The ranchero, not a man to be shackled by a single *senorita,* drank many drinks, wooed many women. His love for Maria faded and he talked of leaving her for a woman of a better class."

"He was a land owner, heir to his papa's many ranches. Big-wig in horses and cattle. People like that don't marry peasants," Isais clarified.

"Yes," the old woman continued, "but he had children. And this was the only thing that concerned the ranchero. Maria resented him, deeply. One day, Maria took her children for a walk along a river so they could play, and so she could clear her troubled mind. They passed a carriage with her ranchero and a beautiful mistress inside. The ranchero spoke to his children, ignoring Maria. He left without saying a word to her, as if she wasn't there at all. Maria was angry at the ranchero, so full of hate and rage that she threw her children into the deep river and left them to drown."

"She was free of burden, and had her revenge on the ranchero…but she felt shame." Isais interjected. The old woman nodded.

"Maria tried to rescue her children, but it was too late. Day and night she mourned for her children, in the same white dress that she had used to attract all the suitors in the village. She would not eat or drink. Her beauty faded to bone, and she died on the bank of the same river where her children were lost. Maria stood at heaven's gate, but when she tried to enter, the angels told her she could not. They demanded to know where her children had gone. They said she could not enter heaven without her children, and so she returned to look for them. Now she cries for her children within the whispers of the wind, '*Donde estan mis hijos?*'"

"Weeping woman," Isais pointed out.

"Yes," his grandmother agreed. "She is locked between this world and the spirit world. They say she marks wandering children with a single tear, and takes them when they are near her shores. Others say she appears on her eldest child's birthday and calls for him, and taking those she has marked, returning to the world between worlds. Her son was 14-years-old when he died, like you are now." She paused. "So many tales, who knows what to believe any more."

"Do you think I'm one of those children? And her world between worlds, is that the key-worlds?" Dorothy asked.

"No. You are not one of those children." The old woman replied simply.

"Then why tell me this?" Dorothy asked in frustration. She sat back in her chair, folded her arms, and sighed. This was all looking like a huge waste of time.

"I tell you this, because all tales are similar, even in the many different cultures which tell them. This key is a mark, of that I am certain. But it is not yours. The key, like our Maria, calls when it wants to be found."

"And that's exactly what happened!" Dorothy retorted.

"No, little one. You called to the key. Now it rejects you."

"The key doesn't want me?" Dorothy's heart sank into her stomach. It couldn't be true. She found the key right there in the barn, where anyone could find it. Anyone! Did it call to someone? No. She found it, and by God it was hers. Not her fault the rightful owner didn't listen.

"If this isn't my key, then whose is it?" Dorothy asked.

The old woman closed her eyes and placed her hand on the key. She frowned and shook her head. "Someone close, I think. Perhaps someone in your school, maybe someone who visited the farm before you arrived. That is for you to find out, after..." she said, and her expression grew dire.

"After what?"

"Your tormentor, this Spintwister. He is not the demon who marks these trinkets. He cannot make them." She ran her thumb along the base before flattening her palm along the length of the key. "He was close to that which does. A spirit who has passed beyond the worlds between, and he has taken up their rule by claiming himself king. He is not *La Llorona,* but he knew her well. He..." Isais's grandmother lowered her head.

"He tricked her, and poisoned her. He poisoned many, as he plans to do to you, Dorothy. He now knows your key can be used by anyone, and he will stop at nothing to retrieve it. I think, now the key is calling, desperately calling to anyone, any—soul, willing to take it."

The old woman lifted her hand, leaving the glass key glinting in its box. Dorothy didn't know what to say, and her heart sank deep at the thought of it wanting to be rid of her so badly. It didn't seem right. Didn't seem fair.

"You saw this?" Isais asked. The old woman nodded.

"He talks to me, here, sitting before you. He doesn't like me. He fears me, I think. I ask him, 'Fiend, why do you torment this girl?' He says he does not, 'for she is no-girl'. I ask him what he means. How is this girl sitting in my chair, in my kitchen, not a girl? He says, 'You know why. Because she is not sitting there at all.' He says, 'She is a thief. She has stolen all you see, and he will get his property back."

"I'm not here?" Dorothy asked.

"No child. You are here. You simply shouldn't be."

"Because I do not exist," Dorothy said, repeating the Spintwister's words. Isais's grandmother nodded. At last she poured three cups of tea and passed them around.

Dorothy sipped nervously.

"Do you think he's one of her children? The *La Llor...* The Weeping Woman's?"

"I suppose. Anything is possible. Who knows? Child, we are specks of dust in this universe. Purity is rare, and vanity flourishes. Vanity breeds evil, and evil feeds upon the downtrodden." She touched her forehead, ran her hand to the nape of her neck, then touched each shoulder before kissing the knuckle of her index finger. Isais followed suit.

"I don't understand. What vanity?" Dorothy asked.

Isais's grandmother shook her head. "Leave the philosophy to the old, dear. You have bigger problems."

Dorothy shuddered. "I do?"

The old woman nodded. "He cannot touch you, not while you claim the mark," she said while patting the glass key. "But he can touch those who have been rightfully marked, and he is going to use them to get to you. He will use the key against you. You, and those two boys he feeds on."

"Charlie and Ragesha."

"You've seen the pain he causes them."

"I've seen him take their pain in your vision that you showed me, but not cause it." Dorothy said, without conviction.

"What he takes is more than their pain, dear. Pain is who we are as God's children. Pain defines you, just like happiness and love. Pain is the teacher of will and control. Without the one, you lose the others."

Isais sat up, and took his grandmother's hand. "What do you mean, Nana?"

"She needs to face this fiend, Isais."

"No, she can't. She cannot go back, Nana. Can't she fight him here? With you? Me? Please, Nana!"

"She has to, *mijo.* If she does not, those two children will die, and he will become strong enough to take what is rightfully his. He will take it from her, and give it to another. One who does exist. One who can feed him. And when he is full again, he will give it to another child, then another."

"He's going to kill Charlie?" Dorothy asked. The woman nodded.

"Yes, my dear. Just as the sun will rise, so will your friends fall. Both of them, and," she shut her eyes, "one is very close." Dorothy could see her eyes moving beneath closed lids. "The

189

other fights. He is losing, but he fights, and he is waiting for you." She opened her eyes. "Go home, Dorothy. Talk to your father. Talk to your uncle. Prepare yourself. You are not fighting for your life anymore. You are fighting for all the children."

Chapter 11
Home Again, Home Again

Dorothy and Isais spent another hour with his grandmother, and true to her promise, she never offered Dorothy her name. Dorothy wanted to feel insulted, but in an odd way, she didn't blame her. Could she? She was the no-girl after all. Or perhaps the old woman was stark raving mad, and she and Isais had simply fallen into her story-trap. A pleasant thought, but inaccurate, Dorothy suspected. Either way, she could always ask Isais when leaving.

Before the two departed, Isais's grandmother asked Dorothy to step outside so she might cleanse her grandson. She observed the ritual from a respectable distance, and quietly chuckled as the old woman swatted Isais with a head of lettuce, all the while blowing smoke from a cigar up and down the length of his body. The smell on the ride to home proved to be amply nauseating.

As they clambered into Isais's F-150, Isais's grandmother returned to her knitting project. She didn't look up from her work again.

"Why didn't she offer to cleanse me?" Dorothy asked. She thought she knew the answer and guessed that the old woman didn't see her as a worthy recipient. Neither did she, truth be told. Still, it would have been nice to be asked.

"Nana said you'd ask. She was worried you might release the soul that you borrowed before finishing your work. She said come see her after."

"Why does everyone keep saying that? I mean for frig's sake, how exactly do you steal a soul? It's stupid!"

"I don't know. Might have something to do with how you cheat death, right?"

She sank as he said this. He had a point, and she had no counter-argument. A thought occurred to her, though, and she sat up straight and blurted, "Do you think…do you think I was like this when Mom died?"

"Hmm? You mean like, would you have survived the fire?" Isais asked.

She nodded, and whispered, "Dad could have saved Mom. I could have walked out on my own."

"Maybe, but didn't you say you passed out from the smoke? You also said you were hurt when Charlie tossed his key at you. Doesn't sound like it, you know?"

"Yes, I suppose. But still, she could be alive right now, and we could be home. No Spintwister, no—" She did not finish the thought. No, Charlie was a bit more than she could say out loud.

Outside, trailing them distantly in the darkening night sky, she could sense him, how tickled he had become by her new sense of purpose. She wanted to scream at him, challenge him, show him he couldn't hurt her. Somehow, she suspected he knew this. He would follow her to the ends of this world and those between, until…well, until her key decided that enough is enough. She could almost feel it reach out and beckon someone, anyone who isn't her. Did the Spintwister sense this? Is he simply lying in wait, patiently awaiting the day Dorothy could no longer bear the weight of her key? Dorothy slumped into her seat and sighed. Her eyes grew heavy, and her mind settled.

Dorothy spent the rest of the ride lost in a strange absence of thought. She felt if she devised a plan, the Spintwister would sense it somehow. She wasn't quite sure what she wanted translated to what she was going to do and guessed the creature would view desire and action separately. For now, she was stuck with the annoying monster. She had to get rid of him.

They arrived home shortly after nine, and joined her father and uncle at the table. Isais started to excuse himself, but Dorothy asked him to stay. She had something to say, and wanted him there for it. Dorothy sat at the kitchen table and looked her father in the eye, unsure as to how she would begin. Thankfully, he began the conversation for her.

"So, spirit all spic-and-span? Make right with the good Lord?" he asked beneath a wavering mustache. Al chuckled, but quieted abruptly when he saw Dorothy's lip quivering.

"Good God, Dorothy. What happened?" her father sat next to her and looked at her intently. She raised a hand and gently

192

nudged him backwards a couple inches, then placed her backpack in her lap. She reached into the pack for the key box, and placed it in the center of the table.

"Well, I'll be," her uncle said, as she lifted the lid. "Where'd you find this thing? I haven't seen it in years!" He lifted the key and tossed it about his hands. "You remember this, Pete? We were going to give it to my mother as a Christmas gift, thought we could drill a hole through the center, and mount it on a plaque. Damn thing broke three bits before we gave up."

"Yeah," her father replied warily and shook his head when her uncle offered him the key. "I thought we threw it out years ago." He turned to Dorothy. "Your mother hated it, said it was the ugliest dang thing she had ever seen."

Al chuckled, "If memory serves, she tossed it in the garbage more than a few times. Always wound up back in the barn somehow." He gave Dorothy a mischievous look. "I suspect your dad kept fishing it out and put it there to prank her. Where did you find it Dorothy? Let me guess, the barn?"

"Yeah. Mixed in with Mom's things."

"See, damned thing is magic," Al mused.

He had no idea.

Dorothy intended to explain everything that had happened over the last couple of months, but cut herself short when her father blankly reached across the table and took the glass key in his hand. He inspected it with tempered fascination, lifting it, then laying it on the table and staring it down while stuffing his hands between his legs.

Isais and Al noticed the change in his demeanor and sat in silence while he sorted through his troubled assessments. Dorothy called his name and, when he didn't respond, touched his shoulder. He jumped, then returned to the key as if she were a mile away.

"I know this key," he said, and ran two fingers over the edge of his mustache.

"Was this…" He looked at Dorothy. "You found this with your mother's things?"

"That and a bunch of pictures," she added. "Mostly of you three. She was in them, sure enough."

"Al, was this hers?" he asked. Guess he wasn't listening to the whole conversation, a moment ago.

"Dad. Look…" Dorothy attempted to shift the conversation back to her announcement.

"God, she was beautiful. Me and Al, we'd take her down to the lake, swim for hours. Isais's grandparents always had to come find us. Life was so good during those days…"

He looked down at the key, and Dorothy thought she saw a hint of a snarl.

"Dad."

"You should throw the damned thing in the trash." He tossed the key back into its box. "I don't want to see it anymore."

"Dad!" Dorothy shouted.

He pressed into his chair, and for a moment, she felt as if he intended to hit her. His eyes narrowed to slits, and he balled his hands into fists. In a heartbeat, he softened.

"Dorothy, I'm sorry."

"It's all right. It's the key, I'm almost sure of it. It doesn't…it doesn't like adults. Or me, for that matter."

"That's crazy talk, Dorothy," Al interjected.

"No, boss, hear her out. It won't be so crazy." Isais nodded, and motioned, for Dorothy to continue.

"I've got a story to tell, but before I do, I need to show you something."

She stood and asked her father to push away from the kitchen table. After everyone was clear, Dorothy tipped the key from the box, displayed her index finger to her uncle and father, and pressed against the barrel of the key.

The table groaned against a creaking floor. Al stepped forward, peering beneath the tabletop, and gawking at the strained legs.

"Grab the key, Dad," she instructed, and her father fiddled with the bit, pulling and prodding, yet found that he was unable to wrap his fingers around the glass. She lifted her finger, and he picked up the key without effort. He returned the key to the table.

"I…I don't understand, Dorothy. How did you do that?"

"And what did you do to my table?" Al followed, wobbling the now uneven legs like a seesaw.

"There's one more thing. Dad, can I see your pocket knife?" He glanced at his daughter suspiciously, then retrieved a large buck knife from his front pocket and laid it on the table. The blade was about three inches long, and at least an inch wide. "I

194

forgot how big it is," she whispered, but unfolded the blade and turned her attention to the key. This would be her third demonstration of, well, what she 'was not' if the stories were true, and still she felt her nerves firing wildly with apprehension.

She looked around the room, and, when she was sure all eyes were on the key, stabbed the blade through the back of her hand. Again, no pain, only a faint notion of skin parting around the blade.

"Dorothy!" her father screamed, lunging to retrieve the knife. He pulled her hand to his, inspected her palm, back, and wrist. He repeated the process three times. "It's okay, Dad. It doesn't hurt." And, so she began her story.

When she finished, ending where Isais's grandmother had placed the weight of the world on her shoulders, the three men sunk backwards into their chairs. They were stricken, and—she thought—helpless. How quickly they realized this.

Al stalked from the kitchen and began putting the house in lockdown. Windows slammed shut, doors barred, guns pulled from cabinets. Isais joined him and left Dorothy sitting beside her father. Neither spoke for what seemed like an age.

"This is a little too surreal," he began, then dropped his face into his palms.

"I know, Dad."

"The whole, not a girl, no-girl, whatever-girl thing. You know that's not true, don't you? I was there, Dorothy. I saw your mother give birth to you. You're as real as any other person on this God-forsaken earth."

Dorothy lifted her hand, turning it back and forth displaying both sides. "Can't hurt what's not there, right?" she asked.

"There has to be a better explanation. Something more…"

Dorothy shook her head. "No, Dad, it's this," she said, displaying her uninjured hand. "It's the key, it's the Spintwister…"

"The hell with this damned key!" he roared, grabbed and threw the key against the floor. It sang when struck, and the echo trailed throughout their home. Al and Isais ran into the room, and all three looked to the chipped tile floor, then the undamaged glass key.

Al snatched the key and shook his head. "Not a scratch," he commented, motioned toward a 12-gauge shotgun sitting on the couch in the living room. Isais picked up the gun, and the four of them marched outside.

Al placed a shell in each barrel, slammed the gun home while Isais set the glass key against the bottom of the round yard fence. He offered Peter the gun. Before Dorothy could object, her father raised the stock snugly to his shoulder and took aim.

A part of Dorothy wished that the key would simply erupt into a million tiny shards. She would be done with this whole mess. No key meant no Spintwister. He would return to Charlie's World, never to be heard from again. She'd miss the boys something fierce, but she could live with that. At least something within her would hurt. Besides, with some luck, and time, she might see them again. Older versions of her boys to be sure, but that's a price she'd gladly pay for the sake of knowing they'd live their lives without the Spintwister.

Peter unleashed both barrels in a clap of thunder that echoed off the trees and barn. The wood at the base of the post burst into splinters. The key bounced and landed a few feet from Dorothy. Her father turned the shotgun, gripped the smoking barrels, and slammed the stock against the glass.

Dorothy pulled the handkerchief from her back pocket, and lifted the key, then turned to her father. "It's no use, Dad. The key isn't going anywhere, at least…not without me." Not yet. There would be a point in time where it would abandon her, and reach for another. Whether here, or abroad in the key-worlds, she couldn't say. It would happen eventually, and she felt the need to end this bond between her key and the Spintwister, quickly. Dorothy sighed, and pursed her lips tight.

"Don't do it, Dorothy," Isais pleaded, and took a step toward her. She stepped away.

"Do what?" her father asked.

"I have to. She said I have to help them. I can't wait, Isais, I just can't."

"Who said help who? Isais? What is she talking about?" her father's voice grew strained, and he staggered toward her.

"All the children. If I don't go back, what happens to them?" Dorothy asked, staring hard at Isais. She raised the key and spun the barrel, so the bit pointed up. "What happens when this key won't let me help them?"

"What are you doing, Dorothy?" Peter stepped toward her.

She choked back a sob. "Be ready for me, Daddy. I'm bringing it home. I'm bringing them all home." Dorothy closed her eyes and slid the key into her pocket. Her father's voice cut off in a sudden wave of silence.

There was no grass beneath her feet, nor anywhere as far as she could see.

Charlie's World was dry and desolate. The trees stood as bare eoliths in a blackened sky. The wind turned angry, howled and pushed at Dorothy, throwing black soot into her hair and eyes. She raised her hand and searched for the camp.

Shadows danced along the scarred ridgeline of skeletal trees. Creatures, large and small, skulked between silhouetted trunks, confused by this devolving world. Glinted eyes fixated on Dorothy, and their desperate clicks and tuts lashed at her ears. Dorothy ran a hand over her pocket, pressing both thumb and index finger along the outline of the bit.

"Is this you?" she asked. Could this be the result of the key's desire to move on?

Would it destroy a world to be rid of her?

"Where are you, Charlie?" she whispered. She had hoped, perhaps foolishly, that Charlie would be here, setting up his camp, chewing on candy bars, and waving his goofy wave. Or she had hoped that he was living with his drunken mother, maybe not happy, but safe. He could be, but she had to know for sure. Her visions pointed toward the contrary and sided with the old woman's premonition.

Dorothy guessed she'd arrived in her usual spot at the center of this world. If she had, then Charlie's camp should be off to the right and slightly behind her. She looked and saw little beyond the scar of timber left behind by whatever turmoil had ravaged the land. She prayed that the landscape did not reflect Charlie's circumstances, and wondered, if this was a reflection of Charlie, how bad Ragesha's world must look, or if anything remained at all.

Dorothy made her way to where the camp should have been, keeping a wary eye on the tree line and the skittering clackety-clack monsters prowling within. They clamored along the campsite, jumping from branch to branch, baying and clacking in a panicked rage.

"They cannot hurt you," Dorothy told herself. "Because you do not exist," her mind replied.

As Dorothy neared the camp and her eyes adjusted to the light, her heart sank. The trunk lay in splintered ruins. The tent flapped and whipped on a single string, still tied to a charred stump. Shattered lanterns lay haplessly on the hardpan earth. Scars lined the ground.

The Spintwister's crackling, snapping approach cut through the howling wind behind her, and at a great distance at first, though the savage gale made it hard to discern. She fought the urge to turn, and calmed herself by repeating, "He cannot hurt you. Not here, not there," over and again, until the words skipped in rhythm with her heart.

The crackling grew, expanded, and then settled into a thin sizzle as his cloak and hat appeared at Dorothy's side. The fine hairs along her arms and the back of her neck prickled.

He stood motionless, bony face curled into a vicious frown. His claws were hooked behind his back. His eyes dripped black tar, streaming down to his chin. She shuddered and repeated to herself, "He cannot hurt you. Not here, not there."

The wind suddenly dropped to a gentle breeze. Dust particles danced and lilted to the ground. The Spintwister's cloak snapped and rolled downward, falling into a mist at his feet.

"I know you've been following me." She glared at him.

"Did I make it a secret?"

"I suppose not," she replied, and brushed a foot around in the dirt. "What did you do to Charlie?"

"Oh he's here, my dear. He'll be along soon. He's never far from me now," the Spintwister replied. He looked to the sky, dropped his head, and coyly glanced at her. "It is as if all this is preordained, isn't it? The old woman, she must have told you what these worlds are to become? Or did she hide this, as she hides her name from you?" He popped around to her right, then settled in front of her. "She told me, no-girl. Did she not tell you?"

She held her breath. Gooseflesh rippled across her body, and the Spintwister smiled. "She told me a great many things about you, too, little no-girl."

"My name is Dorothy."

"Not that again," he said, and brushed her off with a wave of his hand. "You never learn, do you? I suppose this is why you are here; that borrowed stubbornness of yours. And, I assume you're here to save my boys from wicked fates and foul deeds. A hero and a thief! How noble of you."

"They aren't yours and I won't let you have them."

"Oh, but I already have them. They were mine long before you arrived. I have taken their pain, and made it my own. They are grateful to me, little no-girl. And you? What have you done for them? Do you think your childish bonds, the Three Key Children, was it? Do you honestly think playtime promises will return my children to your favor?"

Her cheeks grew hot and her mind clouded into a rage.

"I thought not. But I am willing to let you try. My memories are nearly returned, and soon I will be whole again. Three parts—whole. I task you to try, my little no-hero." He balled his claws into a fist. "Turn them to your favor! Make them strong again!" he growled wickedly. "The mighty Musketeers' last stand. Charming, isn't it?"

"Leave my friends alone!"

He hovered to her left, and cocked his head, lips parting in a horrid smile. "Whatever for? Do you wish me to wander aimlessly throughout these lands, with no minds to create them? Make them beautiful?"

"Yea, that's exactly what I want! I wish you dead, a hundred, a thousand times—DEAD! Creating lands with minds, you have no idea what the frig you're talking about!"

"Purpose, no-girl. It is purpose that binds me to you, and to them. It has been this way throughout time, and will be long after time ceases to exist. I thought you would have picked up on this by now." He circled her. "Borrowed time, borrowed key, borrowed soul. Oh, you are the pitiful one. What did the old woman say, I wonder, that brought you back here? She doesn't trust you with a name, I imagine she hasn't trusted you with much else."

"She said I have to stop you."

"Of course!" He leaned closer and pursed his lips, scratching a claw against her chin. "Any idea how?" Dorothy stared defiantly into his eyes. He snapped behind her, and paced. "Do you know you are not the first of your family to visit my worlds?" he asked.

Dorothy nodded. "My Mom." She had suspected someone from her family, mother, father, grandparents, one of them had been the original owner of the glass key, and once they had grown old, they simply grew away from it. Judging by her father's behavior when she presented the key to him, she surmised who the holder must have been. More importantly, she understood the key wasn't stolen. It was inherited. Her mother set her on this path the moment they arrived in Florida. Her last gift to her daughter.

"Well, we're not there quite yet," the Spintwister said, before tapping a claw against his temple. "Need a little more of the ol' memory juice for that."

"You won't touch another drop of their blood!" Dorothy roared, and stomped within inches of the creature. He dropped his pointed chin to his chest and frowned. "Blood...A mere leech? Is this how you see me?"

"Aren't you?"

"Am I? What does that make you, I wonder," he asked, popped behind her in a haunted sizzle, and pushed his claw through her shoulder. She winced, snarled, and folded her arms beneath the protruding claw as best she could. "What indeed." He stepped away and shook his hand, as if tossing mud from his fingertips. Dorothy inspected the fresh hole in her shirt and gritted her teeth.

"I grow weary of you, little no-girl. I want nothing from you, but what you have stolen from me. To do this, I must finish what I have begun." He drifted away from Dorothy, and into the campground. He ran his fingers along the shredded remains of Charlie's tent, and continued, "So, few of you left, and so much to remember. Let's hope my boys will be enough. When I have drained them, when my memories are restored, I will know how to end you, and all of this miserable nattering nonsense. I will take your key, and your world will be mine," he shot a wicked glance at Dorothy. His hand fell to his side, and he slowly hovered away from her.

"As for you, well, the old woman has told me what you will do. Did she tell you? Probably not, she fears you more than she fears me. They call that irony."

Suddenly, he spun and bowed to her. "Your little boy-toy comes. Do your worst, my dear. I look forward to your failure."

He exploded into a cloud of crackling smoke bubbles, and appeared an inch from her nose. The Spintwister drew a claw under her chin, and lifted her face to meet his eye.

He vanished in a wave of snaps and gurgling smoke. Charlie lay on the ground where the creature had stood, curled in a ball. He wore only a greasy pair of tanned shorts. His back was covered in crosshatch pink scars—like a map, with all roads leading to his death. Maybe hers, too.

She fell to Charlie's side, and pulled him into her arms. He felt lifeless and limp, though his warmth at least told her that he was alive. "Charlie, wake up! It's me, it's your Dorothy," she pleaded. He didn't move. She shook him, then patted at his face. No response. She turned to pull her supplies out of her backpack and cursed when she realized she had left it at home. She could go and get it, but her father may not let her return. Or worse, the Spintwister would take his prize, when he learned how the little no-girl had abandoned it. She couldn't risk it.

Looking around the barren landscape, she guessed nothing of use had survived the Spintwister's wrath. She could think of only one thing to do. She turned Charlie onto his belly, and prayed. The bone key sat in his pocket, bit facing up. Dorothy wrapped her key and set it on the ground next to Charlie, letting it roll out of its cloth. She did the same to his, and pondered as to how she would hold these two keys together.

She guessed she could combine the keys, but she was also certain they, like she had with Charlie, must touch glass to bone and both to skin in order for them to work. It might work without the skin, but it also might send the keys off by themselves, and then where would they be? Maybe she could combine them using Charlie's hands, but again, if he dropped them—being unconscious and all—no telling what might happen.

A gust of wind brushed past, and nearly knocked her over. She glared at the ground, where the Spintwister had departed and shook her head.

"Tick-tock, little no-girl," she mocked. She had to do something.

Dorothy inspected her clothing: Black U2 t-shirt titled *Self Aid,* from the 1986 Dublin tour she'd obviously never attended.

Below a yellow-orange silhouette of Bono, printed in large capital letters read the following: MAKE IT WORK. Nice.

Dorothy gnawed through the bottom seam of her shirt and tore off a thin strip, which she stretched across the ground. Another gust of wind kicked up, and she scrabbled after the cloth as it snaked across the black dirt. She wrapped her glass key in the handkerchief, stretched the piece of t-shirt across the ground and placed the glass key at the center. Take that, Spinney.

Dorothy wrapped Charlie's bone key in the cloth next, and hovered the key over the glass, then paused. The wind paused with her. She looked at Charlie's limp form curled next to her, and draped a leg over his. Feeling not quite confident about this position, she shuffled Charlie between her body and the keys, then looped her arm through his. Dorothy inhaled, held her breath, and placed the bone key on top of the glass.

Nothing happened.

Dorothy tied the keys together, double knotted, then tripled, just to be safe. She wrapped both keys in the silk, turned Charlie over, and placed both keys against his belly.

Still nothing.

"Oh Charlie," she said, "I'm so sorry that I have to do this." Dorothy winced, gripped his hand, then placed a finger against the glass key.

The weight pushed against his stomach, his eyes shot open, and he convulsed. She jumped away, landing on her back. She looked up to the bluest of skies, nestled amongst tall, thick strands of grass.

The sight confused her, and for a moment, she thought she might have placed the keys together incorrectly. Charlie coughed, and Dorothy sat up and crawled to his side.

He hunched over with a hand cupped against his stomach, struggling for breath.

Charlie's eyes met hers, and before Dorothy could apologize, he fell into her arms and embraced her. Warm tears patted against her neck. She pulled him in.

"I've missed you," Charlie whispered. "I'm so sorry I sent you away."

Dorothy kissed his cheek, and the two remained in each other's arms for a time she dared not measure. She was home again.

"Are you all right?" Dorothy asked. Dark rings nested beneath his bloodshot eyes, his skin was pasty, almost translucent, and he smelled pretty raw. Despite all this, he assured her he was all right—now, anyway.

"Where are we?" Charlie asked, tearing her attention away. All of their key travels led them to fields surrounded by forests, and each held a distinct perimeter. This world resembled a tremendous valley, no constricting field in sight. There were trees with thick green leaves. Soft grass carpeted the ground beneath them, adorned with giant flowers, some taller than Dorothy. She could see birds of all colors flying between and under the trees, which were laden with fruit.

"I'm…not sure. I think I did the right combination."

Charlie inspected the wrapped keys, and shrugged. "Looks right. Could this be Ragesha's world?"

Dorothy gasped when she heard Ragesha's name. She gripped Charlie by the shoulders. "Wait. First, what happened to you? What did he do to you?"

Charlie lowered his head and shrugged. "I'm not sure. I feel better, I think. He'd visit me at night, you know, after Mum went to sleep. We'd come here, and I'd take off my shirt. He'd do something to my back. Felt like scratches at first, bloody hurt, too," he mused, and craned his neck to see. "But then, after that, I don't know. I just felt better."

Dorothy frowned. She wanted to get to the bottom of what the Spintwister had done to him. Whatever it was, those scars ran deep. She just wasn't sure what it could be.

As she contemplated her next move, a familiar voice sang out from the left.

Charlie gasped, jumped to his feet, and ran toward the figure waving at them. It was Ragesha, though not really as they remembered him. His hair seemed longer, skin…softer, she guessed. He wore cotton khaki pants rolled above his ankles, and a loose, gleaming white button-down shirt. He smiled, not suppressed and melancholy like before. This smile was wide, caring, and warm.

And for the first time in any of these odd worlds, the sun was visible overhead. The air was cool and sweet. She stood on soft fertile ground and lost herself in the sound of buzzing of insects—small, proper insects.

"Paradise," she whispered. She joined the boys in a state of bewilderment.

Charlie lifted Ragesha into the air, swung him in a clumsy circle, and dropped him again. They both laughed. Charlie showed no signs of trauma, no indication that he'd been curled into a fetal ball only a few moments ago.

"Rags!" Dorothy greeted. Charlie stepped to the side, and Ragesha closed his eyes, extended his arms and pulled Dorothy close. He smelled like cinnamon, and his touch was warm, his muscles relaxed.

"You look great, Dorothy. You both do! I am so glad you could make it to my home!"

"Home?" Dorothy asked. Home as in permanently living here with the Spintwister? Is he for real?

"This is incredible! How? Did you do all of this?" Charlie asked, and Ragesha nodded proudly.

"Not all of it, but we certainly worked on it together. Is it not the most beautiful place you have ever seen? Soon, we will clear land for farming, just…" he scanned, and pointed to the palm tree near Dorothy's entry point, "over there. The soil is full and rich, so my plants will flourish."

"We?" she asked warily.

"You guys did all of this?" Charlie ran a hand through his matted hair. "Wow, my place is like a graveyard."

"Oh, no, Charlie. Here was very similar. Lots of wind, and clouds, and dirt. The ground was covered in milk-bugs and dead trees," Ragesha explained. Charlie began to nod. "We had to tear down the old, you see. But then, we sort of connected. Hand to back, body to mind. We did all this together, through me."

"Yeah," Charlie replied contentedly, "then we must be in the middle of mine."

"Middle of your what?" Dorothy asked. Ragesha looked upon her, as if she were some lowly peasant asking for dinner. He offered a sympathetic smile.

"The procedure, Dorothy. Taking our pain, of course. Didn't he tell you?"

"She doesn't get it," Charlie added.

"No, 'she' doesn't. So please, give a girl a clue."

Chapter 12
Three Parts Now Whole

The no-girl sat beneath a warm, sunny sky, and all she could do, was stare at the land that he and his little brown child had created together. Oh, how it must irk her. Now she would see how little was within her control.

"Created together," he said, and smiled. When the children had first visited the key worlds, the Spintwister was in a sort of remission; a hibernation of the mind. The two boys revived his memory and awakened the lands he had created for these—and countless other children, who longed for a release from their pain. Their lives, nothing more than payment for services rendered. Slowly, the Spintwister regained his fragmented memories while draining the horrors which scarred their tragic little lives. Eventually, he reached a climactic moment of change once hidden within a shroud of dark shadow.

He soon realized his life didn't begin after the great poisoning where he, disguised as a child, convinced dozens of adults to ingest a concoction made from the bellies of what his no-girl called milk-bugs. So concentrated was this mixture, not a single soul, himself included, survived the day. No, he had lived long before this event. But, how far back, how many years upon years? That is the darkness, he now begins to illuminate.

The first boy—Ragesha, yes, that was his name—locked in a small room, crying for his brother, unable to eat or drink…he was the easiest to lure back home. Fear and anger cut so deep, it sliced through the boy's heart. The Spintwister sat with him for two days and did nothing but console the poor lad. Ragesha wanted him to destroy the farmers, who had locked him away and forgotten about him. He wanted them dead, all of them.

"Vengeance is not who I am, child," the Spintwister soothed. The boy then pleaded with him, begged him to find his brother, bring him home. The Spintwister replied, "A messenger is not who I am, child."

The boy cried.

Ragesha then asked the Spintwister to open the door and free him. He asked for water and food. "A servant is not who I am, child," was the reply.

At last the boy asked what he could do to help him. "Return with me and see," said the Spintwister. So, he did.

He ran a claw down the center of the boy's back. Within the river of flowing blood, the Spintwister took the memories of sticks, rocks, and fists that beat the boy into a submissive, useless glob of existence, and eased them far and away. As the wound healed, the boy felt better, if only just a little. The Spintwister drank the pain, as if consuming an old wine, and he savored each precious drop.

For the first time in his newly discovered life, the Spintwister gazed beyond the walls of his mind. He looked upon a moment, just a wisp beyond the limits of his forgotten past. He swam past the poison he ingested, past the minds he'd manipulated into thinking they would transcend into the heavens. He looked to the time before their departure from his world, where dozens of adults—nasty, opinionated, bags of useless meat who trampled his flowers, destroyed his crop, and sullied his purpose.

"They invaded," he seethed. "These adults had somehow stolen a key, and invaded." But how? The keys call when they want to be found. Their song is heard only by the young. A rule which transcended to days long past his meager memory. Yet, they held a key just the same. Just like this no-girl holds a key which doesn't belong to her. He found the similarity quite curious, and drifted deeper into his memory until he looked upon a familiar silver key. He could see nothing else.

His memory couldn't quite journey there, not just yet. So, he drank Ragesha's pain, and when this didn't yield answers, he switched to Charlie. He alternated between boys, allowing each some time to rest. This forced the boys to revisit their remaining traumas, and these festered and rotted into a deep, yearning passion for deliverance. A service which the Spintwister was happy to provide. Between the two boys, he continued to unravel his past.

He recalled a time before the invasion of those meddlesome adults, where children of all walks of life and time had escaped to these realms. He thought he played among them. He didn't believe he charged himself as ruler, and as such, the children hadn't bled for him. They didn't need to. The vast lands were therapy enough.

He drank again.

It was here, nested within his fragmented past, where he could see something of the child, who gave away the silver key. A boy, it seemed, had been the catalyst to all his suffering. He wanted a name and a face to place it upon. He wanted to know why he ruined his lands, why he invited the meat-bags to cross into his realms.

He wanted to know how he, the Spintwister came to be. So he drank, and prayed his two boys would fulfill their purpose. They wouldn't survive the process, that much he was certain of. But if they lived long enough, he might see how the key was given away, and then, he'd understand how the no-girl could have acquired hers. He needed this, before the key severed the tie to the no-girl completely, and offered itself to a worthy child. This must not happen, not if he planned to take her key and offer it to those of his choosing. Time grows short.

Chapter 13
Wake Up, Sleepy Heads

"Still don't get it," was all Dorothy could say. She threw her hands in the air, stomped off to the nearest palm tree, and sank into its shade. After an hour of back and forth with Charlie and the new version of Ragesha, she had given up all hope of the Three Key Children charging at the Spintwister in a blaze of unified glory.

The boys had ventured off to explore, Ragesha leading the tour around his new and improved home. They circled past Dorothy at least twice, even paused to deliver an apple. She refused to bite into it, but Ragesha gave her the stink-eye until she caved. She told him it tasted like a monkey's ass and spit the chunk out at his feet. When he turned around, though, she polished off the rest, giving into the sting of hunger. She'd never admit it, not in a thousand years, but the dang fruit tasted amazing. Nothing like she had back home, not even when she and her mother went north to the orchards.

Whatever she was going to do next, she needed at least one of those brain-twisted dolts to participate in order for anything to succeed. But with the two of them stroking each other's egos and frolicking about like love-struck rabbits, it seemed an impossibility. Her head hurt, and she sighed heavily. Somewhere, she knew the Spintwister was laughing at her.

The boys were taking their sweet time, and Dorothy found herself dozing under the lilt of a cool afternoon breeze. The boys' jovial shouts blurred into memories of happier days not too long past. She dreamed of her mother.

"Hey," Charlie whispered, and her eyes shot open. He sat on his heels, barely able to control his breathing. She met his gaze. "So. How do we fix him?" he asked, jerking his head backward over his shoulder. Dorothy sat up, confused but hopeful.

"I thought you two were chumming it up, patting each other on the bum and all."

Charlie turned, and watched Ragesha for a minute. He was plucking fruit from a tree near his campsite. He sat down in the grass, then fell backward, arms raised. He began to laugh and cheer, until he bit into whatever it was he'd picked.

"He's gone bonkers. And…I don't think there's a whole lot of him left. I asked him about his brother, you know, the one who went off to fight?"

"He didn't know who he was, did he?" Dorothy asked.

"Doesn't have a clue about anyone other than us, and Mr. Spintwister."

"Mister?" Dorothy asked. Charlie shrugged.

"Look, I like it here, really. It's a heck of a lot better than home, and it's nice to eat real food once in a while." He frowned. "But still, I don't want to forget anymore. I can't remember what my father looks like. I don't remember any of my old friends. Aunts and uncles? No idea." He looked at Dorothy earnestly. "He's doing this to me, isn't he?"

"Yeah, I think so. And if I understand it, he's not done."

"Right. So, what's your plan? We're going to give him a fight I hope."

"Yeah," Dorothy acknowledged. "Not here, though. I think he's too strong here."

"Then where?" he asked.

"My time. My home. I've got people there who know what's going on. I think they can help us, if we let them. Maybe the Spintwister's weaker there, I don't know. Maybe? I mean, it's gotta be worth a shot, right?"

"Can we do that? All of us go to your time?" Charlie asked. "Cause if we can, then we need to do it soon. He's not here yet, but time's almost up."

"What do you mean?" Dorothy asked.

"Well, far as I can tell, he can only take a little bit at a time. My sessions last an hour or two, no more. Then, he goes away for maybe a day, maybe a half a day, and starts over. Whatever it does to him, it takes time to, well, you know. Stick."

"When did he visit you last?" she asked.

"Some time yesterday."

"Well, for frig's sake, Charlie, why didn't you say something?" she shouted, then stood. Charlie grabbed her wrist. "Wait. He's watching us, you know that, right? I'm sure he doesn't want us to leave."

Dorothy set her jaw. "No. You know what? He thinks he's got this all wrapped up in a tight little bow. We're going to show him, Charlie. By God, we will!"

They approached Ragesha with determination, and stood over him, one on either side. He met their eyes with a warm smile. He patted the grass invitingly, and Charlie—to Dorothy's dismay—hastily obliged, and flopped down next to him. He stretched across the grass and pressed his shoulder against Ragesha's, and the two of them giggled like a couple of schoolgirls. Ragesha pointed to the sky and outlined several clouds with his fingers.

"Did you make those yourself?" Charlie asked. Ragesha nodded.

"Charlie?" Dorothy asked, fearing she might have lost him in a matter of 30 seconds.

"Sit with us, Dorothy!" Charlie blurted gleefully, throwing her a quick wink. She sighed, and crouched to Ragesha's right.

Ragesha sighed and placed his hands behind his head. "It's wonderful having the three of us together again. And this," he continued while jerking his chin to the sky, "is everything we ever wanted. It is why I built all of this."

"You did all of this for us?" Dorothy asked.

Ragesha leaned on his elbow, and faced Dorothy. "Of course, Dorothy. We're the Three Key Children, aren't we?" He shook his head and lay back down. "Who else would I do it for?"

"That's sweet of you, Rags." Dorothy said earnestly.

"Well, I love you both. You should have the best," he replied simply.

"Would your brother have liked this?" she asked, casting a sidelong glance. He said nothing. "I bet your mother would love to pick flowers here. I know mine would have."

"My mum would, heck she'd love anything outside of London these days." Charlie added.

"I bet she would!" Ragesha commented. "But I don't think she would be allowed here. No one is, just us," he sang, then sat up. "I think I want to swim."

"Wait!" Charlie exclaimed. He looked at Dorothy with wide eyes, then jerked his head toward Ragesha, when she didn't quite pick up on the problem right away.

"Oh! Um. It's beautiful, Ragesha," she fumbled. "I can't believe you did this all for us. Hey, come here." She stretched her arms, and as Ragesha went for the hug, she signaled Charlie. In a flash, he untied the keys and embraced them both.

"What are you doing?" Ragesha asked. Dorothy squeezed tighter.

"Now Charlie!" she shouted, and he parted the set of keys.

They returned to Charlie's gray world, where a windstorm knocked them to the ground.

"No! Why are you doing this?" Ragesha shrilled, breaking free from the group. His voice barely rose above the cutting streams of wind and sand. Dorothy pushed her way to his side and shook him by the shoulders.

"Rags! We can't stay there. He'll kill you!"

"Kill me? No!" Ragesha hollered over the howling wind. "He saved me! He can save you, too! You don't understand. Come back with me and you'll see. Everything's different." He displayed his key.

Charlie seized the opportunity, wrapping his arms around Ragesha's waist and pinning his hands to his side. Dorothy jumped in and hugged them both, as Charlie slid the glass key into her back pocket.

The wind dropped to a whisper, and the three stood in pale moonlight at the edge of the ranch. Isais, her Uncle, and Dorothy's father sat by a campfire a ways away, though they all turned to face where the children had entered. They stood, and Dorothy collapsed to her knees.

"Buggers," Charlie exclaimed, as Ragesha tried to wriggle himself free. Dorothy carefully placed a finger on Ragesha's key, which was then ripped from his hand and fell to the charred ground. He moved to complain, but Isais's large form loomed over him like a mountain over a pebble. Charlie released him, and retrieved the key.

Peter approached, and Dorothy fell into his arms. He scanned each child with concern, but said nothing. He knelt, kissed Dorothy on the head, and took the three keys Charlie handed him. He gestured to the chairs by the fire.

"Did you leave that thing behind?" Isais asked.

"I don't know, Isais. I hope so." She shifted gears. "So, this is Charlie, and this is Ragesha."

Ragesha waved weakly, and Charlie managed an unenthusiastic "Pleased to meet you". Al leaned back, tilting his head. "You're not from around here," he said to Charlie.

"No, sir. I'm from England. Rags is from India."

"I'm glad both of you are safe, and thank you...for keeping my little girl safe." Peter stepped forward and offered his hand to Charlie, who shook it eagerly. Ragesha stared blankly.

"You all right, kid?" Al asked.

Ragesha turned to Dorothy and spoke...but she couldn't understand a word. He turned and jabbered incoherently to Charlie, who only shrugged.

"I guess he doesn't speak English," Al offered.

"You already know what's going on?" Charlie asked. Ragesha thundered over toward Peter, shouting and pointing at his key.

"Sit down, son. You'll get it back, don't worry." He raised his hands to his chest, then lowered them again. "I know some of it, Charlie. Can't say I understand a lick of it."

"If he comes back, it'll be for Charlie," Dorothy began. Charlie turned and displayed his scars, then sat back down. Al gasped, turned a shade paler, and excused himself. He trotted to the house.

"That's what the Spintwister does," Charlie explained. "He says he's taking my pain away. But...I think there's more to it than that."

Dorothy continued, "We think it's tied to his memory somehow. Like, by stealing Charlie's memories, he revives his own. Charlie can't remember his father, and Ragesha can't remember anyone. He only knows us."

Ragesha perked upon hearing his name. He pointed at the key again, then presented his hand, and boldly stated in broken English, "Key, mine!"

Dorothy's father frowned, and twitched his mustache. He pointed sharply at Ragesha, then to the ground. Ragesha sat obediently.

"Dorothy said you could help," Charlie blurted. All eyes turned toward Dorothy.

"What?" she asked. "You asked if there were guns in the house," she reminded her father. "And you grabbed a bunch of them! And Isais, isn't that why you took me to see your grandmother? To help me?"

Isais nodded before lowering his head. "I don't think she'll help you. Maybe them," he said, and motioned to the boys.

"Well, of course, Dorothy, of course we're here for you...wait, why won't she help Dorothy?" her father asked.

"Because she doesn't think I'm...real."

"That's absurd," her father stated irritably. "I was there when you were born, Dorothy."

"I know, Dad," she said, and tapped the back of her wrist. "But the knife, remember? I don't know what I was, or what I've become. I might have always been this way, I mean, I don't ever remember being sick. Never a broken bone. Few cuts and bruises, sure..."

"Which healed pretty dang quick, come to think of it," her father added.

She thought about the day of the fire, then asked, "Can I ask you something?" Dorothy's father dipped his head. "About the fire. How bad was my room when you pulled me out of it?"

He slumped and closed his eyes, cringing at the thought. "Dorothy. Come on, sweetheart."

"How bad?" she reiterated.

He sighed, looked to Al as he was handing Charlie a tee-shirt, then to the three children. "I was surprised you were still alive."

"And Mom?" Dorothy asked.

"There was no way to get to her," he said.

"Did you try?"

He lowered his head and pressed two fingers against the bridge of his nose. Al brushed a hand over his back, and her father waved him off. "The roof caved in on her. I tried Dorothy, I really did."

"You went to her first, didn't you?" she asked solemnly. He nodded. "And when you came to get me—" she asked, and he interrupted in a gruff, emotional tone.

"The room was so hot, kid. I had to wrap myself in a wet a towel just to walk inside. The fire roared along the wall next to you...you couldn't have been more than three feet away..."

"I should have been burned."

"Worse," he admitted. She nodded.

"Mister Dorothy's Father," Charlie interjected.

"Just call me Pete."

"Mister Pete, did you get burned?" he asked.

"You know, he can take that pain from you," Ragesha suddenly interrupted in perfect English. All eyebrows raised and turned to him. "If you let him, Dorothy, he can take the pain from you. You never have to relive that moment again."

"I thought he couldn't speak English," Al asked.

"I don't," Ragesha replied.

Dorothy pulled a sharp breath in through her nose and swung to face Charlie. His face was frozen with the same terrible recognition. Ragesha pulled in a deep breath and clapped.

"He's here! He's here!" he cried. He stood and stretched his hands into the cool night air. "Take me back! Let's go back, just you and me!"

Dorothy and Charlie jumped to their feet and ran to Peter's side.

"Isais, I think you'd better get these kids inside," Peter said, grabbing his arm, and adding, "and get those guns." Isais nodded.

Wood snapped in the distance, crackling closer, and then a thundering crash shook trees just beyond the campsite. Dorothy squinted into the darkness. A faint popping sound fizzled from right to left, and back again.

"Come on. Inside," Isais said.

Ragesha walked out into the darkness. Dorothy's father ran for him, grabbed his shoulder and spun him around. "What in God's name are you doing, kid?"

Ragesha smiled calmly. "There's no hiding, good sir. He's here, and he's here for me."

Chapter 14

Awakened

"Al, grab that kid!" Dorothy's father yelled. Al lunged at Ragesha, wrapped an arm around his waist and lifted him off the ground. Ragesha dangled from his arm like a limp sack. He laughed, lifted his head, and said, "You are wasting your time. He is here, and he…"

"Oh, shut up," Al grumbled, and hastily tromped to the porch.

"Isais, go! I got these two. Get the guns." Peter ordered, then ran to Dorothy's side. The air sizzled behind them.

"Dad!" Dorothy shrieked. She reached for her father's hand and gripped tightly, pulling herself to his side.

He rolled his head around, and when his eyes met the Spintwister, he drew in a short, choking breath. "What in the hell is that?"

The Spintwister stood directly between the fire pit and the porch door. The space between his misty cloak and the ground snapped like firecrackers. His head was bowed, hands behind his back, eyes hidden beneath a smoking brimmed hat.

Dorothy pulled frantically at her father's hand. He stumbled, pulled away, and took a step toward the Spintwister.

"Charlie…" the creature crooned. "Time for your medicine…"

Isais burst from the porch with two rifles and a pistol in hand. He lumbered over to Dorothy and her father, calling breathlessly, "Pete, I've got them!"

The Spintwister raised his arms, flexed his claws at his sides, and slowly levitated off the ground. It advanced, a careening specter of shadow, its slow charge charring the earth black at its heels. Thin whips of crackling smoke trailed down blades of grass, turning the greens yellow, each withering into an ashen river which flowed upward to the dark haze below his knees.

Charlie slipped behind Dorothy, frantically tugging at her shoulders. "Run Dorothy! Please, for the love of God!"

"*Dios mio!*" Isais breathed.

The world around Dorothy slowed. Isais, her father, even the boys stood breathless, each eyeing the massive shadow drifting above a darkened sea of emptiness, as if each looked upon the very pit of hell where life itself did not—could not—escape. The soil swelled, expanded, and split around him.

"Guns..." Peter's voice was distant. "We need bigger guns..."

Lost to himself, to Isais, to his daughter, he raised a hand and absently fished for a weapon, any weapon. He blinked, but otherwise remained fixated on the Spintwister, who loomed ever closer.

Isais gasped and stepped away. Dorothy pulled at her father's hand and begged him to turn. To run.

Ragesha slipped from Al's grasp and fell to his knees. He raised both hands in welcome, then lowered his face to the ground, arms extended. He sobbed and clenched both hands to fists.

"We can't fight this, Dorothy!" Charlie screamed. "Let's go!"

Charlie reached for her hand, then gasped. She turned and stumbled, wanting and unable to scream.

The grass at Charlie's feet blackened, twisting around his feet, then burst upward, snaking around Charlie's head, turning his body before pulling him to his knees.

Another appeared at Peter's feet. Then Isais, Al, each snaking arm wrapping around their chests, violently pushing the men into the air, slamming each into the ground.

"No!" she shouted. She lunged for Charlie, then pulled a deep breath as pressure, not pain exactly, clouded her mind. She felt as if standing on air. She couldn't move her head. Raise her hand. Frozen by the same twisted, grappling chains which held her father. Her Charlie.

"Dor-o-thy!" she heard her father cry, struggling against whatever strange tendril held him in place. She felt her body lift and spin, until she met the Spintwister's eye.

He crossed his arms and turned to her disdainfully, its lips curled to a disappointed snarl. "I expected more, little no-girl. There, you might have stood a chance. Even put up a fight." He knelt, turning to Charlie with a sigh. "Now," he continued, Dorothy forced to look at Charlie as the Spintwister unleashed another twist from the ground. She felt the skin break beneath her chin. Her jaw clenched shut. Pressure mounted against the back of her throat, split, and grated against muscle as a smoky blade passed through the back of her neck.

"I suppose I could thank you, no-girl. Handing me all of this," he passed his hand along the outline of trees to the front porch of her uncle's home, "It's a gift beyond anything I could have hoped for."

He stood, paced to Charlie, and stretched a claw toward his back. "I have it all," he smiled, closed his eyes, and chuckled as Charlie slowly inched to the Spintwister's outstretched hand. Charlie's muffled cries threw Dorothy into a panic, yet she couldn't move. Couldn't speak.

"Please! Don't!" she heard Ragesha cry, and Dorothy darted her eyes to the left. Ragesha stood, hands clasped together, just inside her field of view.

The Spintwister sank for a moment, and she thought he turned his head downward, apologetically. He returned his attention to Charlie.

"I must know," the Spintwister whispered, reared, and ran three of his claws deep into Charlie's back. Charlie's eyes widened, and he thrashed in a mad effort to break free from the twisted nether holding him. Two threads appeared below each waving arm like a hangman's noose, wrapped around his wrists and secured him. Charlie shook his head, cheeks puffing into spheres as he soundlessly begged for his life. His voice, nothing more than a muffled hiss.

The Spintwister raked his claws down the center of Charlie's back. She thought she heard bones snap, air whoosh from his lungs.

The monster lifted his head to the sky and pulled a deep, satisfying breath. He pushed Charlie to the ground, pressing, pulling, squeezing.

Veins pulsed along Charlie's temple. Muscles bulged along his jawline. He swallowed. The Spintwister's claws burst through his chest and into the ground.

Charlie's eyes fluttered, then rolled. His body loosened and sank, soon lost in the blur of her tears. She slowly slipped to the ground as the twist retracted from her neck. She curled and wailed.

"I see it all…" The Spintwister whispered. "I remember all!"

Isais, Peter, and Al tumbled to the ground around her. The three stood, Isais tossing the Winchester to Peter, who caught the rifle by the barrel, flipped it, and chambered a round. He aimed and fired without a second's hesitation.

The Spintwister raised his eyes, and the earth rumbled beneath him. He pulled his hand from Charlie's limp body and flung him aside, then turned his attention to Dorothy and her father.

"You!" His voice rolled through the darkness, and a veil of smoke settled into a fog around Peter's feet.

"Dorothy, go inside." Peter said evenly. He popped the round and chambered another. Dorothy sat up, glanced absently to her father, then to the Spintwister.

"You left me to die!" it raged.

"I didn't! I swear, I didn't!" Dorothy cried, finding her voice above a wave of fear so vast, she felt as if she were floating. "Why did you do that? Why?! "

Isais aimed a lever-action .30-30 and popped off two rounds in a resounding crack-crack! The shots ricocheted, echoed, and trailed around him.

"Pete, it's not working!" he bellowed.

Peter chambered a third round. His voice was square, unwavering. "Al, get them out of here." He leveled the rifle to his shoulder. Al raced to Ragesha, lifted him, then approached Dorothy.

"Dorothy, what did he do to Charlie?" Ragesha looked confused, suddenly broken from whatever ecstatic trance held him to the Spintwister's favor. Dorothy shrugged away from her uncle's grip and stepped behind her father as he fired off two more rounds. Isais emptied his rifle, dropped it, and pulled a pistol.

The Spintwister shuddered, and his eyes receded into deep black sockets. Suddenly, and for no reason at all, as far as Dorothy could tell, Peter dropped, rolled; the whites of his eyes mimicking the Spintwister's. The creature wrapped his claws around his own head, and a vicious light flickered across his face. Peter pressed his fingers against his temples, and curled forward.

"Dad!" Dorothy dropped to the ground next to him, clutching his shoulders, slapping his cheeks. His mouth opened, and he rasped as if struggling for a breath. The Spintwister, panting in time with her father, interlocked his claws around his own smoking face.

"Dorothy, inside, now!" Al said firmly. He took a step, then another, backward toward the house.

"What did he do to Charlie, Dorothy? Why isn't Charlie moving?" Ragesha whimpered, squirming under Al's tight grip, and staring helplessly at Charlie's limp body.

The Spintwister lurched forward, sprawling face first against the grass, turning the blades into darkened threads. Dorothy's father collapsed into her arms. She cried frantically, incoherently, brushing his hair from his eyes, and pushing against his shoulders and chest.

The creature punched the ground, which quaked and rolled, throwing Dorothy and her father apart. Al stumbled and dropped Ragesha, who rushed to Charlie's side.

Dorothy forced herself up, fighting through a fog sealing her mind. A halo of darkness pressed her vision into a tight tunnel, and she stumbled, then crawled feebly toward her father.

The Spintwister struck the ground again. Dorothy flipped upward and landed on her back. Her father was thrown further from her, and Al went to his knees. Isais tripped over his own feet while trying to reload. "You did this," the Spintwister said again, slow and ominous.

Dorothy began to object, then quieted suddenly. The Spintwister wasn't looking at her. He crept across the yard toward her father, gouging his claws into the dark earth and pulling his body forward.

Isais aimed the pistol and snapped five rounds. The shots passed through the Spintwister as though he were a cloud, stirring up puffs of dirt behind him. He turned and met Isais's eyes. Isais stumbled backward, spun, and ran for the house.

Dorothy blundered to her feet, and leaped between the Spintwister and her father. It was all she could do. Her energy bled from her body, and she grew weaker by the second. The Spintwister shoved her to the ground, and disappeared in a twist of smoke, reappearing over her father a moment later.

Peter raised the gun to the Spintwister's head and pulled the trigger. The rifle erupted and fell to the ground. The Spintwister growled and raised his claw above his head.

"You…did this to me!" He slammed his claws downward, digging into Peter's chest.

"NO!" Dorothy cried, and mustered the strength to jump to her feet.

The Spintwister lifted Peter into the air, grinning broadly at Dorothy. He curled the two fingers protruding from her father's back and threw him down. The earth swelled and cracked from the impact. Trees splintered and snapped, and the porch collapsed into rubble.

Peter moaned. He wrapped his hands around the Spintwister's wrist and pulled. The creature lifted him so their eyes met. Peter dropped his hands, and the creature flung him aside.

Dorothy ran to her father and hunched over him, frantically checking his chest and back. She found nothing, not a scratch, nor a hint of blood.

Peter propped himself up, wearily glancing at the Spintwister. He squinted, gasped, and, as if a door had suddenly unlocked within his mind, said, "Max?"

The Spintwister turned, and locked his claws behind his back. "Good God, Max, what the hell are you doing?" Dorothy's father sat up, then nodded to Dorothy, gently moving her to his left.

"You're not hurt, Daddy. How are you not hurt?"

"Hold on, sweetie." Peter slowly pulled himself to his feet, took a step toward the Spintwister, who, to Dorothy's surprise, stepped away.

Isais and Al approached, keeping a dozen yards berth between them, each with a gun raised.

"Max, why?" he asked, and motioned toward Dorothy. "This is my family! She's my daughter!"

Dorothy's eyes darted between the two, and when her gaze landed upon the Spintwister for a third time, she saw a boy in his stead. A boy not so dissimilar to the blond-haired kid whom she met in the bathroom at school. He had shorter hair, but the same icy eyes.

"You did this, Pete. You reap what you sow," the boy replied. His voice was tiny and soft, and it hurt Dorothy, just hearing it.

"What did I do?" Dorothy's father raised a hand to his chest and clutched at his own shirt. "Christ, Max, I was happy! We were—all happy! It's what you wanted, son. All of this was your idea!" Peter gripped his temple and madly shook his head. "Why can't I remember?" He turned to Max, "Why in God's name did you make me remember?"

The boy was sobbing. "You forgot about me, Pete. Why didn't *you* remember me? Us, together, always…that's what you said."

Peter lowered his head. "I just didn't. Couldn't, I guess." His voice became a whisper. "Not until now, not until…" He turned to Charlie's lifeless body, then shuddered.

Dorothy raised her hands as if to say, "What the frig, Dad?" He brushed his hair out of his face and flung his arm in the boy's direction. "Well, this is Max. He and I did what you and these chuckleheads still do." He paused. "The glass key is his."

"Was mine. You stole it," the boy corrected.

"Dad?" Dorothy whispered. Charlie was gone. Her mother, gone. Ragesha? Who knew where his mind was at. And now her father, the one solid bit of reality she clung to…she crumpled to the ground, reeling.

"I didn't know, sweetheart. I mean, when you showed me the key, I kinda knew what it was, but I couldn't get a clear thought in my head. Not until this," he whimpered sadly. "God, it feels like a damned Mack truck rolled over me."

Al still had his rifle trained on the boy. He edged sideways and tapped Peter's shoulder.

"It's all right, Al. You remember Max, don't you?"

Al lowered his gun a couple inches and peered at the boy. "The kid who went missing?" He cocked his head. "Shouldn't he be our age?"

Dorothy's father nodded. "Yeah, should be." Peter dropped his hands across his knees.

"Dad, what the hell is going on? How do you know him? Why do you know him?"

Max straightened. Peter slumped and began to shake. Max addressed Dorothy, but never moved his eyes from Peter.

"Tell her, Pete. Tell her who you really are. Tell her why, Peter. Tell her why she doesn't, shouldn't exist."

Dorothy dropped to his side, and gently gripped Peter's wrist. He smiled, and ran his index finger down the length of her cheek.

"Pete, what in the Sam Hill is going on?" Al asked.

"This is just a mess, sweetheart. Just a mess that should have gone away when we moved to Macon."

"Tell her," Max reiterated. Pete raised a hand and nodded.

"Tell me what, Daddy?"

"Me and Max. That pink key of yours used to be his. Least, until he gave it away."

"You stole it," Max argued.

"Oh, come on, Max! You know you that's not the truth! It was *you* who set this up. My God boy, don't you remember? Your dad, right? Don't you remember what he did to you?" When Max didn't answer, he turned to Dorothy and desperately continued, "His father was a monster. Beat the kid constantly. Not just hurt, mind you, but *beat* him; cut him, broke his bones. That's how the key found him, and that's how I met him, in, you know, that place. The key-world."

Dorothy slumped to her heels, dropped her hands to her side. She sadly looked to her father, then to Max, finally settling on Charlie's body.

"For a while, it was fun, you know? Everything was new, and different. I never had a worry or a care over there. Heck, I don't think either of us did. But we always went home…it was like the place didn't want us there at night. Well, one day, Max asked me to come home with him and stand up to his dad, you know, together. Hell, I didn't think traveling to his time would even work, so sure, I agreed.

"We got in late, real late. Time from there to here was always off, but for some reason, when we traveled back together, it was way, way off. Must have been after ten when we went up to his room.

"His dad came home some time later. I hid in Max's closet, and he waited for him on the bed. I think I fell asleep. I remember the sound of that door creaking open, and back then, it had to have been the scariest noise I had ever heard. Just slow, and achy, seemed to go on for days.

"I peeked through, I couldn't see all of him, just his body and the back of his head. I could see Max, poor guy was trembling…he looked right at me. I was supposed to jump out and grab his dad, and while I did this, he'd tackle him."

Max turned to Peter and grimaced. "And what did you do, Pete?"

"Christ kid, I couldn't move. I was so damned scared, Dorothy. It was his voice. Just seemed to shake the walls. He said, 'Where you been, boy?'

"Max told him, every bit of where he was, and what he was planning to do to him. 'You won't hurt me again,' he said. 'I'm going to hurt you, for all the times you hurt me. For all the times you hurt Mom. She'd still be here if it weren't for you!' That made his dad mad, crazy mad. He began to punch him, Dorothy. Just beat him down, again and again. Max yelled for me, 'Help Pete! Get him now, Pete!' and that sent his dad into a rage. He tore Max's clothes off and raked his nails down his back. The more Max screamed, the deeper he cut him, until Max didn't make a sound.

"I curled up into a sweaty ball, and all I could do was cry. In the morning, I pulled us both back to the key-worlds."

"And you left me to die," Max harshly added.

"No, that's not what happened at all!" He gripped Dorothy's shoulders and continued, "That's not what happened. He was so banged up, he could barely speak. So, I went home, grabbed my mother's meds, pain killers, and antibiotics, and took care of him. I couldn't leave him, not alone, not there. So, I stayed with him, for days at a time. And no matter what the key-worlds threw at us; bugs, monsters—I stayed *with* him, until they didn't bother us any longer. It was like we became a part of their world, and the one where I was from… Just memories.

"When I went home for the last time, my father was waiting for me. He gave me a fierce licking, beat me silly. I dropped my key and ran. I ran until I collapsed. I had to use Max's glass key to get back. 'Cept, I put the dang thing in the wrong way, and wound up in Max's yard.

"His father was there, and when he turned, I took off running. I didn't know where I was going or how long I ran. I just knew I had to get as far away from his dad as I could." He chuckled, "That's when I ran into your mother. Literally, knocked her to the ground." Peter sighed, picked up a pebble and tossed it to his side. "I lost my key, so the only place I could return to, was here. Not a whole lot of anything around here for a 14-year-old in the fifties, but I did what I could with what I had. I found where your mother lived, and started using the woods near her house to cross. Turns out, your uncle's farm wasn't too far off, so I went there, stole a few things, food mostly, and nursed Max back to health. I told him about your mother, and the boy I met," he pointed to Al, "and how I lost my key. He gave me his…"

"I did nothing of the kind!" Max roared.

"We made a deal, he and I," Peter added, ignoring the outburst. "He'd stay in the key-world, and I would slip between this place and there, at least until we found something that resembled food."

Ragesha knelt beside Dorothy and took her hand. "You both are from this now? This time?" he asked. Her father shook his head.

"No, he was. I was born," he thought for a moment, and ran his fingers through his hair, "I was fourteen in 1996. Found a key sometime in May or June."

"Your pain? It was your father?" Ragesha asked.

"Pain? Yeah, I suppose. My father sure had a heavy hand, no arguing that. Mostly, I was a dumb kid, picked on a lot, played Nintendo all dang day. That's a video game, kid. You'll see it in the next few…oh never mind. Anyway, yeah, Al and me, became pretty good friends back then. Hell, he thought I was living in the woods, which I kind of was, come to think of it. Pretty soon, I spent more time here, then there. The longer I stayed, the more I seemed to forget, until everything kinda slipped away."

"You left him there?" Ragesha asked.

"He left me to die." Max's voice was deeper now.

"I didn't leave you to die, Max! You didn't want to come back! What was I supposed to do? I lost my key!"

"You left me to die!" Max roared, and the ground trembled as his small voice grew monstrous. Three windows burst from their home and showered the ground in a dance of reflective shards. The horses bucked against the walls in the stable. "You were supposed to come back! Every day!"

"I did, Max! All the time! I think…" Peter scratched his temple. "I did, didn't I?"

"Oh someone came, Peter. It wasn't you," he paused and glared at the group. "They were too old to be my caring friend, too many in number. They did have a key, Peter. A silver key—just like yours."

Peter took a breath, then sank. "What are you saying?"

"I had to deal with adults who entered our world, Peter. Adults who ravaged *our* lands, Peter. Adults who stole from *us,* who hurt—*me*." Max smiled and took a step.

"A silver key? My silver key?"

"Your key," Max confirmed.

"Oh Mr. Dorothy's father, what did you do?" Ragesha asked.

"You stayed here and left me to die there. You were never supposed to stay, Peter. You weren't supposed to get married." He looked at Dorothy. "Never have given birth to a no-child, Peter."

"Oh, come on, Max! What was I supposed to do? You were gone, and I loved her. I really, truly loved her!" He turned to Dorothy, and she backed away. "I did, Dorothy. You have to believe me."

"Wait, I'm older than you?" Dorothy stumbled back, raising her hands to her chest. Heat drained from her cheeks, and she felt suddenly cold.

"Do you *look* older than me?" he snapped, then turned again. "Max, please!"

"You are abominations, both of you, living in a time that was never meant to be your own. You stole your existence from me, and birthed this thief. You never belonged here, Peter. She should not exist. She should not have-my-key!"

Ragesha tugged on Dorothy's shoulder, "Oh, he is not happy at all."

"It was your family who entered my world, looking for you," Max said, and his voice dropped into a deep, thunderous growl.

"Pete! We need to move, buddy!" Al shouted, stood, and inched forward. "You, kid! Or—whatever you are. Don't take another step."

"It was your family I returned with, Peter. To your time. Your mother—poisoned," he continued.

Peter's mouth dropped. "You…"

Max shook his head maniacally. "Your father, Peter. So many, oh yes, and I murdered them all! Your family, your friends, gone! The threads, severed! Your line ends here, with you!"

Max burst into thick, black smoke that stretched around them, erupting in a sizzle of explosions. The dark cloud lingered, then shot against the ground at Peter's feet and swelled upward around him. A second later, the Spintwister reappeared.

He stretched his hand backward, a few feet at first, then ten, and then twenty. He balled his claw into a fist and his arm folded as if it held no bones at all. His balled fist sped past the Spintwister and slammed into Peter's chest, throwing him across the yard, through the collapsed porch, and into the rear wall of the house.

The Spintwister extended his left hand and wrapped it around Dorothy's head, pulling her close. She thrashed and hit and clawed at him, but he squeezed all the tighter. Her mind blackened and her hands fell helplessly to her sides.

"Now you see, little no-girl, don't you? You are born from lies. Given life beyond the strings of time. You should not exist. I will do this world a favor, and see that you never do again."

"Please!" Ragesha begged, looking piteously at Dorothy and gently touching the Spintwister's arm. "Please, can't we simply leave these people? Just you and me? I'll never leave you. Never!"

The Spintwister laughed, low and severe, and dropped to a knee, Dorothy still dangling from his raised hand. "My dear boy, you must see the picture now, don't you? This no-girl is a broken thread in time. She knows it; her key knows it. Why do you think it weighs so heavy in her hands? Because she should not exist. It rejects her, as this world, all worlds, reject her. She is but a weed in these sands, don't' you see?"

"And you shouldn't have given her father your key," Ragesha added solemnly. The Spintwister nodded.

"Your key, the dead boy's key, and this thief's key are all that remain." He tossed Dorothy to the ground, and placed his hands in his lap. "There is no key maker. The doors are closing, Ragesha, and only I can reopen them."

"Aren't you the one who closed them?" Ragesha asked.

The Spintwister considered this, and agreed, he was.

"But we still have each other!" Ragesha said, and opened his arms, beckoning for an embrace. The Spintwister shook his head. "You are a tool, child—a means to a new life beyond this accursed one thrown upon me. I will build my worlds again, Ragesha. You are welcome to live in them if you so choose. But your pain, the last bit of your suffering must be drawn out of your poisoned body into mine." He motioned to Dorothy, and back at him. "She must be wiped from your mind. Wiped from all existence."

"There…has to be another way," Ragesha said shakily. The Spintwister lowered his head.

"She does not exist." He motioned to Peter and added, "He cannot exist. I will set all that is wrong in this time—right." He motioned in the same absent manner toward Dorothy's home. "I will have no more landings in unchosen hands. My key can be the only key, Ragesha. I alone decide who is worthy. Now turn your back to me and let me ease the last of your suffering."

The Spintwister flexed his claws, and Dorothy gasped as pincers extended and inched from tips of his fingers. "Together, we will pull all the children on this earth into the worlds we create," he soothed. Ragesha nodded obediently, entranced once again.

Peter, Al, and Isais burst from the house, stalking toward Dorothy and the Spintwister, guns raised.

"Get away from them!" Peter warned, and chambered a round.

"All the children, together," Ragesha repeated. His voice trembled, and he paused before pulling his shirt over his head.

"Dorothy! Move!" her father commanded, and he increased his pace.

"Give me the last of your pain, and together we will end theirs," the Spintwister continued, unfazed. "Permanently!"

Ragesha lowered his shirt and shook his head. "No. Not Dorothy…"

The Spintwister growled, reared, and pressed his hand forward. Dorothy vaulted between them, not knowing what else to do, and pressed her body against Ragesha's back. The Spintwister's claws dug deep into her shoulder, spine, and ribs. He jerked as trickles of blood stained her shirt, then disappeared into the pincers buried in her back. He stiffened and croaked. His dark eyes rolled, and he fell, sprawled over the grass, a single claw flailed in the air, shooting tiny spurts of Dorothy's blood from stained pincers.

Dorothy sank in Ragesha's arms. Her head was swimming, and she couldn't focus her vision. She tried to draw a deep breath, but only managed a few short bursts and coughed up liquid—blood, by the taste.

Voices sang in tunnels. She heard her name, and then nothing. Her own voice intoned then, breaking through the silence, asking her to let go, and drift. The pain, her pain, was receding. Memories of her mother slipped from her mind and into a river. Then her father. Then Charlie.

Light returned and she opened her eyes to Ragesha's tear streaked face. She reached for him, and winced as electricity shot up her arm and down her back.

"Don't move, Dorothy. Please don't move."

"But where's…Max?" she asked. Dorothy angled her head and saw her father and another man she did not quite recognize. Familiar, yes, but so distant. He stooped over Max, pointing a pistol at his temple. Her uncle stood at his side. Max shifted feebly and met Dorothy's eyes.

"I'll go with you," Dorothy whispered. "We can exist together, you and I. The key, Max. Listen for it. The key calls when it wants to be found." He held the glass key in his hand. As she whispered, his eyes softened.

Dorothy turned to Ragesha. "Do you have your key, Rags?" He nodded. "Can I see it?"

Ragesha picked up his stone key and presented it to Dorothy. "Do you want me to take you back with me?" he asked. She nodded, then pressed a hand to his cheek. "Not yet," she choked on her words, turned and spat. Blood peppered the ground, and she began to shiver.

"Okay, Dorothy. I'll wait." Ragesha replied, and wiped his eyes on his knuckles.

"You rotten little son of a bitch," she heard the man say. "I'm going to end you once and for all."

She reached for Max, the Spintwister, and fell limp beneath the sound of echoing gunfire. Dorothy ran her hand along the length of Ragesha's arm.

"Still not working, Pete!"

"Now Rags," she spoke distantly, hearing her words as if spoken beneath a pool of water. Dorothy placed a hand on Ragesha's key, then stretched to touch the glass key. The sound of gunfire echoed through the ranch, then through the landscape of her mind. She fell limp in Ragesha's arms, and her eyes twitched upward and off to the left. She felt Ragesha's body and mind as a whole, if only for a moment, then fell silent. She drifted to Max, and pulled him to her. Max rolled his eyes, and lowered his head to the ground. Peter dropped in a convulsive fit next to him. Isais and Al rushed to his side, screaming his name.

Had they turned, they might have seen Ragesha lift his stone key, bit down, and place it in his pocket.

Chapter 15
The Sun Will Rise and Fall

Ellen and Ragesha sat in silence, staring into the fading darkness as dawn approached. Ellen was beyond exhausted. Her head was pounding. Trying to make sense of the story seemed pointless. In her sleepless state, she could only bathe in the experience of the story—grappling with Dorothy's non-existence, aching for her suffering. Experience…just like he said she would. And she had, as if each word were spoken from some distant memory. There, but just out of reach. She turned to Dorothy, then away, choking back a building tear.

"You took her back with you, to your time?" Ellen asked at length, and resumed her seat next to Ragesha. He nodded. "Yes, back to 1966. With the Spintwister gone, I wasn't sure what, if anything survived in the key-world."

"So you think he died."

"Then? Yes, I absolutely did. All three, Dorothy, her father, and the Spintwister collapsed simultaneously. Dorothy fell lifelessly in my arms. Peter convulsed, and grew still. And Max, the Spintwister, I think he drank non-existent pain. He took what Dorothy shouldn't have been able to give, and made it his own. He inherited nothing, and in such, that is what he became. Considering this, I've come to believe death is a poor choice of words. Death implies change from one existence to another. I believe the Spintwister existed, and then did not. And there is of course Dorothy, in this state," he said, and gripped Dorothy's hand.

"When I returned to my little closet near Naxalbari, my neighbors tried to take her from me. They beat me with sticks, rocks, and fists. None of this affected me, whatsoever." He sat up, and leaned toward Ellen. "I think the Spintwister took more than just memory when I underwent his treatments. Each blow

230

thrust upon me was met with silence. Uncaring and absolute. I lost compassion for anything and anyone that was not Dorothy."

"Were you immune to it? Like Dorothy?" Ellen asked.

Ragesha shook his head. "No, in point of fact, I was not. I just didn't know it at the time. They beat me, and turned on Dorothy, and began to strike her too. Can you imagine? What kind of people would do such a thing? She was bludgeoned once, and never again. I…" he paused for a moment, then cupped his hands beneath his chin. "I want you to understand, all that I was had been taken from me. I was a shell. A body and mind with a singular purpose. I had to protect Dorothy at all costs. She was all I had left. The only reminder of who I was. Everything else had been stripped away."

"He took it from you. Anyone would understand that," Ellen replied. She believed this wholeheartedly, no matter how strange the words sounded coming from her lips. "And you hurt them, didn't you?"

"I did. And not just those who struck me. I found their families. *We,* found their families. For two years, I hunted every last one of them. I took their properties, their fortunes, and their lives. There was no remorse. No fear. I believed what I was doing was right, and needed to be done in order to care for Dorothy.

"Within a year, I amassed enough wealth to live comfortably. Where I once lived in a hut, I now lived in a small apartment in the town of Goa.

"I found work in a hospital in 1967, and studied under a doctor who would later adopt me as his son, and Dorothy his daughter." Ellen began to phrase a question, and Ragesha held up his hand to silence her. He continued, "I don't know how he managed, other than to say state identification wasn't a big priority in those days. I studied, I applied all I learned to Dorothy's care." He smiled. "And I cheated—slightly."

"How so?" Ellen asked.

"Valium, Ellen. I recalled Dorothy mentioning the drug her mother took the day she died. Two pills of a medication called Valium. I described what I thought the drug did, and researched similar medications. We found a drug, and more importantly, a supplier of Valium, then known as Diazepam. Together, with a few outside investors, we built a small factory, and produced the drug Depipam Plus, and sold this as an anxiety medication. You

231

can imagine how popular this was back then. My factory grew, my wealth grew, my status grew."

"The birth of Dutta International."

"Yes, but then it was Dutta Pharmaceuticals. It wasn't until I invested in a small card company called Nintendo. Leave luck to heaven, as they say."

Ellen laughed. "You didn't forget much, did you?"

"Well, no, not when it came to the night of Charlie's death. Dorothy's father described himself as 'a dumb kid who played Nintendo'. After the success of my first endeavor, how could I not look into the second? I pooled and invested millions in the Japanese company, and well, the rest is history."

"You did all this for Dorothy?"

"Yes. You see, as I grew older, I decided," he shook a finger, "no matter the cost, I would find a way to help her, even beyond my limited years upon this earth. I believed I could bring her home."

"How? Why?" Ellen asked. "Nothing of the end of this story even hints at her returning here. She's gone."

"Yes, I would agree. Except for one very important factor. You remember when I told you, we grew up together?"

"Of course. You said, 'in a way, we grew up together'. Meaning you took care of her when you returned." Ellen said.

Ragesha nodded, then added, "Yes, from 1966 until today. And yet, here Dorothy is, 20 years younger."

"She didn't age?"

"Not a single day from 1966 to 1986. She remained 14. Only when she passed the date of that fateful night, did her years resume. I was in my thirties. I thought it was a sign from God at first. Since then, I saw it as a sign of what could come. I changed my studies from medical, to metaphysical."

Ellen exhaled. When she looked at Dorothy, she felt a pull at her chest. A weight, wanting to grow heavier. As if something called to her and wished she'd open her eyes and see. But what? She's aging, so that means what? The clock is ticking?

"That's why you insist she is 26."

Ragesha smiled. "It took some time to see how she aged. I fear that may accelerate."

Ellen dropped her head. "Then why all of this? Why bring her here, why give away your last moments with her?"

"Time, Ellen." Ragesha stretched, bent forward, and touched his toes. He sat up and swallowed. "Time is the root of all her problems. I find it quite difficult to explain, but I will do my best." He took a breath, and looked at the ceiling. "Peter, Dorothy's father, is nearly 14 by now. My history would have him traveling back to 1954, wooing Dorothy's mother, and making a bigger mess of Max's current life."

"Do you think he is? Do you think time works that way? One big, infinite loop?" Ellen asked, shuddering at the thought of another version of Dorothy going through the same nightmare.

"No. Not a loop. As a child, I believed life revolved around me. As if I were the center of my universe." Ellen knitted her eyebrows, but Ragesha raised a hand, and nodded. "Now hear me out. It's not so strange when you think about it. When you are young, life exists within a singular, personal universe."

"Like the key-world?"

"Yes, very much like the key worlds. I never understood life beyond my own little bubble of experience. In my mind, I am the one driving force behind every occurrence and interaction— from my family to my farm, and my village. Life in that sense is directional, following only my movements. Everything else is nothing."

"That's a limited point of view."

"Is it? Or is it a young mind grasping at the concept of consciousness? I am me and I know this, so how can you be you? If we exist on a similar plane, shouldn't we have access to the other's thoughts? At nine or ten years old, not such an unreasonable question."

"Obviously, you moved away from that line of thinking."

"Actually, quite the opposite. I've returned to it." He raised a brow, and Ellen thought he suppressed a laugh.

"Oh, fine, I'll bite," Ellen mused. "Why?" Ragesha leaned toward Dorothy and smiled. When he did not answer, she continued wearily, "You do know we've been at this for nearly 24 hours?"

Ragesha slapped the armrest of his chair. "I will say this. I do not think God allows such chaos. Time does not loop. I believe time, on its own, is linear and very personal. Be it this year, next year, or 20 years ago. No loops, just lines." He parted his fingers and ran imaginary lines in the air. Ellen could almost see them, like sheet music, floating in a space between space.

"Your line, your life-line, is not identical to mine. It is personal to you. As Dorothy's is personal to her. As Peter's is to him."

Ellen paused, fighting to make sense of Ragesha's theories, but her mind was so addled. How is something so universal, also so personal? Point A to Point B. One second to the next. There's nothing personal about it, is there?

"Think of it this way. Rather than time, call it a reality. My reality as a survivor of the key worlds is the same as Dorothy's reality. When we were together, our personal timelines intermingled. Two became one. Yet, when I took her with me and returned to 1966, her reality changed. It flipped from one side of a mirror to another. Her body waited, and when her time collided with mine, she continued to grow."

"You mean she began to age." Ragesha nodded. "But she didn't. Because she isn't in there, right? There's no soul inside her, isn't that what you've implied? Somehow, she left along with Max, the Spintwister, and this shell is what stayed behind. So how is that personal?"

"It is personal to me." Ragesha replied. "This is my reality. My personal timeline, intermingled with Dorothy's shell. A shell that would not exist for 20 more years."

Ellen looked about the room. Dorothy, Ragesha, the rug, two stools and two chairs. All here together. All real. "But isn't it mine too?" she said distantly, and whispered, "I can't exist in your timeline, not if it is personal only to you." She paused.

"Can I?"

"Our timelines are pathed in the same direction, as long as we are together."

"Okay, I understand the theory, I guess. Personal reality that expands with interaction. Like a law of attraction."

Ragesha nodded. He stood, and walked to the kitchenette, keeping his back to Ellen. He returned to his seat, cupped his hands on his lap. He turned to Ellen, and sweat beaded across his brow. She could feel his energy, pulsating outward.

"You're not telling me everything."

Ragesha slowly shook his head. He turned his palm, revealing a small booklet with the same 3-K symbol depicted on the throw rug at the center of the room.

"What is that?" Ellen asked.

"Proof, that time is indeed personal."

"How's that?"

"In 1956, a 14-year-old boy should have met a 14-year-old girl in Ocala, Florida."

"Peter and Dorothy's mother," Ellen said.

"Correct. But they did not meet. Because Peter, in this—my reality, has not journeyed back in time, not yet."

"Because he would do that in 1996." Ellen said. Ragesha nodded. "Because time is linear."

"And personal. He is the future, Ellen." Ragesha smiled. "I can change the future."

"You can stop Peter." Ellen suggested. She considered the implication, then turned to Dorothy. "That would mean she wouldn't be born."

"Correct."

"And so, Dorothy doesn't exist."

"Again, correct. More importantly, if Dorothy doesn't exist, then the chain of events which led to her demise, will never happen."

"That's paradoxical." Ellen said.

"Yes."

She turned to the box, sitting on the floor beside Ragesha. Inside, a gateway to other times and worlds rested in the form of an innocent piece of something that she might call decorative art. A trinket she'd hang on the wall, if it were her taste, and forget about between cleanings. Did she believe it?

"You didn't happen upon Elements by chance, did you?" Ellen asked.

Ragesha ignored the question. "In 1986, I scoured Ocala and Orlando, to confirm my theories. I believe I found her uncle's farm. From there, I searched for her mother's home, which, from what she told me, was only a few miles up the road. What Dorothy never told me was her mother's maiden name."

"So, you didn't find her?"

"Nothing concrete. Not then. I did however, locate the trailer park where Isais's grandmother sat with her needles and yarn. And much like Dorothy's experience, she was expecting me."

"You visited her?"

"Oh yes. I enjoyed a glass of tea with her. She looked tired, worn down. Nothing like the feisty old woman Dorothy had described to me. When she looked at Dorothy for the first time, she cried, and apologized to her."

"But you said these events didn't happen yet." She was getting a headache.

"Premonitions, I suppose. I guessed the old woman had vision beyond personal reality. But yes, she did recognize Dorothy. And she explained why I could not find Dorothy's mother, who lived just a few miles from the farm. She convinced Dorothy's grandparents to move out of Florida, in 1953. Three years prior to Peter's arrival."

"They moved?"

Ragesha nodded. "The old woman has been watching her family ever since."

"She changed her reality. Dorothy's mother, I mean."

"No, Ellen. She changed my reality. She altered my life-line, so we could finish what the Spintwister ended so abruptly."

Ellen shook her head and turned to her reflection in the window. Her curls were matted to her forehead. Black crescents framed her eyes. Oh, how she wanted a shower, just 20 minutes of warmth to wash her mind and body clean.

Dorothy sat to her left. She couldn't see the girl's eyes reflected in the window, just pits of black on pale white skin. She felt a pang in her gut. A forgotten heroine, lost in someone else's time.

"What do you see?" Ragesha asked.

"I…I don't really know." She turned to him. "It's me, right? Not this facility? You're here because of me."

Ragesha laughed softly, and nodded.

"What am I to her?" she asked. A chill raced down her spine. "I'm not…like her? You're not here because I'm Dorothy version two, are you? Is that what the old woman told you?"

"No, Ellen. Though you do bare one similarity to Dorothy."

"I do? What is it?" When Ragesha didn't immediately answer, her voice escalated into a shout. "Tell me!"

He raised a hand. "Ellen, I told you I needed you to listen. Do so now, please."

"Listen to what?" a sense of panic welled up in her gut. Ragesha raised a hand, then removed the lid on the stone key's box.

"Close your eyes, Ellen."

She shook, and stepped away from him, fixating suddenly on her reflection in the window. The image faded as night slowly drained into the dim light of morning. Ragesha disappeared behind her.

The key on the floor beside her pulsed a dull, white light, as if suddenly calling to her. As if it wanted her to find it; to own it. In one instance, Ellen wanted to run from the room, race home and pull the covers over her head and wish this all away. In another, she envisioned a young boy racing across a road and knocking her to the ground. She could see the same boy leaning on an old wooden fence. He smiled sweetly, lowering his head with pink-blossomed cheeks. Ellen's heart swooned, and she reached for him. He disappeared from her mind.

A beautiful girl, young, wearing white shorts, pink tee, golden hair in pig-tails, overlapped Ellen's reflection. She clapped, turned, and ran, fading into the still form of Ellen's silhouette against the glass. She seemed so familiar, yet so utterly strange.

"I've tried to return to the key world so many times," Ragesha said, pacing to the kitchenette. He folded his jacket over the crook of his arm, and returned to Ellen's side. "I've placed the key in Dorothy's hand. I had hoped she might pull us both back. But the key doesn't call me anymore." He slipped his arms into his jacket, then adjusted his tie. "You hear it, though. Don't you?" Ellen's mind reeled.

"The key calls when it wants to be found," Ragesha said softly, his breath chasing up her neck, even from across the room. She wobbled on her heels, ears filled with unrecognizable whispers, as if carried by wind.

"You never married, Ellen?"

"Mama always said I was a career-first kind of gal." She whispered this as if speaking from a dream, hearing the words long after she spoke them. No, she never married. Her mother always seemed to be a roadblock in her love life, even to this day.

"Do you hear the whispers?" he asked.

She nodded blankly, lost between Ragesha's voice and distant weeping. She wanted to reach out to whomever was crying for her.

Ragesha lifted the box, removed the stone key, and wrapped Ellen's hand around the shank. Ellen whimpered. "Please don't."

"The key calls when it wants to be found," he repeated.

"Come home," Ellen whispered, as though echoing an unheard call.

"The key calls when it wants to be found."

"It's not my key." Ellen's eyes rolled upward, then to the left. Her body stiffened.

"The shaman has seen this, Ellen. You need to go to her now. She cannot return here." Ragesha paced around Ellen, his body trembling, eyes wide. "Listen, Ellen. Hear what the key says and heed its call." He placed the small booklet in her hand. "The story must finish…"

Ragesha moved to the window. He stood quietly, and did not turn when Ellen gasped, nor when she stumbled away from Dorothy's wheelchair.

"Time, Ellen. It is personal, and so easily stolen. That's what the shaman told me. Wonderful woman, so dedicated to Dorothy. She spent two lifetimes in search for answers, a means to this end. She moved you from Ocala, you know. Showed your parents what might happen, should you meet Peter again in this life-line. She promised no harm would come to you for as long as they lived, should they do as she asked."

Ellen gripped the key and sank to her knees. She dropped her head into Dorothy's lap, and cried.

"I hope our paths cross again, in this time, or another, Ellen. Time has been so unfair to us. So unfair to you." He shook his head.

It was only when the room grew deadly quiet, that he turned around. Dorothy sat motionlessly at his side. Between her chair and the door, a large circle cut through the rug, digging deep into the concrete below—charred black.

"Go meet your daughter, sweet Ellen," he whispered, and turned off the lights. He stood for a time, staring at the corn-silk hair draped over the back of the wheelchair.

Dorothy didn't move, but he didn't expect her to.

"Be at peace, sister." Ragesha turned, nodded to his man, and walked down the hall. His footfalls faded to silence as the door clicked shut, leaving Dorothy alone with the few beams of sun peeking through the canopy.

She blinked, and her bottom lip twitched into a smile.

THE END

CPSIA information can be obtained
at www.ICGtesting.com
Printed in the USA
LVHW081252010319
609189LV00017B/174/P